Pug Actually

MATT DUNN

Pug Actually

Recycling programs for this product may not exist in your area.

ISBN-13: 978-0-7783-1123-2

Pug Actually

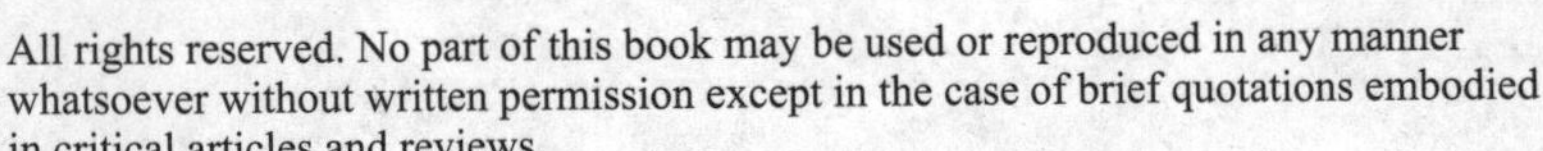

This edition published by arrangement with Harlequin Books S.A.

For questions and comments about the quality of this book, please contact us at CustomerService@Harlequin.com.

Mira
22 Adelaide St. West, 40th Floor
Toronto, Ontario M5H 4E3, Canada
BookClubbish.com

Printed in U.S.A.

For Ian and Marta
There is a light that never goes out.

Pug Actually

1

According to Luke, he's "about to leave the office."

Despite what he just said to whoever is on the receiving end of the furtive cell phone call he's making, Luke's actually sitting in his car right outside the house I share with my best friend Julie. Which proves he's lying. It wouldn't be the first time.

Julie hasn't heard his latest lie, of course. Her hearing isn't as good as mine. She has heard the car pull up, waved to him, acknowledged his "on the phone" mime through the window, and left her front door ajar so she can return to the particularly gripping part of *EastEnders* we've been watching, where a mean-looking bald gentleman has just instructed the pasty-looking character he's been threatening to beat up that he "ain't worth it." An appraisal that—if it referred to *Luke*—Julie and I would have wildly differing opinions about.

I take the opportunity to sneak out through the open door, trot along the path, and sit just the other side of the garden gate, where I can eavesdrop on what's sure to be the latest twist in a saga way more complicated than the television shenanigans in Albert Square.

"Sure," Luke says, after a moment, "Chinese or pizza?" which makes my mouth water, especially when he adds, "Chinese *and* pizza it is." Then I'm brought sharply back to reality, because at his, "Love you too, sweetie," I realize he's talking to his wife, and remember that not only is he a liar, but he's a philanderer, as well.

Luke finishes the call and checks his hair in that reflective device stuck to the car windscreen that Julie only ever uses to help her apply her makeup when she's driving, smells his breath in his cupped hand, and peers up and down the street as if looking for someone. Then he climbs out of his car, walks a pace or two away from the curb, and swivels around quickly to click the vehicle shut with the remote, as if he's firing a gun in the opening credits of a James Bond film.

With a frown, he walks back up to the driver's door and wipes a barely-visible smudge from the paintwork, then he takes a step backward and admires the vehicle—one of those sporty-looking coupes that, mechanically, is the same as the "family" model. *Style over substance*, as Julie's dad would no doubt point out. Therefore pretty much the kind of car you'd expect Luke to drive.

With a last check of his cell phone, he switches it off, slips it into his pocket, and strides confidently toward Julie's gate, hesitating when he spots me waiting for him in the garden.

"Doug," he says.

It's an observation rather than a greeting, so I give him a look, reluctantly step to one side so he can get past, then tail him back toward the house, nipping in through the front door before him, just in case he tries to shut me outside.

"Sweetie?" he shouts, as he regards me warily, and it occurs to me I rarely hear him call her "Julie"—a sensible tactic if you're seeing multiple women, I imagine.

"In here," replies Julie, from the living room, and Luke strides along the hall, peering around the house like a potential burglar, though if I know him, there's only one thing he's interested in getting his hands on.

I follow him into where Julie's sitting expectantly on the sofa, taking up a defensive position at her feet as she switches off the TV. This is worrying: *EastEnders* isn't over yet, and under normal circumstances, even if the house were falling down, she'd probably try to hang around, dodging falling masonry, until the end credits were rolling. Then again, as Luke's all-too-regular off-hours presence here often reminds me, he and Julie aren't exactly "normal" circumstances.

"This is a pleasant surprise!"

"Couldn't stay away." Luke collapse-sits onto the sofa next to her, then hoists his feet up onto the coffee table as if he owns the place. "You know me."

I exhale loudly as I take up a guard position beneath his legs: if she really knew Luke, I doubt she'd let him in the house, let alone on the sofa. It took *me* long enough before I was allowed to sit there.

"Can I get you anything?"

"Just this," says Luke, leaning across to plant a wet one (as Julie's dad describes the way I do it whenever anyone raises me to face level) on Julie's lips, and I have to look away. I don't know why, but I find this "kissing" thing Luke and Julie insist on doing unsettling—possibly because of the weird hum of pleasure he makes every time. "I was just passing. Realized how much I missed you."

"Passing?" says Julie, dejectedly, then she does a double take, and a look flashes across Luke's face, and Julie's expression mirrors it. Then I realize why he's come round, and it shocks me so much it's all I can do not to let out a disgusted bark. From what I can work out given his earlier phone call, he's going to have a "quickie" with Julie, then calmly pick up takeout and bring it home to his *wife*.

"Yeah." Luke licks his lips, an action which makes me shudder. "I'm not interrupting any plans, am I?" he asks, though I'm pretty sure he already knows the answer to that question. Julie rarely has any plans. Mainly because—given Luke's situation—she can't make any.

"No, just..." Julie nods at the TV. "Priya's going to be here in a bit. *Game of Thrones* is on."

"Oh yes. The Dragon Lady." He rolls his eyes, and I'm not sure whether he's referring to a character from the program or Priya. Luke's not her biggest fan. And the feeling is definitely mutual.

"I can call her," says Julie, already reaching for her phone. "Tell her to come later. We can watch it on DVR."

"Don't worry. I can't stay."

"Oh." The disappointment in Julie's voice is so obvious, Luke can't help but give a little victory smile.

"For long," he adds, looking pointedly at his watch.

"Oh," says Julie, again, followed by another, but this time, an I-get-it one, which makes me suspect she's "up for it," as I'm sure Luke would probably describe her. It's at that moment I decide I can't just stand idly by and let him get away with this. So as Julie shimmies across the sofa to straddle him, and Luke reaches up and starts unbuttoning her blouse, I squeeze myself out from underneath his still-outstretched legs, leap up onto the sofa, and force my way between the two of them.

"Doug!" Julie gives me a stern look. "Down!"

I'm wishing I could say the same thing to Luke, but before I can decide what my next move's going to be, he picks me up—rather ungently, it has to be said—and sets me back on the floor.

"Yes, Doug, down!" Luke sniffs his fingers, makes a face, then surreptitiously wipes his hands on a cushion, which irks me even more, particularly since I've already had my bath this month. "Now, where were we?" he says, reaching for Julie's buttons a second time.

As he busies himself with the contents of her blouse, he simultaneously blocks my route back up onto the sofa with his legs, and I fear I might be stymied, until I remember a tactic that Eddie, the Jack Russell star of the reruns of *Frasier* Julie and I love watching, often uses. I dart under the coffee table, leap up onto the armchair opposite the sofa, position myself in Luke's direct eye line, and fix him with my most disapproving stare. After a moment my strategy works, because he opens his eyes midkiss (which is even creepier than the noises he makes), catches sight of me over Julie's shoulder, and breaks away from her.

"Something the matter?" asks Julie.

Luke glares back at me. "It's Doug."

"What about him?"

"He's staring at me."

"What?" Julie turns to look at me, so I hurriedly put on my best, most irresistible pug eyes, wrinkle my forehead to the maximum, then angle my head for good measure.

"He's not *staring.* He's a pug. That's just how it appears."

"It's disconcerting."

"Well, just shut your eyes."

Julie leans down to kiss him again, and Luke does as instructed. But sure enough, a few seconds later, he half opens one of them, to find I've resumed my visual assault.

"He's doing it again."

"Luke..."

Luke wriggles out from underneath her, sits upright, and places a cushion in his lap. "I'm sorry. I just can't. Not with him…"

Julie sighs, then she gets up from the sofa, picks me up and carries me through to the kitchen.

"Sorry, Doug," she says, depositing me on the floor by my bowl, before tipping some food into it, hurrying back into the living room, and shutting the door behind her.

"Now, where were we?" I hear her say, perhaps a little impatiently, then everything goes quiet, so I pad over toward the door. It's one of those opaque-paneled ones, so all I can see is the outline of the two of them cavorting.

I sit down and fix my gaze on my best guess of where Luke's face is, and stare as hard as I can at him through the frosted glass. And it seems to work, as it's only around thirty seconds before Julie says, "What *now*?"

"He's still doing it."

"Pardon?"

"Doug. Staring at me. Through the kitchen door."

"What, with his X-ray vision?"

"You know what I mean."

Julie sighs in a way that demonstrates that it's evident she doesn't. "What do you want me to do? Put him outside?"

"Would you?"

I whimper at the prospect so plaintively that it's only a matter of seconds before Julie opens the kitchen door, picks me up, and carries me over to the armchair. Though my victory is fleeting, as she heads straight back to the sofa, and resumes her straddling of a somewhat disgruntled-looking Luke.

"Tell you what." Julie walks her fingertips suggestively along the arm of the sofa. "Why don't we take this into the bedroom?"

Luke frowns, perhaps wondering whether Julie's suggesting some light furniture removal, then the penny evidently drops. "Good idea," he says.

"Right. I'll just nip into the bathroom, and you..." Julie nods in the general direction of the bedroom.

I sit there innocently as she jumps up from the sofa and heads off along the hall. But the moment she shuts the bathroom door behind her, I leap down from the chair, sprint out of the living room, and—almost losing it on the sharp corner thanks to the combination of my short legs and Julie's polished wooden laminate flooring—get to the bedroom ahead of him. And I'm already sitting defiantly on Julie's bed by the time Luke appears in the doorway.

"For fu...!"

He narrows his eyes at me, then glances at his watch again, perhaps working out just how late he can get away with arriving home by blaming it on the length of the wait for the takeout. Then—and admittedly it's the one flaw in my plan—he raises both eyebrows in a *gotcha* way, and shuts the bedroom door, trapping me inside.

Hurriedly, I jump back down from the bed, run to the door, and place an ear against it. From what I can work out, Julie's finished in the bathroom, and I hear Luke tell her that, actually, the sofa's just fine with him. There's a giggle (Julie), then the sound of a belt being undone, then silence, followed by some sounds that I'd rather not report. Aware that I've run out of options—and I'm not proud of myself—I begin to whine. And whine. Then I start to bark insistently, upping the volume every third-or-so bark, until finally there's a frustrated-sounding "For crying out loud!" from Luke, quickly followed by footsteps, and a slightly-flushed-looking Julie opening the door.

"What's the matter, Doug?" she says, as she picks me up

and carries me back into the living room. "How did you get yourself shut in there?"

I glance pointedly over to where Luke is sitting on the sofa, adjusting his clothes while giving me what I believe is known as "the evil eye," but Julie misses the inference.

Luke sighs resignedly, in the manner of someone who's realized he's not going to get what he wants. "Right. Well..." He glances at his watch a third time, then hauls himself reluctantly up from the sofa. "I ought to..."

"Don't go." Julie sets me gently back down on the floor, then takes a pace toward him. "We haven't even..."

"Yes. Well. Whose fault is that?" huffs Luke.

He's meant that it's mine, but judging by the look on her face, Julie appears to have taken his last comment personally. "Sorry. No. You're right," she says, sulkily. "You get off home to your *wife* like a good boy!"

As Luke swallows loudly, I snort as incredulously as I can. There's only one good boy here, and (spoiler alert) it's me.

"Sweetie, don't be like..."

Julie shrugs off his attempt at a hug, and I brace myself for the inevitable. They've had this conversation—or rather, argument—several times before, and each time Luke tells Julie he just can't leave his wife yet, I sense a little something die inside her.

True to form, she's got tears in her eyes, and though I'd like to rush over and comfort her, I stop myself. She needs to feel bad about Luke, and sometimes you have to be cruel to be kind.

"Don't 'sweetie' me!" she snaps. "You *promised*!"

"And I will." Luke perches on the arm of the sofa. "I told you, now's not the right time. I just need to get all my ducks in a row, and..." He fires off finger pistols in rapid succession, and I can't help but snort again. "But I understand," he continues. "If you can't wait, then perhaps we ought to..."

"No, I didn't mean…" Hurriedly, Julie takes his hand, as if *she's* the one who should be apologizing. "I get that this is hard for you. Really, I do. But you can't blame me for wanting us to be together?"

She smiles down at him, a pleading expression on her face, and Luke kisses the back of her hand, as if bestowing some kind of papal blessing. Then he stands up and sighs dramatically as he takes her in his arms. "It's what I want too," he says. "But try to look at things from my point of view. I just want to do right by everyone, you know? You, me, *and* Sarah…"

At the sound of Luke's wife's name, Julie winces, then she nods, though if you ask me, the only person Luke has ever intended to do right by is himself.

"Okay," she says, reluctantly. "So I'll see you on Monday?"

Luke looks shocked for a moment, as if there's some important date he's forgotten, then he lets out a short laugh. "You mean at *work*?"

Julie nods again, and Luke grins like someone who knows he's still in the driving seat—and not just of the showy coupe parked outside. "Right," he says, patting his pockets to locate his car keys, his mind probably already on which pizza topping he's going to choose. "Well, say hi to Priya for me."

"Sure," says Julie, though all three of us know she won't, unless she wants a lecture.

"I'll see myself out," Luke says, and even though that's probably directed at me, I still make sure to escort him off the premises. I wouldn't want him to take anything. Especially advantage of Julie.

Though my fear is, that's exactly what he's doing.

2

"Was that Luke I just saw driving away?"

Julie's other best friend Priya has just arrived. This is good because a) she's brought wine and snacks (though I'm not a fan of the former given how much of it Julie drinks on an all-too-regular basis, the more of it she consumes, the more of the latter I get), and b) given the amount of wine Priya's brought, and the fact that she's just seen Luke leave, she and Julie are inevitably going to have a pretty heavy conversation about Luke at some point this evening. And maybe—just maybe—this time, some of it might sink in.

"Might have been," says Julie, then she hurries off to fetch a couple of glasses from the kitchen, to avoid further questioning. Ever since Luke became a feature in our lives, Priya's been pretty vocal in her disapproval, mainly of Julie's ongoing belief that Luke will eventually leave his wife for her.

"Right. Only he didn't seem that happy."

Julie seems to be considering trying to explain what happened, then evidently thinks better of it. "Probably because he was going home to *her.*"

"Oh, Jules, I'm sorry."

"What are you sorry for? We haven't split up or anything."

"That's what I'm sorry about!" Priya lets out a slightly over-the-top laugh, then, with a super-friendly "Hey, Doug!" she kneels down to scratch the wrinkles on the top of my head, following it up with an impressed-sounding "Big stretch!" when I perform my usual warm-up move. "And?"

"And nothing. He was just passing by. Called in for a quick..."

Priya holds a hand up as if she's going for a high five. "If you're about to add an *i* and an *e* to the end of that last word, then that's way too much information!" she says.

"Visit, I was going to say."

"Right." Priya gives me a final pet, then hauls herself back to her feet. "Not had an argument, have you?"

"Just a difference of opinion. That's all."

"Do I want to know?"

"Don't you always?"

"Sorry, Jules. I just don't want to see you get hurt. And I'm afraid Luke is *never* going to leave his..."

"P!" It's Julie's turn to do the high-five thing. "I don't want to hear it."

Priya gives me a look as if she and I are in on a secret, then she nods at the wineglasses, so Julie pours them both a drink, then empties a packet of Kettle Chips into a large bowl, which she sets down on the sofa between them. I take up my usual position on the rug in front of the sofa and stare expectantly up at the bowl. Julie picks up the TV remote, stabs at a couple of buttons, unmutes the volume, and the familiar *Game of Thrones* theme tune blasts out into the room.

"Winter is coming," she says, in a funny voice, and Priya frowns.

"We still talking about you and Luke?" she says, and Julie does that openmouthed thing that's supposed to indicate both disbelief and displeasure.

"Priya, just drop it, will you?"

"Okay, okay." Priya takes a huge gulp from her wineglass. "It's just..."

"He *will* leave her. He promised. He said it again tonight. He just has to get all his ducks in a row, and..."

"That's ducks with a *d* instead of an *f*, right?"

Priya's very quick-witted. She comes out with a lot of this kind of thing, and possibly despite herself, Julie smiles.

"P, please. Not all of us have it as easy as you and Sanj, you know?"

Sanj is Priya's husband, and the point Julie's making is that Priya didn't have to lift (or even swipe right with) a finger to find Sanj. Their parents introduced them, and it's why Julie quite often tells Priya she doesn't have "a leg to stand on" when commenting on her and Luke. Although to her credit, Priya won't be put off.

"Maybe so," she says. "But just tell me this—how long are you going to give him?"

Julie helps herself to a chip, and while I hope I might be getting one too, she's too preoccupied with Priya's question to think of me.

"As long as it takes."

"And what if it takes forever? You want a family, right? Kids?"

Julie chews thoughtfully. "Eventually," she says, in the same way you might say "obviously," and Priya leaves a dramatic pause before tapping the face of her watch.

"It *won't* take that long," Julie says, sounding a little less confident than before.

"But what if it does? How many more excuses can he come up with?"

"He's promised me. Told me we're going to grow old together."

Priya shudders. "I'm suddenly seeing Luke as this funny little wrinkled thing, sitting next to you on the sofa, alternately snoring and farting, and you've already got one of those!"

For some reason, Priya nods down at me, then she smiles sympathetically. "He either wants to be with you, or he wants to be with her. He can't have you both. That's not how it works. Although…"

Julie reaches for the remote and stabs at the mute button. "Although what?" she says, though in a tone that suggests that—despite killing the volume on *Game of Thrones*—she doesn't really want to hear Priya's answer.

"It's exactly what he's got right now."

"Priya…"

"Two women, two shags…"

"He doesn't sleep with her anymore."

Priya throws her head back and roars with laughter—to me, it looks like she's putting it on a bit, but it has the desired effect. Assuming the desired effect is to make Julie annoyed.

"He *doesn't*," she insists, crossly. "He told me."

"And you believe him?"

Julie nods, and Priya narrows her eyes in an I-don't-believe-*you* kind of way, then she takes a sip of wine. She's good at this stuff—sees everything in black-and-white, much like I do. Although of course with me, that's genetic, given how dogs are color-blind.

"What does he tell her, do you think?"

"About?"

"How does he justify them not *doing it*?" Priya passes a chip to me, and I wolf it down almost without chewing to avoid missing anything.

"He… Well…" Julie stares at the screen, where either a fight or some weird sexual encounter is taking place—often on *Game of Thrones* it's hard to tell the difference. "Priya, can we please talk about something else?"

"No, we can't!" says Priya, suddenly angry. "I get that he's charming, and good-looking, and how it can be flattering to have a married man paying you attention, but Luke is leading you on, Jules, and the quicker you realize that and kick him out, the better. Otherwise you're just going to be sitting around wasting your time, listening to excuse after excuse from him as to why now isn't the right time for him to leave his wife, while he gets to have his cake and eat it and all you get out of it is the occasional shag. And if you're not careful, you might wake up one day and find yourself all alone, like that mad lady who lives next door with nothing but a creepy cat for company."

Priya pauses for breath, and I swallow so loudly it makes a sound, my reverie following Priya's reference to cake dissipating almost instantaneously at the mention of the word *cat*. Surely Priya's joking? There's no way I'm going to let something so duplicitous into the house, no matter how desperate Julie is.

Fortunately, my embarrassingly-loud gulp seems to have gone unnoticed. Instead, Priya sees how devastated Julie looks, and all the fight seems to go out of her.

"Sorry, Jules," she says, leaning across to give Julie a hug. "I just worry about you. That's all."

"There's no need. Honestly."

"No?" Priya doesn't sound convinced, nor does Julie, and to be frank, neither am I.

"No! It's just…complicated."

"It shouldn't be."

"Huh?"

"Watch." Priya helps herself to another chip from the bowl, then holds it out to me, just out of reach, and though I regard it hungrily I decide not to debase myself by begging. "Just find someone who looks at you the way Doug is looking at this Kettle Chip."

"That *is* how Luke looks at me."

Priya shakes her head. "Doug looks at this chip like he thinks it's the only one in the world for him. It's all he's focused on, the most important thing in his life right now. Luke… He's always going to be thinking about the other bag—no pun intended—he's got at home. And possibly another one in the shop he's got his eye on too."

"That's not true! It's just Luke says it would devastate her if he left *just like that.*"

"But it's devastating *you* all the time he doesn't! Besides, put yourself in her shoes. Would you really want someone who doesn't love you to be hanging around?"

"He does love her. He's just not 'in love' with her."

"I'd argue he's not 'in love' with you either. Especially if he treats you like this."

"He is!"

"How do you know?"

"He tells me. All the time."

"He tells you he's going to leave her all the time too, and that doesn't seem to be happening."

"Yes, well," says Julie, which seems to mean the exact opposite, and also signifies the end of the conversation, given how she's suddenly snatched up the TV remote and is stabbing at the volume button, thus rendering any further discussion impossible.

Priya sighs, and, with a resigned "Here you go, Doug," she feeds me the chip she's been using to demonstrate her point.

I take it gently from her fingers, careful not to make too much of a mess as I crunch it, and as the two of them turn their attention back to the television, I collapse down onto the rug, more than a little troubled by what Priya's said. Because the truth is, like Julie's pointed out, it *is* complicated. Even I can see that. And yet, what Julie *can't* see is that it's in Luke's interest to keep it that way.

Later that night, when I'm having difficulty sleeping, I realize something—however remote the possibility is that Julie and Luke might end up together, the alternative might just be the cat thing. And neither of those options are anything to look forward to.

Then something else occurs to me, something important. I am, in fact, what's known as a rescue dog. My previous owner was very old. Housebound, practically, so what on earth she was doing with me was anyone's guess. Because she was very old, walks consisted of my being let out into a small back "yard," which couldn't have measured much more than that. And as for food—well, perhaps you might not be so quick to judge my current, voracious eating habits if you knew that back then, I had to take my chances whenever I could—something dropped from the stove, or, on the few occasions my human remembered, from a generic bag of value dog food from the local corner shop.

Long story short, one morning, my original human didn't wake up, and it took three days for anyone to notice. You'd have thought *I* killed her, given the home they sent me to after that. But at least I got fed there regularly, was walked a few times a day; had all my basic needs met, until the day Julie and Julie's dad Jim took me somewhere much better. A *real* home. Julie's home.

At the time, it never occurred to me there was a grander life out there than the one I had. I didn't realize the situation I was in wasn't healthy. Had no idea I *needed* to be rescued. A little, I suspect, like Julie feels right now.

And the utterly simple, yet mind-blowing revelation I have about being a "rescue" dog is this.

There's no reason it can't work both ways.

3

Today is something called a Saturday, which is good, because a) Luke never seems to grace us with his presence on either a Saturday or a Sunday, and b) Julie doesn't go to work on a Saturday, which usually means the two of us take a morning walk to the café in the park.

Having said that, the morning's almost over, and Julie's not up yet.

Priya headed home early last night after their little altercation, so Julie finished off the bottle of wine on her own, and then did the same with the second one before stumbling into bed, which I'm suspecting might mean no walk to the café today. Or *anywhere*, if I'm honest.

After half an hour of patiently waiting by her bedroom door, I'm starting to fear Julie might not be getting up *at all*. I'm a pug, so my bladder isn't exactly capacious, and I'm faced with the dilemma of what to do: my options are to scratch on the bottom of the door, bark frantically, or go for a combination of the two. Which—given that I'm too short to use the bathroom—is what I decide to do.

After a minute or so, a bleary-eyed Julie cracks the door open. I'm guessing she hasn't slept too well, given the state of her hair and the pillow lines imprinted across her left cheek.

"Sorry, Doug," she says, as she plods miserably through the kitchen and opens the back door. "You'll have to go in the garden if you're desperate."

I give her another look, and consider going to stand pointedly under where she keeps my leash hanging in the hall. After all, going in the garden means I might not get a proper walk until much later, if at all. But I'm busting, so instead I run out through the doorway, find the nearest bush that looks like it needs watering, and do what I have to, then trot back inside and take up my usual position by my food bowl.

Julie's checking her messages on her phone, and it looks like she's struggling to focus on the screen, so it takes her a while to realize I'm peering expectantly up at her.

"Sorry, Doug," she says again, then she opens the cupboard by the door, retrieves my packet of dog food, and presents it to me, like a sommelier might do with a bottle of wine on *Frasier*. "The usual?"

It's Julie's favorite joke—one she repeats every morning, and something that never fails to bring a smile to her face, though this morning it seems a little forced, so I just wag what passes for my tail and stare at the empty bowl to encourage her to start pouring. In truth, it isn't my preferred brand—Julie only started buying it because it has a picture of a pug on the front, which is weird, because the stuff she eats for breakfast comes out of a box with a picture of a chicken on it.

But then, and annoyingly before Julie can feed me, the doorbell rings, and the way she drops the packet on the kitchen table, rushes down the hall—pausing only to check her reflection in the mirror—then throws the door open, tells me that despite the fact that it's a Saturday, she thinks it might be Luke. But the "Hello, love," I hear from the man standing there evidently isn't coming from the person she really wants it to be from, as Julie replies with a hesitant, "Dad…," then bursts into tears.

I peer up at her, my confusion temporarily overshadowing my hunger. This isn't a common reaction to Julie's dad. Everyone loves Julie's dad. *I* love Julie's dad, in particular, though perhaps I shouldn't, since he's the one who gave me this ridiculous name. Though in his defense, Julie's dad is something called Scottish, and being Scottish means you speak differently to most people round where we live. In particular, Scottish people pronounce the word *dog* like "dug."

Julie's dad takes one look at Julie, then he gives her a hug, and simply says, "Whatshisname?" and Julie sniffs loudly, then shakes her head and hurries into the bathroom.

He gives *me* a look, and I return it in spades. Julie's dad always seems to be able to work out exactly what's going on. He's "on the ball," as he'd probably describe it. Has all his marbles, apparently. This jars a little with what I know about him, I have to say, because I heard Priya tell Sanj a while back that Julie's dad lost Julie's mum a year or so before I came along. Which seems somewhat out of character, given how great Julie's dad is with directions.

"Hey, Doug," he says. "Have you had your breakfast yet?" he adds, crouching down to my level, an action accompanied by a loud, double-kneed pop. Then he spots my dog food on the table just as I telepathically shout, "No!" so he hauls himself upright with the usual accompanying groan, picks up the packet, and shakes a rather generous helping into my bowl.

Fortunately, when Julie emerges from the bathroom, she's still too upset to notice how much I'm eating. Julie's dad gives her another hug, then he says, "I'll put the kettle on," and Julie sniffs again.

"Thanks, Dad," she says, then she sits herself down at the kitchen table while he does as promised.

"Did you want to tell me what happened?"

Julie shakes her head, which I understand means no, though she then proceeds to do the exact opposite.

"Just Priya lecturing me about you-know-who last night."

Julie's dad finds a mug in one of the kitchen cupboards. "And the two of you had an argument?" he says, depositing a tea bag into the mug.

Julie nods. "Yeah. Well, no. Not really. But she...said some things."

"And did they upset you because they weren't true? Or because they were?"

Julie gives her dad a look. "She thinks I'm going to end up like Miss Harris."

"You'll have to refresh my memory, love."

"The woman who lives next door. On her own. Or rather, with her cat."

Julie's dad looks a little confused, perhaps because living with a cat is the *same* as living on your own. "But you're a *dog* person," he says, which reassures me a little, until Julie says, "That's not the point!" and starts crying again.

I'd go over to comfort her, but Julie's dad gets there before me. "Never mind, love," he says. "I'm sure she didn't mean it."

"Then why would she *say* it?" says Julie, between sobs.

"Priya cares about you, is all." The kettle clicks off, so Julie's dad pours boiling water into the mug, and gives the tea the briefest of stirs. "We all do. Don't we, Doug?"

I look up and pause my chewing for a moment. This is one of the things I like about Julie's dad—he always involves me in the conversation. And Julie seems to like it too, because for the first time this morning, her smile appears genuine.

Julie's dad takes his time fishing the tea bag out of Julie's mug, then he deposits it in the bin, and splashes in a drop of milk. "Besides," he says, eventually. "There's nothing wrong with living on your own."

I'm guessing he's meant it as a reference to his own situation, but the way Julie's eyes have widened suggests she's taken it personally.

"You think it too, don't you?"

"Think what, love?" says Julie's dad, though it's clear he knows exactly what "what" is.

"That Priya's right."

"About?" says Julie's dad, in the vain hope Julie might mean something less likely to end in tears.

"About how I'm going to end up as one of those old spinsters, living alone, relying on a cat for company."

"That's never going to happen," says Julie's dad, placing the steaming hot mug of tea down in front of her, even turning the handle round so Julie can pick it up more easily. "A catch like you?"

Julie gives herself a theatrical once-over. "Yeah, sure. I'm a real catch. Like the *measles*."

"You *are*."

"Dad, look at me. I'm thirty-five years old, and my life's going *nowhere*. All my friends are getting on with their lives, and I feel like I'm being left behind."

"You're hardly..."

"I *am*. I've been stuck living in the same place, working in the same job for the past ten years. My last few boyfriends have run a mile the moment I've so much as hinted at making plans for the future." She does her best to blink away a fresh onslaught of tears. "The only reason Doug probably hangs around is because I feed him."

"I'm sure that's not true. Is it, wee man?"

I look up from my bowl, but my mouth's too full of food for me to respond—something Julie seems to take *as* a response, because her lower lip starts to tremble.

"And then I meet someone and fall in love against the odds, despite the circumstances, and—unlike all those emotionally stunted boys I went out with before him—he's someone who actually tells me he feels the same way, but because of those circumstances, since he's so caring, he can't… *We* can't…"

Julie's voice trails off, and she seems to run out of steam, which is possibly just as well given the look of discomfort on Julie's dad's face. "It'll all be fine, love," he says cautiously, like someone entering a booby-trapped house. "Even if things don't work out with whatshisname, Doug would never let you end up like her next door. For one thing, he'd never let a cat in the house."

Too flipping right, I think, as Julie stretches out her foot and massages my back with her toes, not strictly a proper petting, but I'm still grateful for the attention.

"What's he going to do?" she says, miserably. "Find me a boyfriend?"

I freeze. Now *there's* an idea.

"Stranger things have happened," says Julie's dad, and Julie lets out a short laugh, then her smile fades.

"It'll work out with me and Luke," she says, almost to herself. "It has to." She stares into her mug, and swallows hard. "Because if it doesn't…"

"Then you'll meet someone else," says Julie's dad, quickly. "Someone…" He glances down at me, but I pretend I've got an itch in an impossible-to-reach place. I know what's coming, and Julie's not going to like it. "More suitable."

"What do you mean by *that*?"

"Well, not already married to someone else would be a start."

Julie looks like she's about to argue, but instead, she just slumps further down in her seat. "But I might not," she says.

Julie's dad puts his arm around her. "'Course you will, love," he says, giving her a supportive squeeze.

"*You* haven't."

Julie's dad's expression flickers momentarily from its usual, perpetually-sunny one. "I said *more* suitable. Your mother was… Well, she was pretty much perfect. And once you've had perfection…"

"It's been *five years*, Dad. Today, in fact," she adds, with a mournful glance at the calendar on the wall.

"You think I don't know that?"

"That's not what I meant. I just want you to be happy."

"I was happy," says Julie's dad. "For a long time."

"But don't you want someone special in your life?"

"I've *got* someone special," says Julie's dad, giving her another squeeze.

I've nearly finished my bowlful by now, so I can give them both my full attention, but neither of them seem keen to make eye contact back. Julie looks like she's on the verge of crying again, and given how his voice seems to be faltering, her dad's possibly not far behind her.

"Now, are we done crying here?"

Julie nods.

"Good. In that case, drink your tea," he continues, mock-sternly. "Before you set me off."

"Yes, sir!" Julie gives a little salute, then she picks her mug up obediently and takes a sip. "You not having a cup?"

Julie's dad glances up at the kitchen clock on the wall above the back door. "No. Not here, anyway," he says. "Me and young Douglas have an appointment."

"An appointment?"

"That's right." Julie's dad winks at me. "At the café in the park. So why don't you take your tea and go back to bed, and we'll see you when we see you? Sound like a plan?"

"It does. Thanks, Dad." Julie scrapes her chair back, then she stands up and gives him a hug. "Love you," she says, picking up her mug.

"Yes, yes," says Julie's dad, awkwardly, before taking her by the shoulders, swiveling her round so she's facing the door, and setting her off along the hall with a gentle pat on the backside.

He waits until he hears Julie shut the bedroom door, then he smiles, and shakes his head. "You too, love," he whispers.

4

Julie's dad lowers himself into the nearest chair, and lets out the longest sigh, so I pause, midchew, and give him "the eyes," which never fails to elicit an explanation.

"Oh, don't mind me, Doug," he says. "I'm just a bit..." His voice trails off, so I angle my head a little further, and he smiles flatly. "Okay. Well, since you asked..." He nods toward the calendar hanging on the wall by the microwave. "Like Julie said, it's five years since we said goodbye to Jean. That's Julie's mum," he adds. "You never met her. But she was..." Julie's dad swallows loudly.

"Anyway," he continues. "That's why we got you. Julie thought I could do with the company. Funny, really, how it turned out she needed you more than I did. And still does, judging by that Luke idiot she can't seem to shake."

Julie's dad reaches down to scratch my back just in front of my tail—a move that always makes my left hind leg twitch uncontrollably, as if I'm trying to kick-start a motorbike, and something that never fails to put a smile on his face. Except for today.

"She'd have known what to do. Perhaps if she was still around, Julie wouldn't… I mean, sometimes, I just don't know what to do." Julie's dad sighs again and when his gaze returns to me, his eyes are glistening wet. "Not a word of this to Julie!" he says, wagging a finger at me. "She doesn't need to know her old man's a soppy old fool."

Julie's dad hauls himself to his feet, helps himself to a piece of paper towel from the dispenser on the kitchen counter, and blows his nose with such force that the glasses rattle in the cupboard. Then he stands at the sink and stares out of the window, so I pad over to where he's standing, sit down at his feet, and rest a paw on his shin.

Julie's dad snaps out of his daydream. "You done?" he says.

I snort my agreement, then follow him dutifully along the hall, where he collects the set of spare house keys from the hook by the front door, slips them into his pocket, pats the pocket he's just slipped them into to double-check he's got them, and smiles down at me.

"Ready?"

This is almost as funny as Julie's "the usual?" because I'm *always* ready for a walk, as a walk is my second most favorite thing to do, after eating, or maybe my third after eating and riding in the car. And a walk with Julie's dad always means the park, with its smorgasbord of scents, and a chance to mingle with other dogs. All in all, a pretty perfect morning.

Plus, since Julie's dad lost his wife, it gives him something to do every day. A purpose, as I overheard Julie telling Priya once. And we all need a purpose in life—even me. For example, keeping cats out of Julie's garden. Or Luke out of her bedroom.

I big stretch, to the accompaniment of Julie's dad's "Big stretch!", then follow him out through the front door.

"So," says Julie's dad, once we're safely clear of the house, and therefore out of Julie's earshot. "What are we going to do about Julie, then?"

I stare up at him as I walk, pleased to be included, then stick my tongue out, lick my nose, and snort affably, even though I assume the question's rhetorical.

"Trouble is," he says, leading me around the corner. "She'd be better off without that Luke. Though of course, you can't tell her that. You could never tell Julie anything, especially when she was a wee lass. Always needed to find things out for herself, she did. Sometimes the hard way."

I snort again, a little guilty that this is a pretty one-sided conversation, but Julie's dad does live on his own, so I suppose talking to me is better than talking to no one at all. Besides, as I learned from watching sitcoms on the television with Julie, most people already know the solutions to their problems, and it's encouraging them to talk that's the important thing.

"You don't know anyone for her, I suppose?" he continues, as we head in through the park gates and take the path that leads toward the café. "Someone more appropriate? Mind you, that's not asking for much."

I have a think about everyone we know who might be suitable for Julie. There are random strangers, obviously, but maybe I better save them for backup. Which leaves… To be honest, I can't think of anyone, and it's a relief when the café comes into view. As we walk in through the front door, Dot, the café's owner, shouts out her usual, "Morning, handsome!" greeting from behind the counter, and Julie's dad's face turns a different shade. He likes Dot, and Dot likes him, though that seems to be the end of it. Whenever Julie suggests that he asks Dot out, Julie's dad always mumbles something about it being "too early," and while anyone sensible might therefore come back in the afternoon, for some reason that doesn't occur to him.

"Hullo, Dot," he says awkwardly, possibly confused as to whether Dot's "handsome" refers to him or me, then he leads me over to a table by the window. Dot doesn't mind dogs in here—in fact, she actively encourages them. A sensible marketing strategy given the park's clientele.

"The usual?" she calls, ignoring the woman with a walker standing at the counter in front of her.

"Best not. I'm watching my weight."

"What on earth for? You're as fit as a butcher's dog."

Julie's dad does that "face-darkening" thing again, possibly because Dot's just broadcast that last sentence to the whole café, then he reaches down to refasten my leash to my collar and loops it around the table leg, possibly as a diversionary tactic.

"Doctor's orders," he says, a little self-consciously. "I will have a coffee, though. And one of your muffins. For Doug."

"'For Doug.'" Dot's made a pair of midair "bunny ears" with her fingers. "Sure."

She winks at him, and Julie's dad appears not to know where to look, then he catches my eye, and says, "What?" in an embarrassed way, then turns to stare out of the window. But before I can think of a suitably appropriate response, Dot's materialized at our table with a mug of coffee in one hand and a plate bearing a large, delicious-smelling muffin in the other.

"Everything alright?" she says, depositing the two items on the table.

"What? Oh, yes," says Julie's dad.

"Only you seemed to be lost in thought."

"Me?"

"No, I was talking to Doug." Dot winks at me this time. "How's your Julie doing?"

Julie's dad looks up with a start. Dot's no fool, and he knows it, therefore I suspect he also knows there's no fooling her.

"Not so good, actually."

"Boyfriend trouble?"

"You a clairvoyant, or something?"

"I knew you were going to say that," says Dot, and Julie's dad bursts out laughing.

"She's…seeing someone." He pushes out a chair with his foot, and Dot sits down. "But it's…complicated."

"Don't tell me he's married."

Julie's dad stares at her mutely, and when Dot says, "Well?", he smiles and says, "You said not to tell you."

"Ha!" says Dot. "So, he is?"

Julie's dad nods as he peels the wrapper from the muffin. "Apparently so. And even though he keeps promising he'll leave his wife…"

As is *de rigueur* for our visits here, he passes the wrapper down to me, and—deftly anchoring it to the floor with one paw—I begin to lick the crumbs from it. "Between you and me, I fear she's only with him because she's worried she might end up on her own, a lonely old lady, with just a cat for company."

"That's *awful*."

"What is? The fact that she's only with him for that reason, or the chance that she might end up like that?"

"Both!"

Julie's dad picks his mug up and blows across the top. "She needs someone loyal. Faithful. Smart. Someone who's a…" He glances down at me, retrieves the muffin wrapper (which I've licked so clean Dot could probably reuse it), then makes a face as if something's just occurred to him. "Good boy."

Dot nods thoughtfully, then reaches down to pet me. "So you're basically looking for the human equivalent of Doug here?"

"Yup," he says, after a mouthful of coffee that's evidently a little too hot. "Though maybe a bit taller. With a few less wrinkles. And better-smelling breath."

I huff, then lick the remaining muffin crumbs from my nose as Dot and Julie's dad erupt into a fit of giggles.

Dot pauses in her stroking me, and I give her an encouraging tail wag.

"What kind of men does she normally go for?" she says.

"If she was getting that right, we wouldn't be having this conversation." Julie's dad sighs. "Ever since we lost her mum, it's as if she's been scared of change, and now she worries she's stuck in a rut." He throws both hands up helplessly in the air. "Not that you could tell her anything."

"Kids, eh?" says Dot.

"How's your…?"

"Tom?" says Dot. "In the same boat, unfortunately."

"Seeing a married man?"

Dot punches Julie's dad lightly on the shoulder. "Turns out he picked the wrong woman to marry. Not that you could tell *him*."

"Ah," says Julie's dad, as something occurs to me. Tom's Dot's *son*. And by the sound of things, he's not in the healthiest of relationships either.

A plan starts to formulate itself in my brain. Perhaps instead of me doing the rescuing directly, I could engineer things so Tom rescues Julie from Luke, and then Tom and Julie could rescue *each other.*

It's such a great plan that I can't see why Julie's dad and Dot haven't thought of it themselves.

"Like you said. Kids, eh?" says Julie's dad.

It's times like now that I regret not being able to talk, but it's fortunate that I'm a master of unspoken communication. Pointedly, I let out a loud snort, widen my eyes to maximum aperture, and stare up at the two of them, flicking my gaze from one to the other until eventually, Dot gets the message.

"Here's an idea," she says, as if it's hers, although I don't really mind who gets the credit. "Your Julie should meet my Tom."

"D'you think?"

"Why not?" says Dot.

Julie's dad opens his mouth, as if he's already thought of a reason, then—thankfully—he evidently changes his mind. "He's single, is he?"

"He *was* married," says Dot, pointedly. "But his wife… Let's just say she's no longer on the scene."

"Oh. Right. Good. You hear that, Doug?" says Julie's dad, perhaps because I'm still staring up at the two of them, so I snort in an "obviously" way. I hear *everything.*

"He's thirty-two. Drives a Mercedes. Convertible, mind."

Julie's dad makes an "impressed" face. "All his own hair and teeth?"

Dot nods. "And he's nice looking. Not as ruggedly handsome as you, of course."

Julie's dad looks like he's not sure how to react to that. "Sounds promising," he says, after an awkward moment. "And is he local?"

"A little bit *too* local, right now," says Dot, then she smiles. "Seeing as he's just moved back in with his mum."

"Right," says Julie's dad, a little less enthusiastically than before. "And, um, please don't take this the wrong way, but…" He clears his throat awkwardly. "What's wrong with him?"

"What do you mean?"

"He's thirty-two, and still living at home." Julie's dad takes another sip of coffee. "You said it yourself."

"Relax." Dot rolls her eyes. "He's had to sell his flat, so he's moved back home until he can find somewhere else to live. Or so he says. Four weeks and counting..." She grins. "But aside from being a little bruised. Emotionally, I mean..."

"What does he do?"

"Goes for long runs round the park after work, then spends the evening moping around the house, as far as I can tell. Though work-wise..." She glances down at me. "Well, let's just say he's in the medical profession."

Julie's dad sits up a little straighter. "He's a doctor?"

"Sort of."

"Sort of?"

Dot leans down to cover my ears with her hands. "Of animals," she whispers.

"Oh. *Right*," says Julie's dad. "So he's a...?"

"V-E-T," says Dot, and I freeze, suddenly downgrading the brilliance of my plan. I don't like V-E-Ts. Never have. And the thought that Julie might start going out with one is only slightly less horrendous than the idea of her ending up with a cat.

"Kids?"

"No, no kids. But he looks like he needs cheering up, and I'm sure he'd be interested in meeting Julie. And he loves dogs."

Julie's dad looks impressed. "So how do we get the two of them together?"

Dot thinks for a moment. "Well, it's supposed to be a nice evening tomorrow, so I was thinking of having a barbecue. You could come. Just so you have an excuse to bring Julie, obviously." She stands up, and pushes her chair back in. "And

Doug is invited too, of course. Say around six? I'll make sure Tom's there, and..."

She makes a gesture with her hands that I imagine is supposed to symbolize Julie and Tom getting together, and Julie's dad frowns. "And what—they'll bond over their sob stories?"

"Stranger things have happened," says Dot.

As she heads off to serve some other customers who've been waiting impatiently by the till, Julie's dad reaches down to pat me. "What do you think, Doug?" he says.

I hesitate, because Tom *is* a V-E-T, then I remember this isn't about me, so I wag my tail in approval.

"Worth a try, eh? Though I'm not so sure Julie will go for it," he says. "Not while this thing is going on with Luke."

At the sound of his name, I let out a frustrated yap, and Julie's dad widens his eyes. "You don't like him, do you? Luke, I mean."

I yap again, following it up with a low growl, and Julie's dad smiles. "Whereas Tom?"

I angle my head so far to one side I almost topple over, then snort at my own clumsiness, and Julie's dad lets out a chuckle.

"What was that?" says Dot, who's just reappeared at our table.

"Oh, I was just getting Doug's input," he says, and Dot's mouth curls up in a smile, as if there's something funny about the concept.

"And is he in favor?"

"He is."

"Great."

"And as to how we make it happen...?"

Dot mulls this over for a moment. "Julie usually walks Doug here on a Sunday morning, right?"

"Aye."

"In that case, leave that to me."

"Happy to," says Julie's dad, then he runs through a quick summary just to make sure he's got Dot's plan down correctly. "So, barbecue. Your house. Sunday evening. Six."

"Correct," says Dot.

"Address?"

"You can wear what you like!" says Dot, with a grin, then she jots her address down on her notepad, rips off the sheet of paper, and hands it to Julie's dad. "But play dumb when Julie mentions it."

"When *Julie* mentions it?"

Dot taps a finger against the side of her nose, so Julie's dad does a little salute for some reason, before saying, "It's a date." Dot raises her eyebrows, and Julie's dad smiles back at her, a smile which lasts until we're almost back home before it begins to falter. Perhaps because he's suddenly realized it might be a date of the "double" variety.

Quietly, he lets us back into the house, then puts a finger to his lips and makes a *shh* sound just in case Julie's still sleeping off her hangover. He kneels down to my level to unclip my leash, and scratches me under my chin.

"So, fingers crossed for tomorrow night," he says. "Though I wouldn't hold my breath, if I were you."

I think to myself, *fine*, because breathing's tricky for me at the best of times given my compromised nostril layout.

"Oh, and not a word to Julie," he adds, before hauling himself upright again, and slipping back out through the front door.

Silently, I pad into the living room, though I've barely had time to assume my usual position on the sofa when a looking-sorry-for-herself Julie appears in the doorway. I leap back down, skid to a halt on the wooden floor, and rush to meet her, though when even the most enthusiastic of welcomes can't seem to bring more than the briefest of smiles to her face, I realize more than ever that—despite my misgivings—the Luke situation needs fixing, and fast.

And if it takes a V-E-T to fix it, then that's just how it'll have to be.

5

It's Saturday evening, and we're watching reruns of *Frasier* again. Julie's still in last night's pajamas, I'm sitting on her lap, and there's a three-quarters-empty bottle of wine sitting on the table in front of us, when Priya phones. In stark contrast to how she's faced the rest of the day, Julie seems happy to hear from Priya, especially when Priya opens with an apology. Sort of.

"It's only because I care about you," Priya says.

"I know, I know."

"And I want you to be happy. We all do."

"Me too!"

"So we're friends again?"

"We never weren't."

I snort at Julie's poor grammar, then there's a pause, as if Priya's thinking of launching into another anti-Luke diatribe, then she obviously thinks better of it.

"Whatcha doing?"

"Watching TV. With Doug."

"Watching TV?"

"Well, Doug didn't fancy Laser Quest or karaoke, so we..."

"I meant on a *Saturday night*?"

"It's not just any Saturday, is it?"

"Huh?"

"Mum?" says Julie, then she does what she's been doing on and off all day, and lets out a muted sob.

"Oh, *Jules*," Priya says, tenderly. "Want me to come over?"

"No, I'm fine," says Julie, reaching for a tissue from the box on the coffee table and blowing her nose loudly.

"Have you heard from Luke?"

Julie balls the discarded tissue up and adds it to the pile on the table, then helps herself to another one. "Yeah," she says, dabbing at her eyes. "He popped round earlier with a huge bunch of flowers and an engagement ring. Said he'd finally left his wife. Didn't know why it had taken him so long. Practically begged me to say yes."

I peer quizzically up at Julie. Surely I'd have noticed that, seeing as I've been here all afternoon?

"Jules!" Priya laughs down the phone, so loudly that Julie has to move the handset a good six inches away from her ear, and she mouths "sorry" when I wince. "Would you?"

"Would I what?" says Julie, though all three of us know exactly what Priya means.

"Marry Luke. If he asked."

"He's hardly likely to leap out of one marriage and want to get straight into another."

"That wasn't my question."

"Well, he'd have to ask *very* nicely."

"Jules, you can't be serious?"

Julie takes the phone away from her ear again, though this time it's only to frown at it. "That's easy for you to say, P," she says, once she's moved the handset back into position. "You've got a husband."

"So have you. Unfortunately, he's not yours."

"Yes. Well. That's because I'd be all on my own otherwise."

I feel a little hurt at this but decide to let it go. Julie's upset, and evidently going through something of a crisis of confidence.

"Split up with Luke and you won't be for long. Gorgeous example of womanhood that you are."

"Hardly, P. But thanks," says Julie, her voice thick with emotion. "I just... I don't know. It's not like we've had a normal relationship, is it? So how can I possibly tell?" She reaches for her wineglass and gulps the contents down. "But what if...?"

"What?"

"Well, what if this is all I *deserve*...?"

"Hey!" says Priya, though "shouts" would be a better description. "Don't for one minute think this is your fault. Or anything to do with you. Luke's..." She hesitates, as if wary of breaking some sort of unwritten code, then she takes a deep breath. "A cheat. Pure and simple."

"Priya!"

Priya sighs loudly. "All I'm saying is, men who behave like Luke does, they're a type, aren't they? Chances are they've done it before. And..." Priya stops talking, but the implication is clear.

"So you're saying even if he does leave his wife, I'll never be able to trust him, so I'm best out of there?"

"Well, you're kind of putting words into my mouth," says Priya, after a moment. "But they're the *right* words."

On the television, a woman is storming out of a bedroom, and a half-naked Frasier looks like he's about to burst into tears. And he's not the only one.

"But I *love* him, P," sniffs Julie.

"Are you sure?" says Priya. "Or are you just in love with the idea of the life you might have with him if he ever left his wife and stopped being a cheating bastard? Because I'm afraid neither of those things are likely to happen." Priya follows this last observation up with another burst of laughter, a little inappropriately if you ask me, perhaps in an attempt to lighten the mood a bit.

"What if he's the one?" Julie says.

"He is. But like I said, someone else's."

"You can love more than one person, you know?"

"You can," agrees Priya. "But you shouldn't."

"I won't give up on him. On *us*. Not until I *know*." Julie wedges her phone between her ear and her shoulder, takes me by the front legs, and adjusts my position in her lap. "Otherwise, I'm always going to think he's the one who got away..."

"...with it?"

"Not funny, Priya."

Priya thinks for a moment. "You know what you should do?" she says, and I prick my ears up for this. "Play him at his own game."

"Huh?"

"Start seeing someone."

"What?"

"I said, you should..."

"No, I heard you. But, um, why?"

"Well, for starters, if Luke sees you interested in someone else—or more importantly, someone else interested in *you*—it might help him make a decision, if you know what I mean?"

"P..." says Julie, wearily, and it's evidently a tone Priya's heard once too often.

"If you're about to say 'I can't be bothered,' I'm going to come round right now and..."

"I *can't*. It's too much hard work."

"You said the same thing about getting Doug. And look how that's worked out."

"Maybe," admits Julie.

"And worst-case scenario, if Luke's decision doesn't go the way you want, you might actually meet someone you *like*."

The implication is "more than Luke," but to my surprise—though perhaps it shouldn't be because getting me has worked out *splendidly*—Julie seems at least amenable to the idea.

"You think?"

"It's worth a try. And might help you get a little bit of the old Julie back."

"The *old Julie*?"

"The one who was beating them off with a stick, rather than beating herself up all the time."

"Okay, okay," she says, though whether in double-agreement, or just to stop Priya going down that particular conversational dead end, I'm not sure.

"So you should totally keep an eye out for any opportunities," Priya says.

"That's a laugh!" says Julie, in a tone that suggests it isn't. "For one thing, I never meet *anyone*," she adds, miserably.

It takes all my self-control not to let out an excited bark. Because I can do something about that.

6

It's the following morning, and we're just heading out to the park, when a gruff voice from the adjacent garden makes me jump.

"He's been barking at my Santa again!"

Julie stops in her tracks, rolls her eyes at me, then fixes a smile on her face. "Who has?" she says, sweetly.

Miss Harris, our next-door neighbor, glowers at me over the fence. "Who do you think?"

"He's a dog, Mary. Barking at cats is kind of what they do. And the only reason he barks like that is because *your* cat..." She nods at Santa, who's staring smugly at us from where she's being clutched tightly in Miss Harris's arms. "Keeps coming into *our* garden."

"She's a cat," says Miss Harris. "It's... Now, how did you put it? Kind of what they do?"

Julie looks like she's doing her best to ignore both the sarcastic tone *and* smile. "Yes, well, she kind of *keeps* doing it.

And peeing here too. She's killed half my plants. Why can't she go in your garden?"

I snort to myself. What's *actually* killed most of Julie's plants is the fact that Julie forgets to water them, and actually, Santa peeing on them is quite possibly the only liquid refreshment they get.

"That would be disgusting," says Miss Harris, as if that's a reasonable response. "Wouldn't it, Santa?"

She's addressed this last comment to Santa in a pathetic baby voice, proof if it were needed that this immoral feline manipulation works. As Santa mews pathetically back at her, it's all I can do not to launch into a barking frenzy.

"Can't you teach her not to?"

"Yes. Sure," says Miss Harris, sarcastically. "Because you can train cats."

As if on cue, Santa wriggles out from Miss Harris's grasp and vaults agilely onto the fence, so I tense up like a coiled spring, ready to leap to our protection. Julie—perhaps sensing I'm ready to launch a merciless strike—grips tighter onto my leash.

"Anyway," Julie says. "If Doug's barking, at least he's doing it inside my house and not in your garden."

"I can still hear him. Through the wall."

I look up at Julie as innocently as possible, though she doesn't appear to be angry with me.

"I'm surprised. Given how loud you always have your television."

"Do I, dear?" says Miss Harris, as innocently as possible, although the *dear* sounds more like an insult than a term of endearment.

"A little."

"That's only so I can hear it over the sound of barking."

"Even when you go out?"

"I leave it on for Santa," says Miss Harris, defensively. "It's company for her when I'm not there. Isn't it, darling?"

Santa mews again, then, with all the poise of an Olympic gymnast on the beam, begins parading along the top of the fence. I'd bump against the post in an attempt to knock her off if I didn't think she'd just perform some sort of effortless midair flip and land on her feet to spite me, and even if she did land on our side, there's no way I'd be able to catch her. Trust me, I've tried.

Miss Harris attempts to grab her, but instead, Santa just wriggles out of reach and gives her a "how dare you?" stare, and it's about now I hope Julie can see how disobedient, untrustworthy, selfish, and disloyal a cat can be.

"Tell you what," says Julie, and I can tell she's considering giving Santa a less-than-playful shove the moment Miss Harris turns her back. "You keep Santa on your side of the fence, and I'll make sure Doug keeps it down."

Miss Harris frowns. "I told you. That's impossible."

Julie shrugs. "I'm afraid that's the deal," she says, as sweetly as possible. Then, with a "Come on, Doug," we head out through the front gate.

"Well!" huffs Miss Harris, then, with a brusque "Come on, Santa!" she storms back toward her front door.

And I don't need to look around to know Santa's heading in the completely opposite direction.

It's mayhem at the park this morning. Perhaps because it's a sunny Sunday, children are there with footballs, and on those scooter things that their parents always seem to end up carrying. Mothers are pushing oversize four-by-four strollers while chatting distractedly on their cell phones. If you're my size, it's a pretty dangerous environment, and for a moment, I think about feigning exhaustion so Julie has to carry me.

On the plus side, though, this high level of park activity means a number of men are around, which also means that if I can work my magic, Julie's problem will be sorted out by lunchtime, and there'll be no need for her to hook up with a V-E-T.

We do our usual circuit round the perimeter path, me pausing to sniff every few meters, though in reality, it's so I can check out what's on offer. I've already set a few ground rules: No men who are already with women (to avoid a repeat of the Luke situation). No men with other men. And—most important—no men with children. I don't want to be treated like some kind of plaything by a little human.

The trouble is, this narrows the field down to almost zero this morning, and I'm contemplating giving up when I spot a man around Julie's age sitting on a bench a few yards along the path by the pond. What's more, he's actually reading a book, rather than just the more commonplace activity of sitting and staring at his phone.

On the pretext of a particularly interesting scent trail, I lead Julie across to where he's sitting, then stop in front of the bench and peer up at him. He's reading some novel with words on the front that I can't quite make out, possibly because it's "in foreign," as Julie's dad is fond of saying. After about five seconds, he lowers the book, and raises his eyebrows at me.

I snort accordingly, then glance back over my shoulder, expecting Julie to initiate a conversation, when I realize the first flaw in my plan. She's lengthened my extendable leash to its maximum, and is therefore standing about twenty feet away from us, staring at *her* phone. Plaintively, I bark to get her attention, and she looks up distractedly.

"Doug," calls Julie. "Stop bothering that man and come over here."

"He's not bothering me. You're not bothering me, are you?"

says the man—Arthur, according to the scrawl on the side of his coffee cup, though I've been into Starbucks often enough with Julie to know that might not actually be his name—as he reaches down to stroke me. "Are you?" he repeats, in a childish voice.

I forgive him speaking to me as if I'm a human toddler, and snort again, but sadly Julie doesn't take the bait. Instead, she presses the button on the handle that retracts my leash, and attempts to reel *me* in like a fish.

I've got seconds to act, so I wait until the leash's tension's off, then put my front paws onto the bench, and—using it for leverage against the spring of the mechanism—leap up just far enough to nudge Arthur's coffee cup over with my muzzle. Something that guarantees Julie's *full* attention now.

"Doug!" she scolds, hurrying over to us, as Arthur leaps to his feet.

"Hey, no harm done," he says, reaching down and righting his coffee cup to prevent any further spillage.

"I'm so sorry!"

"No need. Doug, you said?"

Julie nods. "My dad," she says, giving me a look as I sit at Arthur's feet.

In truth, I don't normally like to do this with people I don't know, but duty calls, and all that.

"As in your dad came up with it, rather than Doug's actually named after, you know, your…?" Arthur smiles hesitantly. "Well, the name suits him. If only because it rhymes. He is a pug, right?"

"Right," says Julie. So far, she's not looking all that impressed at Arthur's attempts at conversation. "Sorry about your coffee. He doesn't normally do that."

"More of a tea dog, is he?"

It's a good line, but even though Arthur is being particularly charming—and very good about the fact that I've interrupted his day and spilled his coffee—Julie doesn't seem to be responding.

"Mmm," she says, which is difficult to decode, then she reaches into her pocket and pulls out a handful of loose change. "Can I get you another?"

"*Get* me?"

Arthur's frowning, as if he's trying to work out whether Julie means she'll get him one, or whether they'll get one together, but it's clear to me from the way Julie's counting out a few pound coins she's meant "give you the money for" as opposed to any accompanied replacement.

"Don't worry," says Arthur, quickly. "I'd pretty much finished it. And what was left had gone cold."

A bit like the mood here, I think.

I know he's probably said that to spare Julie's feelings, but it's mine that are hurting. My plan had been that she'd have to buy him another, maybe they'd have gone to the café together, where he'd have insisted she join him, they'd get chatting over a couple of Dot's cappuccinos, and… Zing!

But either Julie's too wrapped up in the Luke situation to have remembered Priya's advice on the phone last night, or—and it's probably more likely given her recent mood and yesterday's admission—she can't countenance that someone might find her attractive enough to flirt with her.

"I'm Arthur, by the way," says Arthur, after a silence so awkward it occurs to me to just drag Julie away to put him out of his misery. "And you are…?"

"Sorry Doug spilled your coffee. Aren't we, Doug?"

At the mention of my name, I look up again. Unless I do something, things are going to be over very quickly. I reach a paw up and—checking it isn't too muddy—paw at Arthur's shin. All I'm trying to do is encourage him, but in the face of Julie's standoffishness, I wouldn't blame him for walking away right now, something he seems to be actively considering given the look on his face.

But while I'm feeling sorry for him, I feel even more badly for Julie: I've sat on her lap often enough while she's been watching these staged "reality" programs on television to have a basic idea of what flirting is, and I'd presumed all I had to do to make sure Julie got over Luke was to get her in front of someone else who'd find her attractive. But the other flaw in my plan seems to be that Julie needs to find them attractive too.

Up close, it's easy to see that in terms of human attractiveness, Arthur's no Luke. Judging by the park's clientele, not many people are. And if Tom doesn't turn out to be either, this is going to be a lot harder than I thought.

"Right, well..." Julie retracts my leash to its shortest, and nods curtly at Arthur, who's looking a little mystified, perhaps wondering what he's done wrong. And quite frankly, I don't blame him.

As she pulls me away along the path, I look back over my shoulder, and see a more-than-a-little bewildered-looking Arthur sit back down on a dry part of the bench. As he shrugs, makes a face, and returns to his book, I slow my pace, wondering if it's worth another go. But Julie evidently has other ideas, as she quickens hers.

"What's wrong with you?" she says, as we hurry past the pond.

And I wish I could ask her the exact same question.

We're walking past the café when I hear Dot whistle loudly. She's standing beneath a large sign that reads Park Café, which—although it's possibly not the most original of names—to quote another of Julie's dad's favorite phrases, "it does what it says on the tin."

Suspecting this is part of Dot's grand plan, I change direction smartly, give a little tug on my leash, and guide Julie across to where Dot's waiting.

"Hello, love," she says. "How's it hanging?"

"Oh, you know," says Julie, the slightest notch up from miserably. "You?"

"Lower and lower the older I get, unfortunately." Dot cackles a little, then says, "Listen, love, have you got a moment?"

Julie looks at her like someone who's got a lot more than a moment. "Sure," she says, as cheerfully as she can muster, which admittedly isn't very. "What's up?"

"Well… This is a bit awkward, but…" Dot lowers her voice, even though there's no one within earshot. "You know how I've been trying to get your dad to ask me out for ages, but despite me dropping hint after hint, no joy. So I was thinking… I'm having a little 'do' at my house this evening. A barbecue. Nothing fancy. But if you and Doug wanted to come, perhaps you could bring along…" Dot lets her voice tail off, and looks expectantly at the two of us, waiting for Julie to finish the sentence for her.

"A bottle?"

"I was thinking more along the lines of a certain piece of meat?"

"I'm sorry, Dot, I don't?"

"Prime aged steak. Of sorts," says Dot, then she breaks into a grin. "You know exactly what—or rather, *who*—I mean."

I let out a short bark, then hope Julie assumes it was at the mention of steak. This is a *brilliant* plan. However miserable she might be feeling, I know she's desperate for her dad to bounce back. And by Dot shifting the focus to *his* happiness, Julie can't possibly refuse.

As I wonder whether that's something I can possibly exploit in the future, Julie's eyes widen in understanding. "Sorry, Dot. I'm not with it today. You mean my dad?"

"I do. Do you think he'll come?"

Julie gives Dot's arm an affectionate squeeze. "I'll do my best. You know what he's like, though."

"Thanks, love. Maybe tell him you'd feel awkward coming on your own. That sort of thing."

"Good plan. I'll see what I can do. What time do you want us?"

"Sixish?"

"Address?"

Dot doesn't repeat her "wear what you like" joke. "Church Street," she says instead. "Number seven."

"Okay," says Julie. "And, *apart* from my dad, what can I bring?"

"Just yourselves," says Dot, then she smiles down at me and adds, "and a healthy appetite."

And for a number of reasons, I can't help but snort approvingly.

Julie's dad just happens to conveniently pop over for a visit that afternoon. He has obviously missed his vocation as an actor, because when Julie suggests to him that he accompany her to Dot's barbecue, his reluctance sounds pretty plausible.

"Tonight?"

"That's right."

"Where?"

"Dot's house. Well, strictly speaking, her garden."

"Right. Ha. Yes." Julie's dad sighs melodramatically. "I'm not sure, love."

"Why not?"

"It's pretty short notice."

"And you've got something else planned, have you?"

"Maybe."

"Such as?"

"It's the weekend. I've got loads to do before Monday."

"Such as?"

"Well, *things*."

"You're retired. You can do 'things' any day."

"Yes, but, a *barbecue*..."

"Don't tell me you're a vegetarian all of a sudden?"

"Okay, okay. But..."

"But what?" says Julie, exasperatedly.

"You're sure this isn't some kind of setup?" says Julie's dad, employing a classic case of double bluff, like when I run for a ball Luke's cruelly pretended to throw.

"Dot actually invited *me*," says Julie. "I'm only asking you because I'd feel awkward going on my own—no offense, Doug. Plus you're the one who suggested I needed to get out more, Dad."

"So *you're* going?"

"If that's okay?" says Julie, sarcastically. "Though I promise not to play the chaperone."

Julie's dad mock-glares at her, and then, with all the gravitas of someone agreeing to donate a kidney, he nods. "Okay," he says, winking down at me so Julie can't see. "It's a date."

And I can't help but wag my tail. Because it *is*.

7

Dot's house is a neat, white-painted terrace just off the High Street, with the most aromatic lamppost just outside that on any other day I'd like to spend longer sniffing. We've stopped by and picked Julie's dad up on the way—he went home to take a little rest—and he's dressed up for the occasion, which means he's wearing what are according to him his best shorts. When Julie points out they're his *only* shorts, his retort "doesn't mean they're not my best ones, does it?" makes her roll her eyes.

Julie's wearing a pair of jeans with lots of rips in them as if they're really old, despite the fact she only bought them last week, and that I overheard her tell Priya they were *very* expensive.

Julie's brought a bottle of sparkling wine, which is apparently a level up from the regular variety, and her dad's brought some lager, because "it's a barbecue," a choice Julie's tutted at even though there are six bottles to her one. They're both behaving a little strangely, although they're also doing their best to act normal, possibly because they each think the other one's being set up. And while only one of them is *technically* correct, I'm hoping they'll both get more than just some chargrilled meat from this evening.

We're dead on time (thanks to Julie's dad making us stand round the corner for four minutes so as not to be early), and at almost the precise moment he rings the doorbell, Dot throws the door open. She's got sooty hands, and a smudge of something black on her cheek, but it doesn't stop her embracing Julie, and then—perhaps a little awkwardly—Julie's dad.

"You made it," she says, as if we've just crossed the finish line at the end of a marathon, rather than walked less than half a mile to get here.

"We did!" announces Julie, in the same manner.

"We're not early, are we?" says Julie's dad, which is a little strange, given that he's made sure we aren't.

"Right on time!"

Julie's dad beams, as if he's just been awarded a medal. "Great. We brought..."

"Oh, how sweet." Dot takes the carrier bag he's holding out. "My favorite!"

"You don't know what it is yet."

"It's a bag that contains alcohol. So my favorite!" Dot grins at him, then stands back to let us pass. "Come on through."

We troop inside, Dot stooping to give me a welcome chuck under the chin as I trot by, then she escorts us through the house and out into the back garden, where a tall, relatively-regular-looking-from-the-rear-for-a-human man around Julie's age is dressed in an apron, poking at the barbecue with a long, metal fork.

I must admit, I'm a little nervous—Tom's a V-E-T, after all—but this isn't about me.

"Something smells nice," says Julie's dad.

"Thanks. It's my new aftershave." The man at the barbecue spins round, smiling, and takes the three of us in, perhaps spending a second or two longer on Julie. *"Sauvage,"* he adds, elongating the second syllable, pronouncing it in the proper French way.

I look up at Julie as she unclips my leash, willing her to make some flirty response, to no avail. Perhaps I shouldn't be surprised given her earlier encounter with Arthur in the park. Though on closer inspection, it appears that her lack of response is because she appears to be having trouble speaking.

Dot eyes Julie's dad surreptitiously, as if to say *told you*. Then Tom makes a "duh!" face. "Oh, you meant the barbecue," he says, and Julie lets out a rather over-the-top laugh.

"Julie, Jim, this is Tom. My boy."

I peer intently at Tom, wondering whether he's of the good variety. Despite the friendly welcome, it's a little early to tell, and like I said, he's a V-E-T. Besides, Luke can be charming when it suits him.

"Jim," says Tom, shaking Julie's dad's hand. Then he leans in to kiss Julie hello, though he goes for one of those continental, double-cheek-kiss greetings. Julie's had the same idea, though unfortunately she's turned the opposite side cheek to the one Tom's gone for, which means they end up kissing each other briefly on the lips. And then, embarrassingly, each of them tries to correct their mistake by going for the other cheek, which means they end up doing exactly the same thing again.

"Sorry," says Tom, just as Julie says, "Sorry" too, though neither of them actually *look* sorry.

"No... That's..." Julie's cheeks darken, then she takes a step backward and nearly trips over me. "And by the way, you do. Smell. Nice, I mean."

"Thanks." Now Tom's cheeks are matching hers. "Like I said. It's..."

"Savage," says Julie, in the English way.

"And this is Doug," says Dot, nodding down at me.

"Hey, Doug," Tom says, and I immediately like the fact he doesn't make a silly comment about my name, so as he kneels down to pet me hello, I snort encouragingly, and take the opportunity to study him from close up. True to Dot's description, he appears to have both hair and teeth. I lick his hand, and when he doesn't recoil, take that as a good sign, and go in for another, a bit like Julie's "double-kiss" greeting, though for some reason, Julie seems just as embarrassed by my reaction.

"Doug!" she scolds, but Tom laughs it off.

"No, that's fine," he says. "You know, the reason dogs lick us is because they know we've got bones inside?"

Julie widens her eyes. "Really?"

"Er, not really, no," says Tom, with a grin. "That was a joke. My, um, only one."

"Good one, though," says Julie's dad.

"Bedside manner," says Tom, then he answers Julie's frown with: "I'm a V-E-T."

"Oh," says Julie, tilting her head like I often do. "Impressive."

"Thanks." Tom scratches the back of my head. "He's a healthy-looking chap. What is he? Four?"

"Nearly five," says Julie. "We think."

"Oh. Right. Did you adopt him, or…?"

"What, as opposed to Doug being my biological dog?" says Julie, then she lets out a loud (and somewhat superfluous) peal of laughter to underline the fact that this scientific impossibility is, in fact, a joke. "He's a rescue," she says, somewhat unnecessarily.

Tom raises both eyebrows, and nods in an "impressed" way. "Good for you," he says, leaping nimbly back to his feet, then the four of them stand there awkwardly.

"Can I help you with that?" says Julie's dad, nodding at the barbecue.

"With what?" says Tom, as if he's forgotten all about the delicious meaty smells emanating from the contraption behind him.

"Only you look like you've run out of charcoal."

"Oh. No." Tom clangs his knuckles on the bright orange cylinder underneath the grill. "I've got gas."

"Hence the aftershave," says Julie, fanning her nose with her hand, before letting out another identical peal of laughter.

Tom starts to splutter. "No, I didn't mean…"

"I'm teasing," Julie says, punching him lightly on the shoulder, then her eyes flick awkwardly between her dad and Dot, as if she's suddenly remembered they're here too.

"Can I get anyone a drink?" says Dot, quickly.

"Let me help you," says Julie's dad, but Dot waves him away.

"No need," she says, indicating the garden corner to the right of the kitchen door. A large, inflatable paddling pool full of iced water is there, in which are immersed enough bottles of beer and wine to satisfy the whole street's thirst. "In fact, why don't you all just help yourselves? I spend enough time serving drinks in my day job."

Julie bursts out laughing again—a bit overenthusiastically, perhaps, but that's probably as a result of the weird effect Tom seems to be having on her. Despite Dot's encouragement, no one seems to want to be the first to get themselves a drink. I'm thirsty, so—taking advantage of the fact that Julie's let me off my leash—I trot over and start lapping at the icy water, though I've hardly had any before I hear Julie's plaintive "Doug!" I stop what I'm doing and look round at her with my best "what?" face.

"Don't worry," says Dot, laughing again. "I did say help yourselves."

"So, Tom." Julie's dad chinks his beer bottle against Tom's. "Dot tells me you've just moved back here?"

"Yeah." Tom jerks a thumb over his shoulder toward the house. "Back in my old bedroom. You know, it still has the Chelsea Football Club duvet cover I had when I was fifteen?"

"That's depressing."

"It's only temporary. And I think my mum likes the company, given how she's on her own."

"I meant that you're a Chelsea fan!"

"Ha!" says Tom, which is an improvement over the groans that Julie's dad's attempts at humor usually provoke. "Though it *is* depressing. I haven't slept in a single bed since I don't know how long."

"Single, you say?"

Julie's dad raises both eyebrows and side-eyes his daughter, but if Julie has noticed his less-than-subtle gesture, she doesn't show it.

"That's right. Most parents turn their kids' rooms into something else the minute they move out. Not mine. It's almost as if she knew I'd be coming home." He shakes his head. "Back living with my mum in my thirties. If you look closely, you can probably make out the *L* for *Loser* on my forehead."

Julie's dad peers closely at Tom's forehead before realizing the statement's allegorical, and Tom grins, then he suddenly looks appalled.

"Oh. God. Sorry. Didn't mean to offend. You don't…?" He's addressed this question to Julie and accompanied it with an exaggerated flick of his eyes toward her dad, and Julie lets out an embarrassed laugh.

"What? Me? Live with my dad? No way. Like you said…" She actually makes the *L* sign with her forefinger and thumb and puts it up to her forehead, before perhaps realizing that might appear a little rude. "Though I'm sure you've got a good excuse."

"Right," says Tom.

"So, do you?" Julie smiles encouragingly at him. "Have a good excuse?"

I angle my head up at him, fearing the success of the evening hinges on his answer. Since she first saw Tom, it's almost as if Julie's forgotten that Luke even *exists*—and while I'm no expert, her body language is almost the complete opposite to her encounter with Arthur in the park earlier. Which can only be a good thing.

"Well..." Tom swallows hard. "The *D* word, I'm afraid."

I prick both ears up. I can think of lots of words beginning with *D* that might be appropriate here.

Both Julie and her dad, though, evidently jump to the same conclusion as each other, because they make sympathetic noises.

"What happened?" asks Julie's dad, prompting an embarrassed "Dad!" from Julie.

Tom sighs. "No, that's fine. My, um, wife... Well, she..." He picks the barbecue fork up again, prods viciously at what smells like beef, then forces a smile. "Actually, I'd rather not get into it, if you don't mind? I don't want to depress you."

"Of course," says Julie, giving his arm a supportive rub, then an appreciative squeeze, as if evaluating the physique of a racehorse she's considering betting on.

"Even more than your 'Chelsea' admission has, at least," Julie's dad says, as he puts a hand on Tom's shoulder. "I lost my wife a few years back. So I know what you're going through."

"Right." Tom looks a little awkward, though that could just be down to the physical attention he's getting. "Anyway," he says, as Dot emerges from the house carrying a bowl of something leafy and unappetizing-looking.

"Who fancies a piece of steak?" she says, handing everyone except me a plate.

Tom spears a blackened piece of something from the barbecue and holds it out proudly, as if he's just hunted it down and caught it, then narrows his eyes and gives it the once-over, as if he's trying to work out whether it is, in fact, steak.

When I manage to reluctantly tear my eyes away from it and glance up at Julie, she seems to be peering at Tom in almost the same way.

And I can't help thinking that's a good thing.

Julie and Tom are getting on like a house on fire, a metaphor almost replicated in real life when a stray spark from the barbecue lands on Dot's lawn, causing Tom to leap up athletically and reach for the garden hose as if trying to save the deciding penalty in a World Cup final. There's only been the one slightly awkward moment, when Tom topped Julie's glass up for the umpteenth time, then helped himself to yet another beer, excusing himself by saying he doesn't have to drive home seeing as he lives here. A somewhat tipsy Julie giggled and blurted out, "Yeah, with your *mum*!"

But given how, when she'd made the *L* sign on her own forehead—much to Tom's surprise—then acted as if it were the funniest observation in the world, and he'd joined in, Dot's plan seems to be working.

Tom talks about being a V-E-T, lowering his voice and spelling the word out to her each time—which shows a consideration on his part not to upset me, and though it's a bit insulting to assume I can't spell, both Julie and I appreciate the gesture. We've even had an impromptu game of fetch, courtesy of an old, moldy tennis ball I unearthed behind Dot's shed, which Julie doesn't want to pick up, but Tom has no problems handling. And unlike Luke, when Tom throws my ball, he actually throws it rather than just pretending to, while making a face at me as if *I'm* the stupid one. And Julie's noticing.

Then, just as I think things couldn't be going much better, Tom takes a deep breath, checks that Julie's dad and Dot are out of earshot, and leans across and whispers, "So, is this some kind of setup?"

"Dot told you?" Julie says.

"No, but she told me there'd be loads of other people here this afternoon, hence all this food. And apart from my mum and your dad, there's just the two of us. No offense, Doug," he says, passing me a bit of sausage that I've been eyeing on his plate for the last ten minutes.

"Well, you're right. And from what I can tell, it seems to be going pret-ty well," says Julie.

She's emphasized the two syllables of *pretty* for good measure, and Tom does a double take. "Okay," he says, followed by a nervous "So…" but before he can add anything further, Julie grins, and nods in Dot's direction, where Dot's doing the same, absentminded "touching her hair" thing that Julie does whenever she sees Luke.

"Little bit weird, though, don't you think?"

Tom feeds me another piece of sausage. "What is?"

"Seeing my dad and your mum…" Julie does a sideways nod toward them. "Flirting."

"What?" Tom's eyes follow the direction of her nod, then he does a sort of slow-motion nod of his own. "Right. Aha. Of course."

"Hang on," says Julie, her eyes narrowing, then she shakes her head as if to clear it. "You thought? I mean, this was for…?" She points at Tom's chest, then back toward hers, then back at Tom's.

"No! Well, *yes*, but…" He suddenly seems as interested

in the contents of his plate as I've been for most of the afternoon. "Isn't it?"

Julie glares across the garden at her dad, who suddenly seems fascinated by one of Dot's pot plants. "Tom, I'm flattered, and I'm sorry if I've given you the wrong impression, and you seem very nice and everything." She rests a hand on his arm, letting it linger there for a moment before reluctantly removing it. "*Very* nice, in fact, and perhaps under different circumstances..." Julie hesitates, and I allow myself the briefest hope that she'll realize that circumstances *should* be different, that she has the power to change those circumstances, but it quickly becomes evident that she's not there yet. "But just so we're clear, I'm kind of seeing someone. So..."

"Hey." Tom makes like someone's just pointed a gun at him. "I wasn't... I was just making..." He halts, midsentence, and narrows his eyes. "What do you mean, kind of?"

"Huh?"

"You said you were kind of seeing someone. Which is either an attempt to let me down gently, or..."

"What? Oh. No. I am. It's just complicated."

Julie's said it in a "leave it alone" kind of way, but Tom looks like he won't be put off.

"How so?"

"How so what?"

Tom hands me another bit of sausage. "How is it complicated?"

Julie's eyes flick away from Tom's, and focus on something on the ground instead. "He's married," she says, and all of a sudden, if you'll permit me to carry on my "house on fire" metaphor from earlier, it's as if the fire brigade's just arrived and directed the world's largest hose at the flames.

"Married," says Tom, flatly.

Julie nods, her face a mixture of guilt and disappointment.

"Ah," says Tom. "But separated, right?"

"Nearly."

For a moment, Tom looks at her, his mouth flapping open, then he says, "I'm sorry?"

"Me too," says Julie. "It's only a matter of time, though."

Tom holds a hand up. "No, that wasn't an apology," he says. "Don't tell me—his wife doesn't understand him?"

Julie's eyes widen. "Exactly."

"And they haven't slept together for ages? In fact, they're living like strangers under the same roof?"

"Wow. It's amazing to meet someone who understands…"

"Understands."

"Yes." Julie reaches across and squeezes Tom's hand. "People can be quite judgmental when they hear you're seeing a married man. But with me and Luke…"

"Luke, you say?"

"Yeah. He's my boss, and… What?"

Julie stops talking. Tom's expression has been gradually morphing into something, and she's suddenly realized what it is: Disgust.

"You're having an *affair* with your boss?"

Julie gives a nervous laugh. "Not really. We're more…" She wrinkles her nose as she tries to think of the right word—an expression a lot of people might think was cute. But Tom looks appalled, and as if he's already thought of a word that's appropriate. And one that isn't very nice.

"He's married. He's your boss. You're seeing him. It's an affair. It takes two to have one, therefore you are too. At least, I think that's close to the dictionary definition."

"Hey, I'm not proud of it, but I'm actually the innocent party here."

"Really."

"Yes, really."

Tom sighs, puts his drink down, and folds his arms. "Well, I disagree."

"What? Why?"

"People wouldn't have affairs if there weren't the kind of people around that they could have affairs with."

"The *kind of people*?"

"Here's a thought. Someone who's married to someone else should perhaps be off-limits, at least until they're not married anymore."

"Yes, well, it's not always as simple as that."

"Yes, well, perhaps it should be."

Tom's looking quite angry now, and I worry my supply of sausage is about to be cut off abruptly. "Did you ever think about her?"

"Who?" says Julie, though I suspect she knows exactly who Tom is referring to.

"The *actual* innocent party. Your fancy man's wife."

Julie bristles a bit at the term *fancy man*, though at the same time, she possibly realizes she doesn't have a leg to stand on. "Of course! But Luke and I, we're right for each other, and he and his wife...aren't. And I know it's not ideal, and that some people might disapprove, but..." She stops talking at Tom's rapidly-raised eyebrows. "Besides, it's not like she's a friend of mine or anything. In fact, I've never actually met her."

Tom looks like he wants to say something, then he appears to change his mind. "Well, that makes it alright, then," he says, with more than a hint of sarcasm.

"That's not what I meant!"

"Right," says Tom. "But you're sure she exists?"

"Of course she exists!" Julie sighs exasperatedly. "I'm sorry. Is there a point to this...lecture?"

"Just that he might have made her up. To avoid having to

commit to you. And if he hasn't… All the lies he's been telling you? He's probably lying in exactly the same way to her."

"Rubbish."

"How else does he get away with it?"

"They live separate lives."

"Really?"

"Yes, really!"

"Completely separate?"

"Well, not completely… It's complicated!" says Julie, again, as if repeating the phrase again might make Tom finally understand.

"So where is he now?"

"*Now* now?"

"Yeah. Why isn't he here, with you, at this barbecue? If they live separate lives, then why is he spending the weekend with her?"

"He… Isn't!"

"No?"

"Well, yes, but only because…"

"Exactly!"

Julie harrumphs, and Tom should be gloating, but he looks like gloating's the last thing he wants to do.

"And how long have you two been 'together'?" Tom's done the bunny ears thing around that last word, which evidently makes Julie cross, because her expression darkens.

"None of your business!"

"I'm just trying to establish why he hasn't left her for you." He pauses, like a comedian waiting to deliver the punch line to a joke. "Yet."

"Yes, well, he can't leave her yet, because…" Julie stops talking abruptly. I'm not sure even she knows the answer to that.

"Don't tell me. For the sake of the children."

Tom's given a sarcastic wobble of the head during those last six words, but Julie doesn't notice. Mainly because she's busy staring awkwardly at her feet.

"They, um, don't have any."

"Right," says Tom, in a drawn-out way. "So the *actual* reason he can't leave her is…?"

Julie doesn't say anything.

"Or is it *won't* leave her?"

Julie folds her arms defiantly, and Tom mirrors her, and you don't have to be an expert in body language to understand this isn't a good thing.

"What's it to you, anyway?"

Tom looks at her incredulously. "It's…" He stares at her for a moment, then all the fight seems to go out of him, so instead, he picks up his beer bottle and takes a swig, then realizes it's empty, much to his disappointment. "That thing I said earlier," he says, quietly. "About my wife. And the *D* word. I meant *D* for *divorce*."

"She's not dead?"

"Why ever would you think that?"

"Well, because *dead* begins with…"

"Well, she isn't. Though she is to me."

"I don't under…"

"She had an affair, alright?" says Tom, though it's more of a shout, and Dot and Julie's dad look up from their cozy little tête-à-tête on the other side of the garden.

"Cheated on me with a friend of mine. And I couldn't forgive her, even though she begged me to. My pride just…" Tom stares off into the distance. "So we got divorced. And she was the love of my life. So it broke my heart."

Tom glares at Julie, then he glances down at me, and despite me leaping to my feet and giving him the full, usually irresistibly cute, pug eye treatment, he doesn't calm down.

Instead, he hauls himself to his feet, and stalks off to retrieve another beer from the paddling pool.

"Tom!" Julie jumps up too and hurries after him, but he doesn't turn around. "I'm sorry. I had no idea. But Luke and I…"

"Please don't try to justify what you're doing. Because you really can't. Not to me, anyway. And I'm sorry, and I know you probably don't want to hear this, but all this stuff he's telling you…"

"You don't know him," says Julie, quietly.

"And nor do you. Not really." Tom hunts around for a bottle opener, before realizing his beer's one of those screw-top ones. "You're best out of that situation, if you ask me."

"Well, I didn't!"

"Do you really think he's going to break up his marriage for…"

"*Your* wife did!"

Julie immediately goes pale, as if she knows she's majorly overstepped the mark, and Tom stares at her, openmouthed, for a moment or two.

"Right," he says, as Julie stares at her feet again, perhaps hoping the ground will open up and swallow her.

To his credit, Tom just forces a smile. Then he peers round the garden before rolling his eyes and tutting loudly, like someone looking for his jacket then remembering he didn't bring one. "That's my cue to leave, but I live here, so…"

Julie stares at him for a moment, and I'm hoping she's about to apologize or say something to lighten the mood, but she just purses her lips defiantly.

"Well, Tom, I'd like to say it was nice meeting you…"

I sit between them, waiting for Julie to do exactly that, but instead, she glances over to where her dad and Dot are doing a bad job of not listening in, and without a word to anyone, she scoops me up, carries me back through the house and out the door, then strides home so quickly that I can hardly keep up.

Maybe Tom's words have hit home. Perhaps Julie's in a rush so she can get back to our house, call Luke up, end things, and embark on a whole new relationship with someone who's, well, *not* Luke. Though it's only after she's raced into the house, slammed the front door behind us, collapsed face-first onto the sofa, and burst into tears, that I realize it's possibly not as straightforward as that.

It's apparent from both the introduction I arranged for her in the park and from what she just told Tom that—despite Priya's suggestion—Julie's actually *not* looking to meet someone else. Plus Tom is obviously bitter about what his ex-wife did to him, and it sounds like he's not sure he'll ever trust a woman again. So perhaps right now—especially while Luke and Julie are still together—isn't the best time for Tom and Julie to gel.

Trouble is, Julie's (admittedly rather cruel) comment might be something she's holding onto like a life vest, in that if Tom's wife left someone as patently nice as him, then there's a definite chance Luke will leave his wife for her. Which would be a shame, though, because at the back of my mind, I can't help thinking that Tom gets a great big tick for the following reasons:

Firstly, people always say you can tell a lot about someone by the way they treat animals, and Tom's made a profession out of it. If that's not a glowing recommendation, I don't know what is. Whereas Luke doesn't even seem to like *me*, even though *everyone else* likes me. Except Miss Harris.

Secondly, Tom has a Good Job, as Julie's dad would describe it. Being a V-E-T takes years of training, and you have to be clever. This means Tom also has money, probably, and a lot of it (I know this because whenever Julie takes me to the V-E-T, she always complains that it costs her a fortune. If they were together, it wouldn't). Whereas on the odd occasion Luke's been at our house and Julie's ordered takeout, he always seems to have forgotten his wallet.

Thirdly, Tom is slightly younger than Julie. Human females tend to live longer than human males. So if Tom and Julie get together, with any luck, they'll die at roughly the same time, which is a good thing, because neither of them would be lonely (and of course because Julie won't have to get a cat).

Fourthly, and despite his job, I like Tom. Julie's dad seemed to like Tom. Whereas I've only ever met one person who seems to like Luke, and that's Julie. Though I still can't figure out why.

Fifthly, at least, up until the "affair" affair, Tom seemed to like Julie. *Really* like Julie. Maybe not as much as I do, but still. Luke, on the other hand, doesn't seem to like her very much at all—if he did, he surely wouldn't treat her as badly as he does. And I may be mistaken, but Julie seemed to like Tom too.

Finally, but perhaps most important, Tom is single and available. And after what he pointed out today, I'm even more sure Luke's only pretending to be.

8

The following week's pretty uneventful in terms of Luke Incidents (zero, apparently because he's away on a work thing, according to what Julie tells Priya on Friday night). There are also no Tom Encounters, though that's perhaps not surprising given how the last one ended. Twice I spot Santa parading through our garden as if she owns the place, and the second time, as she's in clear breach of the deal Julie negotiated with Miss Harris the other day, I decide I'm well within my rights to bark frantically at her from my vantage point on the windowsill.

By Sunday lunchtime, and after a late start thanks to Julie "self-medicating" the previous evening with a couple of bottles of Chardonnay and a film about someone called Bridget Jones (which was supposed to be a comedy, but for some reason had Julie in tears on more than one occasion), we're standing outside a shop called Boots on the High Street. I'm doing my best not to get run over by strollers that to me seem the size of trucks, or assaulted by sticky-fingered, snotty-nosed toddlers when a familiar but unwelcome scent makes my nostrils flare.

It takes me just a moment to locate the source of the scent, and it's coming from a little further along the High Street. Sure enough, when I narrow my eyes and peer through the legs of the other shoppers, I spy Luke making his way toward us along the pavement. What's worse is, he's not alone. There's a woman with him—about Julie's height, and with the biggest stomach I've ever seen, carrying a couple of bags with JoJo Maman Bébé printed on them—so I glance anxiously up at Julie, because you don't need to be a bloodhound to work out that the woman with Luke is probably Luke's *wife*.

Going on what she told Tom the other day, Julie's never met Luke's wife, and from what she's said to Priya previously, she's never wanted to. While I can understand why, it suddenly occurs to me that this might be the perfect opportunity to drive a big enough wedge between Julie and Luke to enable Tom to squeeze in through the gap. All I have to do is steer Julie toward them.

Luke's glued to his phone, and evidently he hasn't seen us, so I start tugging Julie away from the window.

"Doug!" she says, giving my leash a light yank.

I try again, this time adding an insistent whine for effect, though it doesn't seem to make any difference.

"What's the matter?" she says, though I can tell by the way her brow is furrowed, she's not far from adding "with you" to the end of that sentence.

Anxiously, I peer along the pavement. I've lost sight of Luke and his wife among the melee of shoppers, but his scent is increasing, so I do the same with my tugging, hoping Julie will think I'm desperate to go to the toilet. After a second or two, my plan works, and Julie begins walking obliviously toward them. I trot ahead of her, and all of a sudden Julie freezes, and I'm jerked to an unceremonious stop.

"What the f…!" she says, under her breath, followed by a louder, "You have got to be *kidding*!" presumably as she registers the size of Luke's wife's stomach and the associated purchases. Then she scoops me up off the pavement so quickly it makes me feel a little light-headed.

To my surprise and delight, she begins marching purposefully toward Luke and his wife, as if she's planning on confronting him. Though when they're almost upon us, she evidently loses her nerve, because she spins ninety degrees and carries me into the nearest shop, taking up a position next to the window where she can stare out at the pavement without us being spotted. Then, a loud throat clearing is followed by an indignant "Excuse me!" from behind us. Which perhaps not surprisingly, makes us both jump.

It's evidently not Luke, and the voice is a little too old-sounding to be Luke's wife. Even so, at the sternly-uttered words, Julie swivels nervously round, to find an older, haughty-looking woman staring pointedly in my direction, as if she expects *me* to say something in response.

"Hi?" says Julie, phrasing the greeting as a question.

The woman's gaze momentarily alights on Julie, then returns to linger on me. "Didn't you see the sign on the door?"

Julie narrows her eyes. I'm not sure she even knows what shop she's walked into, such was her hurry to get off the pavement. "What sign?" she says, and the woman does a pretty good impression of one of my indignant snorts.

"The one that says, No Dogs."

"Oh. Right." Julie glances nervously back at the door, then out the window, evidently worried Luke and his wife must be nearly here by now.

"No. Sorry. Obviously. Otherwise I wouldn't have…" Her

voice trails off, and she half presents me to make her point, but the woman doesn't respond. Instead, she just folds her arms and increases the intensity of her glare, and Julie grins guiltily. "Even though I'm carrying him?"

"*Especially* because you're carrying him. What if he starts chewing the merchandise?"

I snort derisively. Even I have my standards.

"Doug wouldn't do that. He's very well beha—"

"Doug?" The woman looks at me again and shakes her head, and I'm beginning to suspect she's probably got a cat at home. If not a couple of them.

"Did you want me to..." Julie nods at me, and then at the window, just in time to see Luke and his wife draw level, so she hurriedly ducks down behind a rail of suits. When she eventually stands up, the woman is still there, and still wearing the same stern expression.

"Sorry, I..." Julie takes a deep breath, and then another, in an attempt to calm herself down. "I'm hiding from someone."

The woman smiles, though it's hardly sympathetically. "Well, while they're still counting to a hundred, why don't I show you something?"

"What?"

"The way out."

The woman strides purposefully toward the door and hauls it open, then stands there, leaving us in no doubt we're supposed to walk through it.

"No, you don't understand. I..." Julie hesitates, as the expression on the woman's face suggests she doesn't want to understand. Or care.

Reluctantly, Julie carries me back outside, peers nervously along the pavement in the direction Luke and his wife have headed, then breathes an audible sigh of relief, which I'm happy to mimic. After all, my plan has worked to an extent.

Julie's seen Luke with his wife, and the fact that his wife is pregnant is bound to have given her pause for thought.

But Julie doesn't pause at all. While the normal course of action would be to head off the opposite way, I feel my leash tugged sharply as she sets off in pursuit, and we begin tailing the two of them along the High Street.

Luke's wife is walking slowly on account of how round she is, so it's easy to keep pace with them, even with my short legs. After a few minutes, Luke and Luke's wife pause briefly, then after a quick discussion, they head down the narrow lane that leads toward the river. Julie hesitates too—perhaps because it'll be hard to follow them unnoticed down there. Then she looks down at me as if for reassurance, and we set off after them.

Switching to "stealth" mode, I ignore the ducks and pigeons who normally congregate on the riverbank, while doing my best to tone down the loud snort-panting that's my *modus operandi* when out on a walk. Soon we're a mere few meters behind them, although it's not me but Julie who nearly gives us away, when her phone suddenly rings.

We duck behind the nearest tree, and Julie stabs the answer button and whispers a frantic "Hello?" Luke has had his phone glued to his ear since we first saw him, and I'm worried it might be him calling. But instead, and to both of our reliefs, it's Priya.

"Whatcha up to, Jules?"

"Just…shopping. In town."

"Cool! Me too," says Priya. "I'll ditch Sanj and come and meet you. Where…"

"No!" says Julie, a little too quickly. "I'm with Doug, and…"

"What's that got to do with it?"

"And… Well… Luke."

There's a pause, and then: "You're with *Luke*? In public? And on the *weekend*?"

"Sort of."

I frown up at Julie. "With" would suggest a distance of considerably less than the twenty or so yards currently separating us. Not to mention our hiding behind a tree.

"Jules..."

"We're kind of following him. Them."

There's a pause, and then: *"Them?"*

"Yeah. He's out with his wife, so..."

"His *wife*?"

"That's right," says Julie, a little hysterically. "His *pregnant* wife."

There's another, longer pause, and then: "Say that again?"

"His pregnant wife," says Julie, softly, and I hear Priya swallow hard down the other end of the phone line.

"Oh, Jules. I'm so sorry," says Priya sympathetically, followed by an urgent, "Stay where you are. I'm coming to get you *right now*."

"No, that's fine. I'm just going to..." Julie's voice trails off, possibly because she's not sure what our next steps are.

"Don't do anything silly," warns Priya, though in a way that suggests that ship has already sailed.

"I just want to see them together. How they are with each other. That's all," Julie says.

Priya suddenly adopts a serious tone. "Jules, listen to me *very carefully*," she says. "This is not a good idea, and..."

Julie makes a funny *hcarr* noise. "Sorry, Priya, my reception isn't so good, and I can't quite..." She does the *hcarr* thing again, ends the call, then gives me a mischievous glance as she switches her phone to silent.

"Come on, Doug!" she says, and I'm only too keen to

oblige; if this helps Julie see what Luke's really like, then Priya's wrong—this *is* a good idea.

We duck behind another tree as they make for the pub on the riverside, and after a moment, Julie checks how she looks in her "selfie" camera, flattens down a stray hair or two, takes a deep breath, and we follow the two of them inside.

From the safety of behind a pillar, Julie peers around the pub's interior, then heads for the far end of the bar. Luke and Luke's wife have already gotten drinks, and are heading toward a table by the window, so Julie quickly gets herself what looks like a goldfish-bowl-sized glass of white wine, and picks up one of the pub's huge laminated menus. Then we take up position at a table directly behind Luke at the opposite end of the room, which is ideally placed so Julie can check out Luke's wife without him seeing her.

I peer up at Julie, who's studying the two of them with the same intensity David Attenborough demonstrates on *The Blue Planet*, though I can't yet work out what she's hoping to achieve by being here unnoticed. Maybe Julie doesn't have a plan: she might simply finish her drink and leave, file the information away, reflect on it, leaving Luke none the wiser until she decides to confront him with it at a later date.

What *I* want to achieve, however, is some sort of confrontation, and luckily, hanging on the wall behind where Luke's wife is sitting is a large, vintage mirror, angled slightly downward, and in which Luke keeps checking out his own reflection.

Careful that Julie doesn't spot what I'm doing, I inch sideways, until I'm right in his reflected line of sight. Which means it's not long before he spots me giving him "the evils" from my position under Julie's table.

Luke does a double take, then shakes his head briefly, perhaps having just decided there must be a lot of pugs in the world and that they all look the same. Then, as he takes a sip of his lager, he swivels round in his chair, as if casually checking out whether the bar's busy, and his eyes track along the length of my leash until he catches Julie peering at him from behind her menu. As he splutters noisily into his beer, nearly choking on it, Luke's wife looks up from where she's been scrutinizing the menu and frowns at him.

"You okay, hon?"

It takes him a moment to stop coughing, then he nods. "Sure. Just went down the wrong way."

"Right." She smiles sweetly, reaches across the table, and briefly squeezes his hand, leaving me in no doubt things aren't anywhere nearly as bad as Luke tells Julie they are.

As Luke's wife turns her attention back to the menu, Luke uses the cover of another coughing fit to shift his chair to where he can stare at Julie and me in the mirror, evidently trying to figure out what's going on. It's possible, I can almost see him thinking, that we're just in here at random: it's a small town, after all, and if you've been out shopping then here's as good a place as any to have a restorative drink. But whatever the reason is that's brought us to the same pub at the same time, Luke doesn't seem that happy about it, and what's more, he looks like he doesn't have the faintest idea what to do now, except to perhaps try to wait it out.

Eventually, Luke's wife puts her menu down, then hauls herself inelegantly to her feet, a pained expression on her face. Luke hurriedly drains the rest of his pint and stands up too, but she frowns.

"I'm only going to the toilet," she says, so he sits back down again, his expression like someone who's just missed out on the opportunity of a lifetime.

As Luke's wife nears our table, Julie does her best to avoid eye contact, but I do the opposite, and, in fact, give her the full head-tilt, tail-wag treatment. Unsurprisingly, it works because she bends awkwardly over to take the paw I'm offering, then angles her smile up at Julie, like mothers do when they see another woman with a cute baby. I imagine the polite response would be for Julie to smile back, perhaps invite her to pet me, then nod at Luke's wife's stomach and ask something like, "when are you due?" or maybe even "who's the father?" but she's evidently too scared to do anything but stare into her glass.

After a moment, Luke's wife shrugs, gives me one last smile, then resumes her journey toward the Ladies'. Luke's still watching in the mirror, holding his breath until he's sure his wife's passed us without incident, then—as soon as she's squeezed herself through the door that leads to the toilets, and is therefore safely out of earshot—he leaps out of his chair and marches angrily across the pub.

"What are you playing at, for God's sake?" he hisses to Julie, trying to make himself heard above the sound of my growling.

"I'm not playing at anything," she says sweetly, although her hand on my leash is trembling. "I was just out walking Doug and fancied a drink. I didn't know you'd be in here with..." She narrows her eyes. "Who *is* that?"

"You know very well who it is." Luke's gone pale, as if he's just realized he might be in a bit of trouble. "Listen, we'll talk about this another time, I promise, but right now, I'm begging you, please leave."

Julie indicates her glass. "I haven't finished my drink yet."

Luke frowns down at the table, and for a moment, I think he's considering picking Julie's wine up and downing it himself. "Right, well..." He reaches into his pocket and retrieves his wallet. "How about if I pay for it?"

Julie smiles innocently, then picks her drink up and takes the smallest of sips, leaving Luke in no doubt that he'll be paying, one way or another. "You're alright," she says, although he plainly isn't.

"Julie, *please*." Luke glances anxiously toward the toilet door. "Sarah's *pregnant*..."

"Really," says Julie, her voice heavy with sarcasm. Even so, Luke pales, as if he's just given away some vital piece of information.

"Yes, and I can explain the..." He mimes having a fat stomach, then glances at the toilet door again, grimacing at the sound of the hand dryer starting up. "Just not right now."

I find myself hoping Julie's enjoying his discomfort, but for some reason, judging by her expression, I suspect not—perhaps because she's realized Priya's been right all along, and that Luke *is* a liar. And if he's lied about his home life...

"Darling?"

Luke freezes.

Sarah has emerged from the toilet, and is waddling over to join us, so Julie leaps out of her seat as if she's the one who's been caught doing something wrong.

"Finished?" he says to his wife, somewhat inappropriately, and the four of us stand there awkwardly until Luke realizes he's supposed to explain why he's talking to us. "Oh. Sorry. Sarah, this is Julie. Julie works for me. At, you know, the office."

As I snort in derision at his nervous, overly-elaborate explanation, Sarah smiles. "Nice to meet you, Julie," she says. "Luke's told me all about you."

"He has?" says Julie. Frantically, her eyes flick across to Luke, in an I-doubt-it kind of way.

"In that you're invaluable to him. A key member of the team."

"Oh. Right."

"And what is it you do for him?"

Julie almost drops the glass she seems to have forgotten she's holding, though it appears she's temporarily forgotten her occupation, as well. "I, um..."

"Julie's our events organizer. She, um..." Luke looks like his mind's gone blank too. "Julie?"

Julie clears her throat nervously. "Well, I organize, you know..."

"Events?" suggests Sarah.

"That's right," says Luke, as if Sarah's just come up with the answer to a particularly tricky question on *University Challenge*. Sarah smiles again, then Julie opens her mouth and closes it, so I do a half bark from the floor, seeing as no one has introduced me yet.

"And who's this?" Sarah says, beaming down at me.

Julie seems to be waiting for Luke to do the introductions, though he's probably decided it might not be smart to admit he knows my name. "Yes, who is this cute little fella?" he says, kneeling down to pet me, but when I growl just for his benefit, he gets up again quickly. "I didn't know you had a... French Bulldog, is it?"

I growl again, mainly at Luke's bad acting, and Julie gives me a reproachful look. "Pug, actually. This is Doug," she says.

"He's gorgeous," says Sarah, and I wag my tail to acknowledge the compliment.

"Don't let him hear you say that, or he'll get a big head," says Julie, and Luke lets out a short laugh.

"Bigger than it is already?" Luke lets out another laugh, then stops abruptly when he sees Julie and Sarah scowling at him. "I meant in proportion to his body. You know. On account of him being a..." Luke swallows so hard we can all hear it. "Pug?"

Sarah rolls her eyes at him. "Ignore Luke," she says. "He's never been an animal lover." She nudges her husband affectionately, and Luke's cheeks darken, and, embarrassingly, so do Julie's.

"So..." says Luke, in that way that suggests it's the start of a sentence, but it really means the end of a conversation. Sarah, though, doesn't seem to be on the same wavelength.

"We were going to order some lunch." She jerks a thumb back over her shoulder toward their table. "Did you want to join us?"

Luke's turned ashen again, and for a moment, Julie seems to be considering Sarah's offer—after all, how better to get a window on their relationship? "No. Thank you," she says, after a moment. "I ought to get... I mean, Doug and I... We should be..."

"I get it." Sarah purses her lips. "Seeing your boss, eh?"

"What?"

"Outside the office. When it's bad enough seeing him when you're *at* work..."

"Oh. Right. Yes. That's it!" Julie laughs, a little too loudly, and Sarah joins in, though Luke appears not to be finding any of this funny, and, in fact, is looking like he's wishing the ground would open and swallow him up. "Anyway, like I said, we've got to..." She grabs my leash and starts pulling me toward the door. "Nice to meet you, Sarah, I'll just..."

"But you haven't finished your drink?" says Sarah, confused.

Julie looks down at her glass, which is still about three-quarters full, then, as if making some momentous decision, she takes a step back toward the table, picks it up, and downs the contents in one go. "There," she says stifling a burp. "Anyway, Luke, I'll see you tomorrow..."

"At work," says Luke, a little too quickly.

"Yeah," says Julie, to no one in particular, then she turns around a little unsteadily, waves her free hand vaguely in the air, and drags me unceremoniously out of the pub.

She doesn't say much on the way home, evidently emotional, and while at first I think it's just because she's drunk most of her wine in one gulp, it's obvious meeting Sarah has been too much for her. As has the proof that Luke is plainly a liar, *and* is clearly "with" his wife—though at least now Julie should know she's not going to end up with him, *and* be glad of the fact.

What's confusing to me is that Sarah seems lovely, so I'm perplexed as to why Luke would be cheating on her?

Then again, it's also a mystery why Sarah's with Luke in the first place. Something she and Julie have, ironically, in common.

9

I'm sitting on the carpet the following morning, basking in a patch of sunlight streaming in through the front room window, when Julie marches into the room. "Come on, Doug," she announces, though not with a great deal of enthusiasm.

Automatically, obediently, I get to my feet, big stretch for as long as it takes Julie to comment on it, trot toward her, then freeze. Julie's dressed for work, and normally I'd be waiting for Julie's dad to walk me, so something doesn't quite add up.

"Doug?" she says, again, so I indicate *Come on where?* with a twenty-degree clockwise tilt of my head.

"Have you forgotten? It's take your pet to work day," she explains, grabbing her keys from the table, and even though my initial reaction is to snort derisively, it quickly strikes me as an excellent idea, as several of Julie's coworkers are bound to be men. And though I've heard Priya suggest that office romances are never a good idea, she might have been specifically referring to the one Julie's having with her boss. Let's face it, *any* romance, even a different office one, is a better idea than going out with Luke. So, all I have to do is check out any eligible men there, work that old "pug magic," set the two of them up, and voilà!

With an excited yap, I follow her out to the car, then clamber in and hop up onto the passenger seat. As Julie fastens my restraint, I can't help but pant happily.

Today's going to be a good day. I can already feel it.

When we arrive at Julie's office, something a little weird happens. Julie picks me up, carries me in through the sliding doors, then carts me through a big room toward a large desk at the far end, behind which a man and a woman are sitting wearing headsets that look a bit like the one Frasier sometimes wears when he's "listening." Before I can figure out what they're doing there, she carries me down a short hallway to another set of doors that slide open with a *ping* when she presses a button. We then step forward into a small metal-walled room and the doors rumble shut behind us.

The room shakes, and I get a weird feeling in my stomach, but it's nothing compared to how I'm thrown a moment or two later when the doors slide back open to reveal that in the few seconds we've been in there, someone's changed *the whole space outside* the doors into something different. I'm disoriented, and don't want to move from the spot on the carpet where Julie's just set me down.

Suddenly a large figure looms over me. "Who's this gorgeous chap?"

A woman much older-looking than Julie, who smells of cigarettes, and has a raspy voice that makes Julie's dad sound effeminate, squats down in front of me. In truth, she's a bit scary, and on top of how confused I'm feeling after my *changing rooms* experience, it's all I can do not to run and hide behind Julie's legs.

"This is Doug," says Julie.

I just about manage to stand my ground as the woman extends a hand to me. Normally, this would be my cue to offer her a paw, but I'm still a little discombobulated.

"Hello, Doug," says the woman, patting me on the head. "You're a cute one, aren't you? Aren't you? *Aren't you?*"

I just stare back at her, until I hear Julie chuckle behind me. "Sorry," she says, on my behalf. "I think he's just reeling a bit from his first time in an elevator."

I glance back at the sliding doors as they *ping* shut behind me, and realize I've been stupid. I know what an elevator is—Frasier uses one all the time, and if it's alright with Eddie then it's fine by me.

Julie leads me over to her desk, stopping along the way to say hello to some of her colleagues. I suspect she really just wants the chance to show me off, as I get fussed over at least half a dozen times. Perhaps that's not surprising given the lack of competition.

I'd been expecting her office to resemble the waiting room at the V-E-T's, but it appears not that many people have gone along with today's pet directive. And while I'm relieved to see there aren't, in fact, any cats here, Vinay from accounts has brought his bearded dragon, which he assures Julie isn't an *actual* dragon like on *Game of Thrones*. Tessa in HR has brought in her goldfish, swimming in a half-full plastic water bottle, which she's placed on the corner of her desk, from where the creature is currently eyeballing me suspiciously. Though not as suspiciously as Luke, who's just appeared at Julie's shoulder.

He clears his throat, and she stiffens, just as my hackles begin to rise. Then, following an overly-loud and excessively-formal, "Morning, Julie!"—probably for the benefit of anyone in the office who might have their suspicions—he bends down and pretends to be interested in the spreadsheet on Julie's computer.

"Lucas," she says, her voice formal and surprisingly even, given how her heart's audibly racing.

"Funny bumping into you in that pub yesterday," he says, quietly.

"Yes, wasn't it?" Julie keeps her eyes fixed on her screen. "Really funny. Hilarious, in fact. Doug and I were chortling to ourselves the whole way home."

"Alright. No need to go over the top."

Julie freezes. "Over the top?" she says through gritted teeth, then she swivels her head round and fixes him with a glare. "If you want to see over the top, I can do over the top."

"Okay, okay. Calm down." Luke looks around nervously. "Listen, are we still on for tonight?"

"Tonight?"

"It's Monday." Luke taps the standalone calendar on Julie's desk. It's one of those ones with a new inspirational saying every day, with today's being *You only regret the things you don't do.* Though right now, I wouldn't bet that Julie feels that same way.

"I'm fully aware what day it is, thank you very much."

"But Monday's our night. Our *regular* night," he says, almost under his breath.

Julie narrows her eyes and types some alphabetical letters into the top row of one of her spreadsheets. While it's a little hard to make out from where I'm sitting on the floor, they seem to spell out the word JERK in capital letters.

"It is. Or rather it *was.* Right up to when I saw your wife and discovered she's *pregnant*!"

For a moment, Luke looks like he's considering denying it, which would be a new low, and a particularly despicable one, even for him. "Right, yes, well, I can explain that," he says, with the look of a man who'd actually rather not. Especially right now.

"Go on then."

"I will. Tonight."

"You will now. Or there won't be a tonight. Or any other night."

I'm impressed with Julie's firm tone, until I see how tightly she's gripping the edge of her desk, and realize she's trying hard to stop herself from crying.

"Okay, okay. She's pregnant. You're right."

Julie doesn't say anything, but just looks up at him, and Luke swallows audibly.

"But I'm not even… *If you could get me those figures by lunchtime that'd be…* Sure it's mine."

Luke has whispered-shouted-whispered that last sentence, though it takes both me and Julie a moment to realize it's been for the benefit of Tessa, who's just passed by on her way to the watercooler.

"What do you mean?" asks Julie.

"Just that Sarah…" Luke peers at the screen again for just long enough for Tessa to get back to her desk. "I think she's been seeing someone."

"What?" For a millisecond, Julie looks like she wants to console him, and I snort in disbelief. Then she evidently realizes something, as her face darkens. "Hang on. You said you're not sure it's yours."

"Yeah. On account of…what I just said."

"Right." Julie sits back from her screen and turns to face him. "But 'not sure' suggests it could be."

"Yeah, well, I've got no proof, you know? Just a suspicion that she…"

"Back up a sec. You're missing my point. She's pregnant, you're not sure it's yours because she might be sleeping with someone else. But the fact there's a chance it might be means that despite everything you've told me, you've been sleeping with her too."

Luke looks at Julie for a moment, and whatever color he is normally drains from his face. For a longer moment, I think it's surely game over. Then—and on one level you have to admire this—he nods, and says, "Of course I've been sleeping with her. Or at least, going through the motions."

"I'm sorry. I don't..."

"This is what I wanted to explain to you. Tonight." He shakes his head, as if Julie's done something wrong by confronting him here and now. "Sarah and I are supposed to be married, Julie. I can't not sleep with her, can I?"

Julie stares at him, any pretend interest in her spreadsheet long gone. "I'm sorry," she says, eventually. "I *still* don't..."

Luke does that furtive looking-left, looking-right-with-narrowed-eyes thing, then, under the pretext of pointing out something on Julie's screen, he leans in a little closer.

"I'm going to leave her for you, right? I just can't yet. Especially because she's pregnant. I mean, who knows what that might do to the baby? So I've got to keep up the pretense that everything's okay until she's..." He does some sort of weird mime with his hands that I assume is supposed to indicate the miracle of childbirth, though it could just as easily be someone with a bad case of wind. "And part of that, I'm sorry to say, involves—and on the extremely odd occasion—*sleeping with her.* Otherwise she'd know something was up."

"How do you work that one out?"

Luke sighs impatiently. "If I wasn't having sex with her, she'd assume I was having sex with someone else. And then who knows where we'd be?"

Out in the open, I want to say. *Where you'd be forced to make a decision*. But I can't, obviously, and for different reasons, neither can Julie—or rather, she *won't*.

"And trust me," Luke adds. "It's you I'm thinking of whenever I do."

Julie's mouth drops open, as if she doesn't know how to respond to that last point, and to be honest, I don't blame her. What's worse is how obviously she desperately *wants* to believe him—if only to prove to herself she's not been completely gullible, and that on some level there's been a method to Luke's madness. And if it's obvious to me, then surely it's also obvious to Luke.

"I know it's hard for you," he says. "It's not exactly easy for me either. But I just need a bit more time. Until she…" He looks like he's about to mime the "pregnant" thing again, but obviously decides a crowded office perhaps isn't the most appropriate place.

Then, worryingly, there's a change in Julie's body language, perhaps because Luke has given her an—admittedly vague—time frame for leaving his wife. Even more ominously, Luke picks up on it too.

"Just give me a chance," he continues. "This evening. To explain properly. I owe you that. Then if you decide you don't want us to carry on with…" He lowers his voice a little further. "*Business as usual*, I'll understand."

Even I know he's not talking about what goes on between these four walls. So does Julie, I'm guessing, because after a moment, she sighs, reaches for her mouse, and highlights the *J* word at the top of the columns. For the longest time, her hands hover over her keyboard, while both Luke and I hold our breath. And while I'm willing her to hit Ctrl and B, instead she presses the delete key.

As she replaces them with "my house, 8:00 p.m.," I look up at Luke, already dreading the smug expression he's bound to be wearing. Sure enough, he's mirroring Santa's fence-face from the other day.

"Thanks, Julie," he says, back at normal volume, then he nods at the screen. "That's great."

Though as Julie hurriedly deletes her spreadsheet, I'm thinking the exact opposite.

10

The rest of the day passes pretty uneventfully, apart from when someone pretends to take a swig from Tessa's water bottle, doesn't realize the top's been left off for aeration purposes, and accidentally swallows her fish. I'm also keen to limit my rides in the elevator, so pass on Julie's offer of a lunchtime walk, and it's a relief when Julie sighs, double-checks the time on her watch with the clock on the wall, clicks off her computer screen, then unties my leash from where it's been looped around her desk leg.

"Come on, Doug," she says. "Home time."

Despite the fact that "home time" means "Luke visit," I leap obediently up from where I've been napping, big stretch (to a chorus of "big stretch" from around the office), then happily trot after her and (bravely) into the elevator. On the drive home, just as I'm in the middle of trying to think up an appropriate anti-Luke strategy for later, Julie surprises me by stopping off at the park.

I assume it's because I'm not getting a walk later given

Luke's scheduled appearance, but in the happiest of coincidences, in the distance, dressed in shorts and a T-shirt, along with a cap, sunglasses, headphones, and running shoes, I spot Tom. He's running toward us, though rather than being out on one of the "long runs round the park" Dot mentioned, he appears to be chasing after a large, somewhat manic-looking Alsatian that's headed at breakneck speed toward the pond.

Julie hasn't seen him, so—conscious I don't have much of a window of opportunity—I recognize I need to think of a way to get Tom to stop, and the most obvious way to do that seems to be to get the *Alsatian* to stop. That it's considerably larger than I am presents me with a problem.

I glance back at Julie. She's let me off my leash and is currently engrossed in something on her phone. I quickly decide there's nothing else for me to do, so I sprint off on an interception course, hoping the Alsatian might think I'm interested in playing, or at least might stop and sniff me hello: if not, I'll just have to throw myself in its path and try to bring it to a halt that way. Too late, it occurs to me that the beast might take one look at a smaller, wild-eyed, tongue-lolling cruise missile of a dog barreling toward him, snorting furiously from the effort, and suspect less than friendly intentions, something confirmed by the way the Alsatian suddenly rounds on me. Before I know what's happening, there's a flash of teeth, a shower of saliva, and my left ear's caught painfully in the creature's fangs.

All I can do is whimper pathetically, while desperately looking around for Tom, as Julie screams at the brute to let me go. The blasted devil-dog's not even wearing a collar, and just when I'm at the stage where I'm wondering whether my ear's actually going to come off in its teeth, from behind us there's a purposeful "Rambo! No!" Then Tom swoops in, performs some daringly magical maneuver with his hands in the Alsatian's mouth, and frees me from the jaws of death. In a scene reminiscent of *The Lion King*, Tom scoops me off the ground, lifts me up above his head so the leaping beast can't reach me and shouts, "Home, Rambo!"

He hands me to Julie, and I realize I've never been more grateful to see him. Whether Julie feels the same way, it's hard to tell, as she's too busy examining my ear.

"Are you okay?" she says. She's almost in tears, and though the question's directed at me, Tom nods.

"Yeah. Rambo was just playing."

"Not you!" she says sharply, causing Tom's smile to disappear as if a switch has been flicked. "Doug?"

I whimper quietly, then furtively check the appropriately-named Rambo's whereabouts, relieved to see he's heading home as instructed. My ear stings a lot, but Rambo doesn't appear to be chewing anything, which would assume it's still attached to the rest of me.

"He should be on a leash," Julie says angrily, as Rambo trots off across the grass, perhaps on his way to assault some other innocent canine, and Tom nods.

"He should."

"So why isn't he?" Julie shakes her head angrily. "People like you shouldn't be allowed to own dogs."

"I don't!"

"Don't tell me—no one actually *owns* a dog, they're just staying with you, blah blah blah."

"That's..." Tom looks a little confused at Julie's rant, and he's not the only one. "He's, um, not my dog."

"No?"

"No."

"Well, how did you know his name?"

She's sharp, Julie. Why on earth she lets Luke get away with everything he does and says I don't know. Then again, they say love is blind. And maybe deaf, as well.

"His owner. Emily. She brings him in all the time." Tom narrows his eyes in the direction Rambo's just run. "He escapes a lot. And gets into fights."

"Brings him in?" Julie's still not showing any acknowledgment that she's recognized him, though that could of course be down to how their last meeting went, or specifically, the way they parted.

"To the office," says Tom, removing his cap and sunglasses, though his sunglasses get caught in the cord of his headphones, and end up hanging off the side of his head.

"Oh," says Julie, at the sight of Tom's big reveal, followed by a longer "*Oh!* It's *you*."

"Hi," says Tom. "Tom, remember? We met at..."

"Dot's. Well, yours too, I suppose." She reaches up with her free hand, and for a moment I worry she's going to make the *L* for *Loser* sign like the other day, but it's just to push a strand of loose hair off her face. "Sorry. And apologies for my little outburst. I was just concerned about Doug."

"Understandably so."

"And you, of course. That was very brave of you, wading in like that."

"Well, sometimes you come across a bad situation, and you just have to...intervene."

"Right," says Julie, though it's hard to interpret her tone. "I don't know what got into him. He's normally so...placid."

Tom grins. "I'm sure Doug had his reasons. They're very intelligent dogs, pugs. Originally bred as lapdogs for Chinese monarchs, you know? And loyal. Devoted to their owners. You can trace the breed back some two thousand years."

"Right," says Julie, again. "Well, thank you for the TED talk, but..."

"It's Tom," says Tom, his grin widening. "Not Ted."

After a moment—and it looks suspiciously like a *moment* moment, like in those soppy Sunday afternoon films Julie sometimes makes me sit through—Tom turns his attention back to me. "Want me to take a look at the little chap?"

"No, don't worry. I'm sure he's…" I do a little snort-whimper and cross my eyes, partly because my ear *does* hurt, but also because I'd have to have sustained a brain injury to not comprehend that this is another of those opportunities Priya was talking about the other day. "Perhaps you'd better. If you don't mind?"

"Not at all," says Tom.

Julie carries me over to a nearby bench, where she sets me down softly, then Tom squats down in front of me and gently examines my ear. "Good boy, Doug," he says, and I give the briefest of wags with my tail, in an attempt to convey that I *am* a good boy, but that I'm in a little bit of discomfort here.

As Tom gently fingers the wound, I look up at Julie. She's watching me anxiously, but every now and again, her eyes flick across at Tom, as if she's checking him out, or perhaps even considering forgiving him for his outburst the other day. Either way, I should be celebrating, I suppose, at what's the smallest of victories. Even though he is a V-E-T. And even though it might have cost me an ear.

After a moment, Tom stands back up again, a not-all-that-concerned expression on his face. "He'll live," he says, much to the relief of all present. "It doesn't actually look too bad. Probably best to get it properly cleaned, though, and pop in a few stitches. Just in case."

"Right. Well." Julie looks down at me and smiles flatly. "I'll make an appointment with my…"

"No need," says Tom. "My office is just on the other side

of the park. I just stepped out for an after-work run, so if you want, I could pop them in for you now."

I'm just wondering exactly how you "pop" stitches in, when Julie looks at her watch. "I don't know. I've got to…"

"Ten minutes, tops," says Tom. "And best to get his ear properly cleaned straightaway, otherwise…" He makes a face that I don't like the look of, then smiles, though I don't find it very comforting. This is the kind of thing that happens on the path to true love, if the likes of *Bridget Jones* are to be believed, so if my small sacrifice helps get Julie and Tom together, I suppose it's been worth it.

"Tom, that would be very kind of you," she says, and he smiles at her again, a big, warm smile, that, when it's turned in my direction, radiates all the way down to the tip of my tail.

"Plus it'll be a way for me to apologize."

"What for?"

"For the other day. At the barbecue. I was feeling a little sensitive, and I'd had a beer or three, and I realize both that I have trust issues, and that I need to stop tarring everyone with the same brush, so…" Tom looks like he's about to make some sort of admission, though he evidently chickens out. "Well, long story short, I shouldn't have given you a lecture."

"No, you shouldn't," says Julie, but in a way that suggests she's not really giving Tom one either.

"So?" he says. "I promise not to get on my high horse."

"In that case, it's a deal."

And I'm happy, because even though it's a deal and not a date, she's not making it a big one.

Tom's a good V-E-T. I hardly feel a thing, even though he gives me an injection, shaves the patch where I've been bitten, then pops six stitches in my ear. The one part of the whole arrangement I'm not happy about is having to wear one of those ridiculous plastic cones around my head that make me look like I've become stuck in a lampshade. I spend the whole walk back to the car trying to avoid bumping into things *and* struggling to smell anything, while praying I don't see anyone I know. And while Julie didn't take Tom's number, Tom didn't ask for Julie's, and the only contact they're planning to have is when I go back to have my stitches removed at the end of the week, that's something, I suppose.

As we reach the car, I wonder if this is Luke's legacy. Tom's okay-looking—for a human—with a nice smile, kind eyes, a sense of humor, and he's got a job that women are supposed to find attractive, and yet Julie seemed keener than I was to get out of there.

On the way home we stop off at the supermarket to pick up some chewy dog treats, something that would normally fill me with excitement, though this time I know it's only so Julie can attempt to hide my antibiotic tablets in them. And it occurs to me that perhaps Julie needs whatever the relationship equivalent of antibiotics is, in order to get Luke out of her system once and for all.

Maybe that's a role that Tom can fulfill.

But with Luke due to come round this evening, getting Julie to agree to swallow that particular pill might be even harder still.

11

There's a wonderful smell coming from the kitchen, and I'm just about to trot in and help Julie by offering to take another taste of the chili con carne she's cooking when a different, less-welcome scent assaults my nostrils. Luke likes a particular brand of body cologne that—at least according to the advertisements—ensures you're mobbed by beautiful women, often on a desert island beach, the moment you so much as uncap the bottle, and the overpowering whiff of it I'm suddenly getting can only mean one thing. I race along the hall, and I'm standing, growling, at the front door when Julie narrows her eyes at me.

"Doug!" she says, firmly, so I reluctantly step away from the door so Julie can open it, then scamper back to the kitchen. After a moment, and one thankfully free of the usual sound of Luke's "hum" from their kiss hello (which I'm assuming means no kiss), Luke marches into the kitchen, throws his car keys onto the table, catches sight of me, and grins scornfully at me.

"Nice cone, Doug."

This, I understand, is something called "sarcasm," though I'm not sure what the appropriate response is. All I know is it's frowned upon to laugh at someone's disability, so Luke's not doing himself any favors in terms of karma, at least. I can't exactly bite him, so I just snort as disdainfully as possible. A sound amplified by the conical plastic, I'm pleased to note.

Julie picks up a nacho from the bowl on the table and tosses it toward me, though the cone's quite disorientating, and instead of catching it in my jaws, I only succeed in getting it wedged infuriatingly beneath my chin.

"He got attacked in the park on the way home," she says, reaching in and removing the offending tidbit, before carefully feeding it to me.

"Right," says Luke, who appears to be wondering whether showing concern for me might help his cause this evening, though he quickly decides he can't be bothered. "Having a bad ear day, eh, Doug?" he jokes, though neither I nor Julie find it funny.

Despite this, I march up to him and sit at his feet, pointedly right in between him and Julie.

"So?" Julie says, obviously still mad at him, though Luke has the air of someone who thinks he's already gotten away with it.

"So… You looked hot at work," he says, reaching to take her in his arms, a move my expert positioning makes a little awkward.

"Did I," says Julie, though it's not phrased as a question.

"You did. You always do. Especially now."

"Don't think you can get around me that easily."

"What?"

"You said you'd explain." Julie calmly removes his hands from where he's snaked them around her waist. "About your wife."

"What about her?"

"The fact you're still sleeping with her. Despite what you said."

Luke harrumphs, like he's having to repeat something to a stupid child. "Like I told you, I *have* to. Otherwise she'd get suspicious. And it's not like I enjoy it or anything."

"And the fact that she's *pregnant*?"

"Which is why I can't leave her. Not yet, anyway," he adds, quickly. "I mean, how would *that* look?"

"So you're going to leave her when the baby's born?"

"Yeah," says Luke, then he hesitates, either because that's perhaps not the most honorable thing to admit, or because he's wary about making a commitment. "Obviously not straightaway. I'll just hang around long enough to make sure."

"Make sure?"

"Yeah." Luke spots Julie's wineglass on the table, half fills it and gulps most of that down. "That it's not mine. Then..." He finishes off the rest of the glass, then makes some gesture with his fingers that I guess is designed to show him making a run for it. "Then I'll have a reason to leave her."

"You've got a reason to leave her!" Julie wails, adding a plaintive, "Me!" in response to Luke's vacant expression.

"You know what I mean."

Julie retrieves another wineglass from the cupboard, then waits for Luke to fill it up for her. When he doesn't, she empties the rest of the bottle into it herself. "But, um, at the risk of asking the obvious question..." She swallows a mouthful of wine. And then another one. "What if it is?"

"What if what is?"

"The baby. Yours."

Luke shrugs. "It's not going to be, is it?"

"Why not?"

"Well, because she's been, you know..." Luke waits for Julie to fill in the gap, then evidently realizes the ball's firmly in his court this evening. "Seeing someone else. And even if it is… Like I said, that's her trying to trap me, isn't it? And that's not right. So she can't possibly expect me to stay with her. I mean, I'll do my duty, you understand. Take the thing to the park at the weekend. Make sure it's fed and watered. A bit like you do with Doug here…" He lets out a short laugh, cutting it even shorter when he catches sight of Julie's scowl. "I'm *kidding*."

"Not the most appropriate choice of words, Luke," says Julie, and I snort even more derisively.

"Do we really have to be talking about this?" he says, wearily.

Julie stares at him in a "Yes, we do!" kind of way. "You're the one who said you wanted to explain."

"And I have. Haven't I?" He throws his hands up in the air. "Look, I don't know what more I can say. That's how it is. You can either choose to believe me or not. And if you don't…"

Luke looks pointedly at his watch, and—as if a switch has been flicked—Julie suddenly seems to worry she's in danger of crossing that fine line between telling and pissing him off.

"I'm sorry," she says, even though he's the one who should be apologizing. "It's just… Seeing you and her like that, and the fact that she's…"

"I know, I know. It's tough for us all," Luke says, though by the looks of things, it isn't tough for him *at all*. "It must have been a shock for you. Trust me, it was for me! But just give me a bit more time. Can you do that? For me? For *us*?"

Julie hesitates for a moment, notices Luke's glass is emptier than hers—but not as empty as the wine bottle—so tips half of hers into his, and gives him a small—and rather inappropriate, to my mind—cheers.

"I suppose," she says, crossing the kitchen to check on the simmering pot. "But I'm still mad at you. For lying to me."

"That was because I didn't want to hurt you."

"Well, you did!"

"And I'm sorry," says Luke, though he sounds a bit exasperated. "Really I am. So let's just put this behind us, and..."

He fixes what I imagine is supposed to be a seductive smile on his face, marches across to where Julie's standing, and begins to unbutton her blouse, but she bats his hands away.

"Sorry, Luke. I'm just...not in the mood."

"Well, what am I doing here then?"

"I don't know." Julie throws her hands up in frustration. "I thought maybe we could just have dinner. Talk some more. Spend a normal adult evening together."

The implication is "like a normal couple," and Luke stuffs his hands into his pockets like a sulky teenager. "Fine," he says, glancing down at me, and I meet his gaze. "Only, do you fancy going out?"

"*Out* out?" says Julie, the surprise evident in her voice. "I didn't think we were supposed to...?"

"I was thinking takeout. In the car. We could park up somewhere?"

"Oh," says Julie, suddenly disappointed.

"It's just that..." Luke jabs a thumb down at me, like a Roman emperor ordering a kill. "Doug always seems to be giving me the evils. And it'd be good to be on our own. The two of us. Just you and me..."

He's said the same thing three times, as if Julie's stupid, which she isn't—though right now she *is* doing a pretty good impression of someone who could do with an injection of common sense.

"Right. Only... I've already cooked."

"What?"

"I said, I've already cooked."

"And I said 'what?' as in 'what have you already cooked?'"

It's all I can do not to run my cone at top speed into his shins. This is typical of Luke. Most people would be grateful that Julie has spent time in the kitchen preparing them something to eat—I know I am, even when all she's done is open a packet. But Luke is evidently about to decide whether they eat in or not based on what it is Julie's lovingly made him. Cat behavior, if ever I saw it.

"Your favorite."

"Which is?"

I do the dog equivalent of rolling my eyes. If Luke doesn't even know what his favorite meal is... Then again, he can't seem to decide who's his favorite out of Julie and his wife.

"Chili. Con carne."

"Ah."

"What's *that* supposed to mean?"

"I've, um, never really liked it."

"Chili? But you order it all the time whenever we get take-out from Nacho Daddy's."

"*Your* chili."

Julie's face falls so quickly I worry I might need to leap out of the way. "But..." is all she manages, before her lip starts to quiver.

"Nothing personal, love," Luke says, though not one part of that sentence sounds sincere. "I just prefer...theirs. That's all."

There's silence in the kitchen for a moment, then Julie simply marches over to the cooker, picks up the pot of chili, and empties it directly into the swing bin in the corner. I'm horrified, but Luke, however, just sighs quietly.

"Here we go."

"What do you mean, here we go?"

"I get enough of this at home."

Julie folds her arms defiantly, though to my trained eye,

she looks on the verge of tears again. "You get enough of *everything* at home, by the looks of things."

Luke stares at her. "I knew you still hadn't forgiven me!" he says, maintaining the stare for a moment or two longer, then he glances down at me, and like a bad actor, he suddenly and without warning slumps down at the kitchen table, and puts his head in his hands. "Do you think this is easy for me?"

"Yes, quite frankly, I do!"

"Well, it isn't!" he says, displaying all the debating acuity of a five-year-old. Then, in a classic example of both switching the focus away from him and delivering what you can't help but see as an ultimatum, Luke shakes his head pityingly. "You're going to have to get past this, Julie, if you and me are going to have any chance of a future."

"Get past this?"

"That is what you want, isn't it? You and me? Forever?"

Julie hesitates, and I find myself hoping, *willing* her to say "not anymore," but like a drowning woman who's just been thrown a life vest, she grabs onto Luke's last sentence with both hands.

"*Of course* it is. It's what I've wanted all along."

"Then stop making this about you all the time. How do you think I feel, trying to do the right thing by everyone, seeing you at work every day, knowing we can't be together until…?"

"Luke, I…I didn't think… And I need to…"

Luke holds her gaze for what must be a count of five, then, as if he's the one forgiving *her*, he stands up, pushes his chair backward with the backs of his knees, and holds his arms out wide.

"C'mere."

Julie doesn't move, and for a moment, I think the balance has swung back in her favor. She looks like she's weighing her options, and Luke seems to be fearing this is one argument he's not actually going to win. So then—and it's quite possibly the most despicable thing he's done, which if you think about it, means it's pretty darn awful—he puts on this pathetic face, and says, "I'm not ready to start a family. Not yet. At least, not with Sarah. I'd only want to do something like that with someone…" He leaves the most melodramatic of pauses, then gives Julie a look that leaves her in absolutely no doubt that he's talking about her. "Someone I was in love with."

With the air of someone who knows he's just whacked the ball well and truly out of his court and deep into Julie's, and is fully expecting it to come back, Luke collects his car keys from the kitchen table. Then he strides across the kitchen, and kisses Julie chastely on the forehead.

"I'll see myself out," he says, before wheeling smartly round, and marching back along the hall.

I follow him anyway—because you can never trust what Luke says—and it's right there and then I make myself a promise. Their reconciliation isn't going to happen. Not on my watch.

And trust me, I'll be watching *very* closely.

12

"Been in the wars, have you, Doug?"

Julie's dad is here to take me for my morning walk, and the look on his face—a mix of pity and concern—when he sees me in my cone is the exact opposite of Luke's last night.

"Bit of a tussle with an Alsatian in the park yesterday," says Julie.

Julie's dad looks impressed. "Good for you, wee man," he says. "Though has nobody told you you've got to pick your battles?"

I give him a look. I didn't pick that particular one. Besides, it's the war with Luke I'm more focused on.

"Aren't you going to be late for work?" he asks, but Julie shakes her head.

"Doctor's appointment."

Julie's dad looks concerned. "What's wrong?" he says, placing a palm against her forehead.

Julie laughs. "I'm not really ill. I'm just meeting Priya for a coffee. I'll go in this afternoon. But that means I can walk

Doug, if you don't mind missing your regular Park Café appointment?"

Julie's dad looks at me, then at Julie, then he sighs. "No, that's fine. Probably for the best."

"What's that supposed to mean?"

"Oh, you know," says Julie's dad, but Julie evidently doesn't, because she folds her arms purposefully.

"Dad?"

With a sigh, Julie's dad lowers himself onto the sofa, so I attempt to jump up next to him, but I'm disorientated thanks to this stupid cone, and only succeed in getting my front half up onto the cushion. As I slide almost in slow motion back down onto the carpet, Julie's dad shakes his head.

"I just don't want to give Dot the wrong impression."

"And what would that be, exactly?"

"That I'm, you know…" Julie's dad picks me up and plonks me onto the sofa beside him. "Interested."

"Aren't you?"

"No!"

"Because it certainly looked like you were at the barbecue."

"Okay, yes, then. But it wouldn't be…"

"What?"

"Appropriate."

Julie lifts me up and moves me a foot or so along the sofa, so she can sit next to her dad. "She'd want you to be happy, you know?"

"Huh?"

"Mum." Julie reaches across and grabs his hand. "You still think about her, don't you? Still miss her."

Julie's dad nods. "Every day. Pretty much every hour of every day, in fact. Your mum was my life. Until you were."

"Even so."

"Besides." He pats the top of Julie's hand. "I *am* happy."

"But you could be happy-*er*..." Julie looks at him pleadingly. "Time, the great healer, and all that."

Julie's dad smiles in a flat-lipped way. "If it was that great, your mum might have got better, rather than suffered for all those years."

"That's not what I meant."

"I know, love. But what your mum and I had..." Julie's dad stops talking, and his gaze drifts off somewhere. "All I'm saying is, lightning doesn't strike twice."

"Does it need to be lightning?"

"Huh?" says Julie's dad, again.

"I get it that what you and Mum had was special, and that you might not meet anyone like her again. But that's the point—you might meet someone different. Someone like Dot. And in a way, that'll be better, because you won't constantly be comparing your relationship to what you and Mum had."

Julie's dad stares at her for a moment. "I can kind of see the logic in that statement, but it doesn't necessarily mean you're right."

"Do you really think Mum would have wanted you to be on your own for the rest of your life, especially if you're only doing it as some sort of tribute to her?" Julie glances toward the heavens for effect. "I bet she's up there right now, looking down on you with that same long-suffering expression she always used to wear whenever you'd come home with yet another power tool you'd bought from the hardware store because it was on sale, even though you didn't have a clue what it did, *and* probably wouldn't ever use it."

Julie's dad lets out a chuckle. "I did do that, didn't I?"

Julie nods. "Or that time you decided to start making your own wine, then you worked out it was quicker and easier—and cheaper—just to pop to the corner store, even though you'd bought all the wine-making equipment."

Julie's dad holds both hands up. "Guilty as charged."

"Or that day you..."

"Okay, okay," says Julie's dad, then he looks up and mutters a third okay, then blushes when he realizes Julie's seen him do it.

"Go on. Ask Dot out."

"On a *date*?" says Julie's dad, horrified.

"No, for a fight. *Of course* on a date."

"I can't."

"No, you won't. There's a difference."

"What if she says no?"

Julie half rises from the sofa. "Would you like me to take Doug to the park so I can ask her out for you?"

"Don't you dare!"

Julie smirks as she sits back down, and Julie's dad's gaze drifts off again, as if he's considering everything she's said. So I take the opportunity to scamper across her lap and force myself in between the two of them.

"Suppose I did," he says, then he lowers his voice. "What does a date consist of nowadays, exactly?"

"Well..." Julie hesitates. "I'd suggest you take her out for coffee, but seeing as she works in a café, that might not be the best of ideas."

"No." He reaches across and strokes me absentmindedly. "How about this 'Netflix and chill' I've been hearing about?"

Julie's jaw drops open. "Maybe not as a first date. And do you even *have* Netflix?"

"I'm not sure," says Julie's dad. "Do I?"

"So that's a no, then." Julie laughs. "Why not just ask her for a walk along the river one afternoon. Take Doug. He'd be a great ice-breaker. You could stop off at a pub on the way, have a drink..."

As Julie's dad mulls this over, I do too, pleased by the idea.

"I'll think about it, love," he says, eventually.

"Promise?"

"Promise."

"Because you'll never know, otherwise."

"Okay, okay."

Julie leans over and gives her a dad a kiss, then she says "great," and it occurs to me that "great" is exactly what it is.

Because if her dad can move on from a mistake as big as losing his wife, then surely Julie can move on from the mistake she's making with Luke?

Priya's already waiting at a window table in the café at the far end of the High Street, sipping what smells like a latte from the largest mug I've ever seen. She waves us over, takes one look at me in my cone, and it's all she can do to envelop the two of us in a hug before Julie bursts into tears.

"Oh, *Jules*!" she says, when Julie eventually stops crying, though it's in the same way as you might say "What *now*?" and provokes another outburst that even me nuzzling her leg can't stop.

"Luke... We had a fight."

"Another one?" says Priya, perhaps trying to imply something, and Julie nods.

"Last night," she says, between sobs. "He'd come around to explain about, you know..."

"The fact that he was still shagging his pregnant wife?"

Julie nods again, in time with her sobbing. "And he told me he'd never liked my chili..."

"The *bastard*!"

"...so I threw it in the garbage, then he said he wanted to have a baby with *me*, not his wife..."

"Bit of an extreme reaction."

"...and Doug got bitten on the ear..."

"By *Luke*?"

"By Rambo! In the park."

"Hold on," says Priya, eyeing me desperately. "Start from the beginning."

"Which beginning?" wails Julie.

"Sunday. When you saw Luke and his wife in town."

"It was awful," Julie says, once she's eventually caught her breath. "He was just walking along the High Street with her as if…as if…"

"They were husband and wife?"

Julie shoots Priya a look, then grabs a bunch of napkins from the dispenser on the table. "And then in the pub, they were just sitting there like…" She blows her nose so loudly it makes Priya's cup rattle in its saucer. "Like they were a couple. And there was me, having a drink with *Doug*…"

"Here." Priya puts down the muffin she's been unwrapping and slides the cappuccino she's already taken the liberty of ordering for Julie across the table.

"Thanks," Julie says as she picks the cup up, blows across the top, takes a few breaths to calm herself, then takes a sip. "Sorry, P. It was just the shock of seeing them together like that. And then, when she came over to my table…"

"She came over to your table?"

"She'd spotted Doug on the way to the toilet, and you know the effect he has on people, so she had to stop to give him a stroke."

"I bet you nearly had one too!"

"That's not funny," says Julie, though the look on her face suggests otherwise.

Priya nods as if to acknowledge her own joke, then she reaches down into my cone and scratches me behind my good ear. "Well, you do own the cutest dog in the world. Even when he's wearing a lampshade round his head."

I snort in acknowledgment, and Julie smiles proudly. "Anyway," she continues. "When she was in the loo, Luke came over to warn me off..."

"Bloody cheek!"

"Then she came back, and Luke told her we worked together, and she invited me to join them for lunch..."

"The bitch!"

Priya's obviously meant that sarcastically, because she smiles, and Julie bravely does her best to return it, then bursts into tears again. "That's just it! She was so *nice*."

Priya reaches over to pat the back of Julie's hand, then she peers around the café and lowers her voice.

"Did it occur to you to, you know, *tell her*?"

"Tell her...?" Julie's mouth falls open. "She was *pregnant*, P. How could I have?"

"All the more reason for her to know what she's letting herself in for..." Priya's expression suddenly darkens. "Christ. And he told you the two of them didn't have sex, right?"

"Right. That they were more like brother and sister nowadays."

"Eeew—that's even worse!" Priya makes a face, pauses for effect, then she breaks off a piece of muffin, pops it into her mouth, and picks up her mug. "How far gone would you say she is?"

Julie mimes various degrees of a fat stomach, then shrugs cluelessly. "Five or six months?"

"And when did you and Luke start, you know..." She hesitates. "I'm going to go with 'seeing each other'?"

"Eleven months and two days ago." Julie averts her eyes. "Roughly."

"The *bastard*!"

"Exactly! Unless..."

"How can there possibly be an unless?"

"Maybe like he said, it's not his baby. Perhaps she had an affair, just like he did, and got pregnant, and that was just the two of them meeting up for lunch to discuss what happens now."

Priya sighs, and it's a long-suffering sigh, the kind I've heard her make many a time in Julie's presence. "Yeah. Which was probably why she asked you to join them. Get your advice. Someone she's never met before."

"Or, perhaps he just felt sorry for her one night, and he… lapsed, and she tricked him, and got pregnant to try to keep the two of them together, and…"

"Jules…"

"It could happen."

"Yeah," admits Priya. "It could. But chances are pretty high that it didn't." She reaches down to feed me a piece of muffin. "Face it, Jules. Luke has been lying to you. And if he's lied to you about this, then just imagine what else he's been lying to you about."

Julie rocks back in her chair, then she sighs loudly. "I've been taken for one hell of a ride. Haven't I?"

"Maybe," says Priya, clinking her mug against Julie's. "Though there is one way to be sure."

"How?" says Julie, desperately.

"Ask Sarah."

"What?"

Priya shrugs. "Seems to me it's the only way you're going to find out the truth about him and her."

Julie looks mortified at the prospect. "I couldn't."

"Why ever not? You said she seemed pretty friendly. Even invited you to join them for lunch." Priya sits back in her chair and folds her arms. "You've got nothing to lose—whereas the opposite is true for Luke. Plus it's bound to get his dander up, knowing you're besties with his wife. At the very least, it's going to be interesting. And might even force him into making a decision…"

Julie narrows her eyes in doubt, but I widen mine, realizing this is actually an *excellent* idea. Even though I know it could all go horribly wrong, a part of me can't help but be fascinated to see where it goes. All I need to do is make it happen.

And fortunately, I know exactly how.

13

It's Wednesday, and thanks to an Oscar-worthy, sad-eyed, cone-enhanced performance from Yours Truly while Julie was getting ready this morning, she's working from home today. When she phones her dad to tell him she's going to walk me instead of him, Julie's dad sounds a little upset, and I feel a little guilty, as he won't have an excuse to visit the Park Café, but it's a small price to pay so I can put my plan into action.

"Not that way, Doug," Julie says, when I take a left turn at the end of our street, but I tug insistently on my leash, hoping Julie will attribute my choice of alternative route to disorientation caused by my plastic adornment. After a few seconds of futilely attempting to lure me back the usual way, she tries, "No park today?" but I just snort and keep walking.

I have a rough idea of what street I'm aiming for—I've been there once before, when a drunk Julie decided to engage in a little light stalking on one of our evening walks. I can only hope that she doesn't realize where I'm taking her before it's too late.

Fortunately, Julie's more interested in something on her phone, and seems happy to let me lead her, so it's only when we reach our destination—a large, redbrick, faintly-smelling-of-Luke house in the middle of a Victorian terrace in the posher side of town—that she looks up from her screen and goes pale.

"Doug?" she says hesitantly, as I stop to sniff the gate, double-checking that Luke's scent is actually coming from the house rather than wafting in on the wind. But the odor has an aged whiff about it, a *layering*, as if it's historical, which can only mean this *is* Luke's house. Where, I assume, Luke's wife lives too.

I do my best to pick up Sarah's scent, but before I can get another nostril-full, Julie tugs me away—a little roughly, I have to say, given my injured state. I'm just about to voice my annoyance when I realize my plan's worked, as Julie's desire to flee suddenly evaporates, and she peers curiously at the building.

Stealthily, we cross the road, then Julie presses her phone to her ear, pretending to be midconversation, though all the while her eyes are fixed back on Luke's house. All of a sudden—and my timing couldn't be better—a car pulls up, reverses into the vacant spot in front of the gate, and to Julie's apparent horror, Sarah climbs awkwardly out.

Julie's still on the phone, though her pretend conversation has been replaced by a selection of slightly more choice vocabulary, and in the absence of any other ideas, she drops down behind the nearest parked car, as if hiding from a sniper.

Quickly realizing this won't do, I surreptitiously take a couple of steps to my left and peer round the car's rear bumper, wondering how best to attract Sarah's attention without blatantly barking. As she waddles around to the opposite side of her car, and unloads several large shopping bags, I can't help but whine in frustration, worried that at this rate, she'll miss us. Fortunately, my cone clearly doubles as a megaphone, as Sarah looks up at the sound, then spots me on the other side of the road. She smiles, and then—though I'm too stunned to warn Julie—crosses over toward us.

"Hello, gorgeous," says Sarah. "Are you on your own?"

Instinctively, I turn to look at Julie, who's shaking her head frantically at me while mouthing the word *no*. But Sarah figures out the answer herself when she kneels down to pet me hello, and her eyes follow my extendable leash around to the far side of the car, and she sees Julie sitting on the pavement.

"Are you okay?"

Julie looks up, startled. "What? Me? Oh, fine. I was just, you know…" Julie's face contorts with the effort of trying to come up with an excuse. "Picking up after this one," she says, a little too much like she's only just thought of it and is very pleased with the fact.

"Right," says Sarah, though she doesn't sound totally convinced.

"When I realized he'd only done a number one, so I had nothing to pick up, I suddenly felt dizzy. So I thought I'd sit down for a bit."

"Oh," says Sarah, in the same tone, as she struggles to stand up from petting me.

"Of course, you'll be having a lot of that to contend with," says Julie, as if desperate to fill in the gap in conversation.

"A lot of…?"

"You know." Julie nods at Sarah's stomach. "Sorry, I didn't mean… Haven't we met?" she says, evidently deciding attack is the best form of defense.

"Have we?"

"Yes!" says Julie, as if she's just remembered the answer to a question that's been troubling her. "In the pub. Last Sunday.

You're Sarah. Luke's wife? Sorry, you already know that. I'm Julie. I work for him. And this is..."

"Doug! Of course! How could I forget?" Sarah grins down at me, and I snort in response. "Sorry, I didn't recognize you with your cone on."

"Alsatian," says Julie, by way of an explanation, and Sarah smiles sympathetically.

"This is a pleasant surprise," she says.

Julie makes a face designed to indicate that it's a small world, then says, "Small world," just to back it up.

"Do you live around here?"

"No. The other side of town. Sandycombe Road." Julie leaps up from the pavement and brushes the dirt from her jeans. "I was just taking Doug for a walk. We normally go to the park, but to tell you the truth, I think he's a bit embarrassed about the whole cone thing, so he decided he'd go this way. Probably aiming for somewhere no one he knew was likely to see him."

"That's...impressive," says Sarah, though she looks like it's not her first choice of words.

"Well, they're intelligent dogs, pugs. They were originally bred as lapdogs for Chinese monarchs. Which means they're, you know..." Julie peers down at me, so I wag my tail encouragingly. "Smart."

"Right," says Sarah, then she glances back toward her house. "Listen, I've got some frozen stuff in the car that I really ought to get inside and into the freezer..."

"Oh. Fine. Sure," says Julie. "Well, nice to see you again. We'll just..."

"No, I didn't mean..." Sarah smiles warmly. "Did you want a cup of tea?"

"Tea?" says Julie, though I suspect that might not be her

first choice of beverage right now, then a strange expression comes over her face, and I realize my work here is done.

"Tea would be lovely," she says.

We've carried the shopping in, and Julie is begrudgingly admiring Sarah's granite-surfaced, invisible-handled, breakfast-barred, fully-equipped kitchen, perhaps wondering whether it's the kind of kitchen she'll have when she and Luke are together, when Sarah suddenly says, "Whoa!" and sits heavily down on a kitchen chair.

"Are you okay?"

Sarah looks up at her, takes a breath, and nods. "Yes. Thanks. Just a little faint. It happens sometimes." She rubs her stomach, as if to underline how what's in there is the reason, rather than she's drunk in the afternoon or has some debilitating disease. Then she forces a smile. "Don't worry, I'll be… Whoa!" She tries to get up, but the effort's apparently a little too much for her. "Just give me a minute."

"Can I do anything?"

"No. Thank you." Sarah fans herself with her hand. "Though you could put the kettle on. And you'll find a packet of biscuits in the cupboard over there."

"For Doug?" says Julie, doing as instructed with the kettle.

"For Doug. Sure," says Sarah, and Julie grins. "One of the benefits of being pregnant. You can eat what you want. Though as far as I can tell it's the only benefit." She reaches down and scratches me between the ears, and I snort approvingly.

"When are you due?"

"September. Which can't come soon enough, as far as I'm concerned." Sarah puffs air out of her cheeks. "Do you have any? Kids, I mean?"

"God no," says Julie, a little too quickly, then she corrects herself. "I mean, I've got Doug. And besides, I'd need a husband first."

"You can have mine, if you like!" says Sarah, making a face as she rests both hands on her bump, and though I catch Julie's almost imperceptible double take, it's obvious to all of us she's joking.

"Really? Thanks!" says Julie, playing along, and with probably just about the right amount of sarcasm. "Anyway. Tea?"

"Please," says Sarah, then she shakes her head. "I can't believe I've got three more months of this. That's the last time I let Luke anywhere near me, I can tell you."

"Me too," says Julie, then she blushes, and uses her search for the biscuits to hide her embarrassment. "I mean, I can't believe it either. You're *huge*."

"Aren't I?" says Sarah. "Though that's probably because it's twins."

"Twins?"

"You know. Two babies." Sarah rolls her eyes as Julie finally locates the packet of biscuits. "In for a penny, and all that."

"Right. So, did you…? I mean…" Julie spends some time trying to locate the plastic pull tag on the side of the packet, as if desperate to buy time to come up with an appropriate question. "Do, you know, twins, run in the family?"

"Nope." Sarah heaves herself up, walks over to the kettle, finds a couple of mugs on the worktop next to the sink, drops a tea bag into each of them, then tops them up with boiling water. "One of the risks of IVF, though," she says, giving the teas a stir.

"IVF?"

"That's right." She fishes the tea bags out, drops them into the bin, then locates a carton of milk in the fridge, holds it up for Julie's approval, and splashes a bit into each of the mugs. "We'd been trying for ages, but no luck, so we thought we'd give this a go. And hey, presto..." She glances down at her stomach again. "Took me a bit by surprise, I can tell you. But Luke seems made up."

"Right," says Julie, perhaps beginning to understand that "made up" is a phrase that also applies to most of Luke's excuses.

She pulls out a chair and sits down heavily, grateful Sarah's too busy making the tea to notice how white she's gone. From what I can tell, she's close to tears—and if she bursts out crying in front of Sarah, then who knows what'll happen?

Even though it means forgoing a biscuit, there's only one thing I can do. With a loud sigh, I get to my feet, and go and scratch at the kitchen door.

"Everything alright, Doug?" says Sarah, and when I let out a plaintive whine, she looks across at Julie.

"I think he probably needs to, you know..." Julie takes a breath. "Go again. Which means I really should..."

"But you haven't had your tea?"

Julie takes a look at the steaming mug that Sarah's holding out toward her, and I find myself hoping she's not considering chugging it like she did the wine the other day. "Sorry," she says, looking pointedly at me. "But the consequences..."

"Ah," says Sarah. "Another time, then. And thanks for your help with the shopping."

"Don't mention it," says Julie.

As we walk back home, something tells me Julie is going to be mentioning it to Luke. And as far as I'm concerned, that's great news.

Because judging by the look of thunder on her face, if she wasn't sure her and Luke were over before, she's a hundred percent positive now.

14

I'm napping next to Julie on the sofa that evening when a frantic knocking on the front door startles me, so I leap down to the wooden floor, run-skid round the corner, and sprint, barking, down the corridor. Julie's not far behind me, and when she slips the chain on, then cautiously opens the door, my fears (and nostrils) are confirmed. It's Luke.

"What do you want?" Julie says, icily, emphasizing the *you*. She's a lot more composed than I'd have expected, given the bottle of wine she's already polished off.

"You came to my *house*?"

"What are you talking about?"

"This afternoon." Luke is doing his best to squeeze his face through the gap between the door and the doorjamb. "Sarah said."

"I didn't come *to* your house. I was walking Doug *past* your house. Sarah happened to pull up in her car with about half a ton of shopping, so I offered to help her with it, and she invited me in for a cup of tea. What was I supposed to do? Say no?"

"Yes!" Luke scowls at her as he evaluates her explanation. "Down my street seems like a strange place to be walking your dog."

"He was walking me, actually!"

Luke glares down at me, then up at Julie. "I don't believe you."

"Look who's talking!"

Luke stares at her for a moment. "What's that supposed to mean?"

"We don't have sex anymore," says Julie, in a silly voice, which I guess is supposed to be an impression of Luke. *"I'm trying to work out how to tell her. I'm just waiting for the right opportunity to leave."*

Her eyes flash with anger. "If by 'we don't have sex anymore' you meant, 'because I'm jerking off into a cup instead so we can have a baby—sorry, *two* babies—by the skillful use of a turkey baster,' then perhaps you should have been a bit clearer."

Luke's mouth flaps open and shut for a moment or two, then he sighs, as if he's about to do Julie a favor by explaining. "It's a bit more complicated than that."

"You decided to start a family when you'd promised me you were ending one."

"That's not..."

"Do you really expect me to believe that was the first step toward leaving her?"

"It was!"

"How so?"

"Let me in, and I'll explain."

"No way," says Julie, and I let out a low growl to back her up.

"What was I supposed to do? Say no? Tell Sarah we're not ready yet? We've been together for *ten years.*"

"*Yes*, you were supposed to say no! Especially given everything you were telling me. Although I'm not sure that word's in your vocabulary." Julie folds her arms. "If ever there were the perfect opportunity to begin the 'I'm leaving you' conversation..."

"I..." Luke sighs again. "Okay. Here's the thing. I wanted to leave her with something. Sarah had always been desperate for a baby, so I thought it might soften the blow if we... I mean, if *she*..."

Julie's look of incredulity evidently shuts him up, because he stops speaking abruptly. "So you were prepared to get her pregnant and *then* leave her? How is that an upside for anyone?"

"It's..."

"If you say *complicated*, I'm going to..."

"It *is*!"

I look up at him, then at Julie. It's more than complicated. You'd need to be smarter than that Stephen Hawking chap was to work it out. Something Julie evidently isn't, because she frowns.

"Explain it to me, then. Because following on logically from what you've just said—which believe me is difficult—at what point do you leave her now? How old do the twins have to be? I mean, is there an optimum time to abandon newborns? Before they call you daddy, perhaps? Or do you wait a few years until you can explain your disappearance face-to-face?"

Luke tries to shake his head, but he can't, because his face is still pretty tightly wedged. "I don't expect you to understand."

"And I don't. So finally we're on the same page."

"Julie..." Luke reaches a hand through the gap, though frustratingly it's too high for me to jump up and bite.

"Oh, just... Fuck off, Luke!"

"Okay, okay," he says, though in a typical example of him

not following through with his promises, he doesn't. "Just promise me one thing."

"What?"

"That you won't tell Sarah."

"Tell her what?"

"About us. It would devastate her. And she doesn't deserve that."

"She doesn't deserve *you.*"

"Please, Julie." He sniffs loudly. "I'm begging you."

Julie widens her eyes. "Are you *crying*?"

Luke looks like he's realized he might have accidentally hit on something. "No," he snuffles, his acting worse than anything I've seen on *EastEnders.*

For a moment, I worry Julie's going to cave, and I snort derisively in the hope I can make her understand this is all a sham. But as I check out her body language, I see there's something different about her. Something…stronger. As if she understands that finally, *she's* the one holding the leash.

"Don't you think she deserves to know?"

"No," says Luke, desperately. "I mean, yes. And I'll tell her. But it should come from me. Just…"

"What?"

"Tell me you won't see her again."

"Only if you do the same," says Julie, and I fear she's actually giving him another chance, especially when she slides the chain off the door and opens it a little wider. But just as Luke's expression begins to morph into what I'm sure is intended to be a victory grin, Julie's does the same, then she slams the door shut in his face, which—given Luke's shout of pain—isn't quite clear of the gap.

Julie strides defiantly back along the hall and into the kitchen, pours herself the biggest glass of wine *ever,* and then—completely against the run of play—bursts into tears. Huge, shoulder-heaving sobs that I suspect might take a long, long time to subside.

"What have I *done*?" she says, to no one in particular through a river of snot, but all I can do is look up at her proudly.

Because the answer to that is "the right thing."

15

It's a long few days before phase two of Operation Julie and Tom can take place (i.e. until I have my stitches out)—a long few days during which not much happens. Julie calls in sick, and in a rare show of decency, Luke appears to have fucked off, as per Julie's request (or at least, he's not been back to the house). And while at some point she'll have to go back to work, hopefully by then I'll have worked my matchmaking magic.

As an unexpected bonus, and in what could be regarded as a strange, dogs-looking-like-their-owners type thing, Luke's disappearance from our lives has coincided with Santa going missing. I know this for two reasons: firstly, the multitude of Lost Cat posters taped to pretty much every lamppost between here and the park, and secondly because Miss Harris is giving me the evils every time she sees me, almost as if she suspects I've had something to do with it.

"Any sign, Mary?" Julie calls magnanimously over the garden fence, as we head off to the corner store.

Miss Harris pulls herself unsteadily to her feet from where she's been weeding her already weed-free flowerbeds. "Not yet," she says, and the hope in her voice almost breaks your heart.

"Has she gone missing before?" says Julie, probably out of politeness more than anything. I suspect she won't be disappointed if Santa doesn't return either, if only for the sake of her plants.

"Not like this," sniffs Miss Harris.

"I'm sure she'll turn up," says Julie. "Especially with all those posters you've put up."

Miss Harris nods. "Hopefully they'll do the trick," she says, as we make our way toward the front gate.

I try and fail to hide a skeptical snort—after all, it's not as if cats can *read*—and as Julie looks down at me, I do my best to look as innocent as possible.

"Hoping Santa's gone for good, eh, Doug?" she says, and I give a flick of my tail. If only I could be sure the same thing was true of Luke, then all our problems would be sorted.

"Morning, Julie."

Sanj, Priya's husband, and the store's owner, beams at Julie from where he's stacking a shelf behind the till. "Morning, Doug," he adds, so I snort a greeting up at him as we walk in—there's a No Dogs sign on the shop's door, but we've long ago established it doesn't apply to me.

Obediently, I follow Julie to the fridge in the back of the store, then let out a sigh when she picks up a carton of skimmed milk instead of her usual whole. Every time a relationship ends, Julie mistakenly correlates her size with how attractive men find her, and I can only assume somewhere deep inside she feels the Luke scenario has played out this way because of it. What's worse is, Julie on a diet severely limits the number of snacks and biscuits in the house. Just because *she's* trying to lose a bit of weight, I don't see a reason why I have to.

She stops in the vegetable aisle to collect a packet of something leafy, and I realize I'm going to have to rely on Julie's dad's café trips for my treats for the next few weeks—or at least, until Julie and Tom get together and she puts an end to this nonsense. All the more incentive for me to get a move on, I suppose.

After grabbing a box of something I've tasted before called Special K—that isn't *that* special—she deposits her armful of shopping on the counter next to the register, where Sanj takes it all in with a knowing look.

"Priya told me," he says, the equivalent for him of climbing a conversational Mount Everest. Sanj usually prefers to keep out of Julie's love life. And I'm sure there are times he'd prefer Priya to do exactly that too.

"Right."

Sanj looks like he's hoping that's the end of it, although he also looks like he knows it perhaps shouldn't be. "So, um, how are you doing?"

"It's for the best," Julie says, still sounding like she's trying to convince herself, and Sanj nods in agreement.

"You'll meet someone else," he suggests, then a worried look crosses his face. It's justified because Julie's expression has suddenly turned to thunder.

"I don't want to meet someone else!" she says. "At least, I didn't!"

"That's not what I..." Sanj looks down at me, but there's not a lot I can do to help him out of the hole he's digging for himself. "I meant someone different. Someone who wasn't..."

"Married?"

"Who wasn't Luke, I was going to say. But now that you mention it."

"Why does no one have a good word to say about him?"

"Well, perhaps because only bad ones can be used to describe him?"

Sanj has probably meant it as a joke, but Julie doesn't look like she's found it funny in the slightest. "He had his good points."

"Which were?"

Julie stares at him for a moment, then for another moment longer, and then, it looks as if she's having some kind of breakthrough. Either that, or a seizure.

"Why didn't you ever say anything?"

"Like what? None of us like your boyfriend, Julie?" he says, doing bunny ears around the *b* word. "We think he's a total dick? That'd be like me saying I don't like *Doug*," he adds, and I snort at the preposterousness of the idea.

"Well, *yes*."

"Couldn't you tell?"

"Well, yes," Julie says, again. "Though I thought that was because he was, you know..."

Sanj looks at her and smiles. We all know there are a number of words that could complete that sentence. "Come on," he says. "How many times did we ever go out? The four of us?"

"Well, there was that time we went to the pub together. When Luke and I had been dating for a month or so."

"That was by accident. The two of you walked in when Priya and I were already there. And he didn't look at all happy to see us."

"Well, that was because it was..." Julie frowns. "I mean, he was..." She clears her throat. "We invited you round for dinner."

"And we couldn't make it. Ever. What does that tell you?" Sanj shakes his head. "I couldn't stand him, Jules. Sorry."

"Why ever not?"

Sanj takes a deep breath. "Well, seeing as you brought it up, that time at the pub, when Luke and I went to the bar to get the drinks? Aside from his making no move to pay for them…"

"He'd forgotten his wallet, he said."

"…He spent the whole time checking out the other women sitting there. *And* flirted with the bartender."

"I'm sure he was just being…friendly."

"And when I told him Priya and I had an arranged marriage, he said 'yeah, well, Jules and I have an arrangement too, if you know what I mean?'"

I can sense Julie's hackles rising. "Maybe that was just banter. You know, boys will be boys, and all that?"

Sanj just looks at her, and Julie's mouth falls open. "You should have told me," she says, a little testily.

"Told you what, exactly? The man you're seeing is a letch, and never going to leave his pregnant wife for you?"

"She wasn't pregnant then!" says Julie, then she hesitates, maybe wondering whether that makes it better or worse. But Sanj has a point, and Julie knows it. She purses her lips, shakes her head, and nods down at her shopping. "No chance of that now, anyway," she says, curtly.

"No," says Sanj, and the two of them stand in silence for a while, before Sanj remembers what his job is, and rings up Julie's items. He points at the card reader, evidently doing his best not to restart a conversation, though as Julie inserts her card, he clears his throat gingerly. "Did you want a bag?"

"Unless you think Doug can carry it all?" snaps Julie, so Sanj peels one off from the roll behind the till.

"It's, um, five pee." He holds the plastic bag up, then points to a brown material one on a hook behind him. "Or you can have one of these. They're recyclable. You know, save the planet." He does a little dance, though what that has to do with anything ecological I'm not sure. "For the sake of our, you know…" He swallows so hard you don't need hearing as good as mine to hear it. "Kids."

Julie glares at him as she roots around in her handbag for a five-pence piece, slamming it down on the counter before snatching the plastic bag from his hand, stuffing her groceries into it, and storming out of the shop.

And as we walk briskly back home, Julie muttering angrily to herself, I'm even more resolved to get this resolved.

16

Today, finally, is Friday, which I'm happy about, because it's Stitches Out day, which means I'll finally be rid of this ridiculous plastic cone. And though it necessitates another visit to the V-E-T, that V-E-T is T-O-M, and I'm even more determined he's the one who's going to finally get Julie's mind off Luke.

Perhaps in sympathy with my injury, Julie's not been back to work all week, which has helped in that aspect too, as has the fact that Luke's not dared to come around since her ultimatum the other day. This is something I suspect Julie's equally relieved and unhappy about.

"You ready, Doug?" she says, once I've finished my "usual" breakfast, and I snort appropriately in response. Julie doesn't look ready, however. She's still in the sloppy jogging pants and loose-fitting sweatshirt combo she's been wearing all week—hardly the correct attire for meeting her future husband-to-be. Even her ripped jeans might be preferable, but Julie doesn't seem to feel a visit to see Tom warrants the same amount of effort an encounter with Luke used to.

At least not yet.

It's a short drive to Tom's office, which is just as well because the cone makes it impossible to stick my head out of the car window given how it catches the wind. When we get there, the waiting room is the usual mix of subdued dogs, along with a couple of cats in those plastic carrying cases, or "cat jails," as Julie's dad refers to them, and a parrot which keeps swearing, much to the amusement of the five-year-old boy with a cocker spaniel sitting opposite with his mum.

"Name?" says the receptionist brusquely, as we march up to the counter.

"Doug," says Julie, and the woman narrows her eyes.

"Full name," she says, and Julie hesitates.

"Um, Doug… Las?"

"*Your* name," says the woman, not even raising a smile at Julie's faux pas.

"Oh. Right. Sorry. Julie. Julie Newman."

The receptionist taps something into her computer, then frowns. "Any other name?"

"Well, my middle name's Elizab…"

"That you might be booked in under."

"Oh. Sorry. Um, no." Julie leans over the counter and peers at the screen.

"I don't see an appointment," the receptionist says, tilting it out of view, implying she's the only one important enough to look at it.

"Right. No. Well, Tom said we should just pop by today and…"

"Tom?" I can almost hear the boom from breaking the sound barrier the receptionist's eyebrow makes, given how quickly she raises it. "You mean Doctor Armstrong."

Julie frowns. "I might. I don't actually know his name. Surname, that is. He stitched Doug's ear up last week, and..."

The receptionist gives Julie a look that suggests she's accustomed to Tom's shenanigans playing havoc with her booking system. "Right," she says. "If you'd like to take a seat, I'll do my best to squeeze you in. Although there are quite a few appointments to get through before he'll be able to see you."

Julie looks at her watch, then glances at the door, then at me, and then at her watch again, in the manner of someone who's debating the merits of spending a morning in a V-E-T's waiting room versus a bit of DIY surgery back home. For a moment, I fear we're about to leave, then all of a sudden, I hear a familiar voice call, "Doug!" from across the room. The cone's still obstructing my vision, so I attempt a slightly tricky reverse three-point turn, and by the time I'm facing in the direction the voice came from, Tom's kneeling down in front of me.

"How are you doing?" he says, scratching me affectionately on the top of my head.

"He seems fine," says Julie.

"Any problems with him otherwise?" says Tom, gently inspecting my ear. "I'm guessing he hasn't been off his food?"

Julie snorts with laughter at this. I can't imagine why.

"Well, his ear seems to be healing nicely." He climbs back to his feet and smiles at Julie. "I'll just get those stitches out, and..." Tom stops talking.

The receptionist has just pointedly cleared her throat.

"Who was next?" he asks her, though it's obvious it's going to be us.

"Well, Mrs. Waters has been waiting for a while." She nods across to an old lady sitting in the corner, next to a Great Dane who's big enough for her to have ridden it here.

"Right. Thanks."

Tom beckons for us to follow him, then he flashes Mrs.

Waters *that* smile, tells her he'll see her in a moment, and escorts Julie and me into his consulting room.

"So, have you had a good week?" he asks, lifting me up onto the examination table.

"Sorry," says Julie, after a moment. "Were you talking to me this time?"

Tom laughs. "Unless Doug here has suddenly developed the power of speech, I'd better have been. That is unless I'm going a bit..." He puts a finger to his temple, spins it rapidly round, and crosses his eyes. "Anyway," he says, as he unfastens my cone and removes it carefully from around my neck. "Freedom!"

Tom's just mimicked Julie's dad's Scottish accent, and Julie says, "Braveheart?" and Tom grins and nods, and I understand it's a reference to the film rather than an appreciation of how stoic I've been. I snort encouragingly, then shake my head rapidly from side to side, glad to be free of my plastic prison.

"Better?" says Tom, definitely to me this time, then he peers at my ear, and says, "You didn't answer my question," so I give Julie the side-eye to indicate he is, in fact, now talking to her.

"A good week?"

Julie harrumphs.

"What?" says Tom, picking up a pair of tweezers, and gently taking hold of my ear with his other hand.

"Are you genuinely interested, or is this just some bedside manner thing?" Julie says. "You know, small talk to put me at ease, distract me before you pull those stitches out without warning."

As I wonder why on earth Julie's the one who needs to be put at ease seeing as I'm the one undergoing surgery, Tom leans in close with the tweezers and yanks the first stitch out. It smarts, and as I stare at him in shock, Tom grins down at me. "Sorry, Doug. No easy way to do that, I'm afraid."

I let out an exaggerated sigh, then brace myself for the rest.

"It wasn't. You know, bedside," says Tom, synchronizing his conversation with stitch removal. "Because you're not, you know…the one who's technically…in bed." Tom pulls out the last stitch, then produces a cotton wool swab and a bottle of some liquid which I'm not looking forward to him applying. There may be a small logo featuring some bones on the bottle, but there's a skull above them too, which kind of transforms it from potentially tasty treat to a little bit scary. "So?" he says.

"Well, no, actually. Luke and I… We split up."

Tom looks up sharply, an expression of genuine concern on his face. "I'm sorry to hear that."

"No, you're not!"

"I am, if it's made you unhappy." Tom dabs my ear with whatever the liquid is. It smells pretty bad, and stings a little, but I'm far too interested in what's going on between him and Julie to let it bother me. "Did you want to talk about it?"

"Not really. I mean, I know it was the right thing to do, so…"

"Not even over coffee? On me?"

"Isn't that a bit…unethical?"

"Me asking you for coffee?" he laughs. "Again, if I was asking Doug, then maybe. If not a bit weird."

"A lot weird."

"Fair point." Tom laughs again—it's a cheeky, infectious laugh, and I can't help but pick up on the mood, so I wag my tail, and he frowns at me. "It's the strangest thing, but I get the feeling that Doug understands every word I say."

A broad smile appears on Julie's face, and I'm pleased, because it's the first time I've seen that in a while. "He has that effect on people."

Tom turns his attention back to swabbing my ear. "So?"

Julie sighs, and it's one of those sighs she often makes

through her nose that's usually followed by something negative. "Listen, Tom," she says, even though he's already listening. "I've just been through a painful breakup, and I'm sure you're very nice, although if you were then you'd be disproving what I currently think about all men, and it's extremely kind of you to treat Doug like this, and for free, and I'm flattered that you asked me out, even though despite what you said, it might be a bit ethically suspect, but..." She stops talking.

Tom's holding a hand up.

"What?"

"I didn't ask you out."

"Pardon?"

"You said I asked you out. I didn't."

"You just did!"

"When?"

"Just now. You asked me if I wanted to talk about it. Over coffee."

"Oh, that." The smile appears again. "Right. Well, I can see why you might have thought that was me asking you out, but it wasn't."

Julie's cheeks darken. "It wasn't?"

"No. You said you'd..." He hesitates, perhaps not wanting to remind Julie about Luke. "Had a bad week. I wondered if you wanted to talk about it. Over coffee."

"Yes, but asking someone for a coffee has got...implications."

"Asking someone *in* for a coffee, maybe. After you've been out. But..."

"Well, whatever, and I appreciate the offer, but the answer's no. Sorry. I'm not...in a good place right now. And so it wouldn't be..."

"Hey—I get it," says Tom, holding up his hands as if warming them in front of a fire.

"Great," says Julie, followed by a softer, "thank you."

The two of them stand there awkwardly for a moment, before Julie says, "So?" and nods at me, and Tom seems to suddenly remember what he was right in the middle of.

"Right. Doug. Of course," he says, lifting me up off the treatment table. "He might find where the stitches have been is a bit tender for a few days, but apart from that..." Tom narrows his eyes as he inspects me. "All looks good. Although..."

"Although?"

He gives Julie the side-eye. "Someone's maybe a little on the heavy side."

I hold my breath: The one time Luke commented on her weight, it didn't go down particularly well, though to her credit Julie's not looking all that offended.

"This isn't going to be *that* joke, is it?" she says.

"What joke?"

"Where you say you're going to have to put him down, and I get all worried, then you say, because your arms are getting tired..."

Tom looks at her for a moment, then he roars with laughter, and despite the antiseptic he's been dabbing on my ear, his laugh's evidently infectious, because Julie joins in.

"I must remember that one!" he says, once he's regained his composure, which takes a while. "Seriously, though."

"Really? Despite a walk to the park every day?"

"Even so," Tom continues. "I do this thing in the park on Sunday mornings. It's an exercise class. Kind of like Parkrun, but people bring their dogs."

"So, *Barkrun*," says Julie, dryly.

Tom does that slapping-himself-on-the-forehead thing people do when they've been stupid. "I should *so* call it that instead of 'pets-ercise,'" he says. "But it might be a good idea if you and Doug came along? It starts at ten."

"I'll think about it," says Julie, though in the manner of someone who probably won't, and I can't say I'm all that surprised. Her brief attempt at something called Zumba a few months ago, prompted by Luke's comment that he liked "curvy" women as he'd grabbed her backside, didn't last very long.

"Great!" says Tom, as if he's forcing himself to be upbeat. "Right."

"Okay, then."

"Well, thanks for, you know..." Julie peers at where I'm still in Tom's arms, and Tom seems surprised to realize he's still holding me, so he passes me across, and Julie gives me a cuddle, then lowers me to the floor, grunting a little with the effort, and Tom gives her a look.

"Most welcome," he says, then he nods in the direction of the waiting room. "I ought to..."

"Sure."

"You take care of that ear now."

"What do I have to...?"

"I was talking to Doug," says Tom, then he grins. "He'll be fine, as long as he doesn't pick a fight with anyone else. I'm sure he doesn't want to have to go through this again. Do you, Doug?"

I hold his gaze for a moment, then do a top-to-bottom shake to say it was fine, really. In the overall scheme of things, I didn't feel a thing.

Though my worry is, neither did Julie.

17

In stark contrast with Julie's general apathy, Julie's dad couldn't be more wired when he arrives to walk me today, although it's not until we get to the park that I realize what it is: *nervous energy.*

He's also wearing a brand-new shirt—so brand-new, in fact, that it's still bearing the creases from where it's been folded in the packet—plus he's liberally splashed himself with after-shave. *Why* he's gone to all this effort, however, only becomes clear when we near the café, where he slows to a gradual stop, then peers down at me.

"How do I look?"

I give him a customary once-over and snort approvingly, adding a tail twitch or two for good measure. "Thanks, Doug," he says, then he glances across to the café's entrance, and puffs air out of his cheeks.

"Will you look at me?" he says, holding his hand out to show me how much it's trembling. "My heart's beating through my chest!"

I peer up at him, flicking my eyes repeatedly toward the café in an attempt to get him to move.

"Hang on, Douglas," he says. "I just need to..." He takes a deep breath, glances up at the sky, mouths what I think is *sorry*, for some reason, then starts walking purposefully along the path.

I fall into step with him obediently, but I don't notice Julie's dad slowing down again, or that I'm overtaking him, and as I trot a leash-length past his legs, I'm suddenly jerked to an unceremonious stop.

"Sorry, Doug, I can't... I mean, what if she...?"

Julie's dad doesn't finish the sentence. Instead, he does a complete one-eighty and heads off in the opposite direction. I try for a moment to dig my feet in, but despite having double the number that Julie's dad does, find myself being dragged back along the path like a canine water-skier. It's a little painful, and it's not affecting the outcome, so I reluctantly segue into a trotting motion, and—more than a little puzzled—follow him. Then suddenly, I twig what's going on: he's been about to take Julie's advice, and ask Dot for a *date*.

The behavior's certainly similar to the early days of Julie and Luke, when Julie used to take *ages* getting ready for work, always making sure her makeup was immaculate, and I suddenly understand that this is important—not only for Julie's dad's future happiness, but also for Julie's. After all, if she sees her dad with Dot, she might be inspired to get on with it with Tom.

Knowing I have to act, and quickly, and without a thought for my personal safety, I gather some slack in my leash, dart to my left, and quickly circle the lamppost next to the path, then dig my claws firmly into the grass in an attempt to bring Julie's dad to a halt. Which it does. A little too abruptly.

"Doug, what the!" Julie's dad rubs his shoulder. "What are

you playing at, getting tangled round the lamppost like that? You could have dislocated my arm."

I peer back over my shoulder toward the café, throwing in a whine for good measure, and Julie's dad sighs.

"Are you that desperate for a muffin?"

I'm not, but I am desperate for Julie's dad to ask Dot out and kick off a chain of events that should culminate in Julie and Tom getting together, so I increase the intensity of my whine. After a moment, Julie's dad shakes his head exasperatedly.

"Fine," he says, perhaps a little petulantly, as he untangles me, adding, "Anyone would have thought you did that on purpose," as we make our way back along the path.

We reach the café, and Julie's dad stops in front of the window, and I fear he's about to lose his nerve again, but it's only so he can check his reflection in the glass. As he smooths down a stray tuft of hair, I spot Dot watching him from inside, and she sees what he's doing, and suddenly her expression changes, as if she knows exactly why he's here, what he's about to ask her, and the look on her face is priceless.

Julie's dad's obviously happy with what he sees, because he grins down at me and says, "Life in the old dog yet!" which I guess I'm supposed to take as a compliment. Then he says, "wish me luck," so I give him a mental thumbs-up, and lead him inside to where a slightly flushed-looking Dot is waiting by the till.

As I watch them flirting—Dot smiling and touching her hair absentmindedly, Julie's dad standing ramrod-straight and sucking his stomach in—it occurs to me that maybe Julie's problem with Tom right now is the opposite of what her dad's just demonstrated. She doesn't feel good about herself, especially given the wringer that Luke's been putting her through—and if that is the case, then it's no wonder she can't bring herself to flirt with Tom.

Fortunately, though, and not for the first time, Priya and I seem to be on the same wavelength. Because it turns out that—although it's thanks to *me*—she's the one who provides me with a solution to my problem.

18

It's Friday night, and Priya's around for her and Julie's usual *Game of Thrones* session. She's brought pizza, which Julie's turned her nose up at due to her diet, though worryingly, she's eschewed that for more of a liquid one recently.

"Poor Doug," says Priya, picking me up and examining the shaved area where my stitches were, before attempting a kiss on the top of my head.

"No tongues, Doug," says Julie, which sends the two of them into a spasm of laughter that lasts so long I worry we'll miss the start of the program.

"He's a better kisser than Sanj!" Priya wipes her lips on her sleeve. "And your ex, I'd imagine."

Julie gives her a look, but I can tell she finds it funny.

"Speaking of which?" continues Priya, as she sets me down carefully on the rug.

Julie shrugs. "Haven't been in to work, have I?"

Priya follows us along the hall and into the front room,

wrinkling her nose at the state of the place. "All week?" she says, cracking open a window.

Julie shrugs again. "I pulled a sickie."

"I'm pleased he's out of your life now. Personally, at least."

Julie gives her another look, and Priya suddenly seems a little concerned. "You haven't *actually* been ill, have you?" she asks, and Julie shakes her head.

"I just haven't felt..." Julie finishes the sentence prematurely, flops down on the sofa, and picks up a glass of wine from the side table—a glass that's been there since yesterday, I realize, with a mixture of shock and disappointment. "Like seeing him."

"You can just take the week off like that?"

"Don't see why not."

"And you're not worried about Luke taking some sort of disciplinary action?"

Julie gives her another look, though this one appears to be to work out whether Priya's being rude. "Nah," she says. "What's he going to do—fire me, and risk what I might say to HR at my exit interview?"

Priya grins. "Good for you," she says, retrieving a bin bag from the drawer in the kitchen. "Though you can't let him win, Jules."

"How is he winning?"

"You love your job." Priya circles the front room, collecting empties as she goes. "And your avoiding him is stopping you from doing it. Instead, you're just moping around the house. Which isn't helping anyone."

"I just..." Julie drains the glass of wine, then grimaces. "How can I face him, P? I mean, I know it was me who rejected him, but I can't help feeling the opposite is true."

"Well, for starters, you can walk in there on Monday morning with your head held high. Show him he's the loser, not you."

"How? I hardly feel—or look—like that's the case."

"Oh, babes!" Priya sits down next to her, puts an arm around her shoulders, and gives her a squeeze. "Listen," she says, rooting around in her handbag and retrieving an envelope. "I know it's a little early, but I got this for you." She reaches down and pets me briefly. "Well, for Doug, really, for his birthday next Sunday. But it's really for the two of you."

Julie stares at Priya's gift. "What is it?"

"Well, customarily, the best way to find that out is to open it."

"Now?"

Priya nods eagerly, though I don't share her excitement. It's obviously nothing to eat, plus I'm not really into celebrating my birthday—after all, who wants to be reminded they're seven years older?

But Julie takes the envelope anyway, tears it open, then extracts a small printed card with the word *voucher* stamped on the back.

"What's this?"

"It's a voucher."

Julie makes the "Duh!" face. "For?"

"Turn it over."

Julie does as instructed. "Doggy Style? What on earth is that?"

Priya taps the card with her fingernail. "It's that new pets-and-their-owners beauty salon on the High Street. They were advertising this makeover promotion thingy in the window, so I thought to myself, what do you get the dog who has everything? And this was it!"

"Pets and their owners," says Julie, suspiciously.

"That's right," says Priya, excitedly. "You go there and have your hair and makeup and nails done, meanwhile they do the same for Doug. Minus the makeup part, I imagine."

"Right," says Julie, unenthusiastically, and Priya's face falls. "Don't you like it?"

"No, I do, and it's a lovely idea, P, but..." Julie stares miserably into her empty wineglass. "You know how I don't like change."

"It's a voucher for a makeover, not gender reassignment surgery."

"Yes, but... What's the point?"

"So you can show him what he's been missing!" She gives Julie another squeeze. "You're going to have to go back to work at some point, and you can either go there looking like you do now..."

"Thanks a lot!"

"I didn't mean it like that. I just meant..." Priya sighs in a matter-of-fact way. "The better you look, the better you'll feel. And the worse he will."

"I'm not sure, P."

"Why ever not? What's the worst that could happen?"

Julie shrugs, and I freeze. Because the worst that could happen is that Julie ends up looking fabulous, Luke sees *exactly* what he's been missing, and convinces her to give him another chance. And if that's occurred to me, then it's quite probably occurred to Julie. A suspicion I'm worried is confirmed when a strange look crosses her face.

"Fine," she says.

All I can do is keep both sets of paws crossed that it will be.

19

Whatever her motivation, Priya's pep talk yesterday has obviously had the desired effect, because Julie virtually leaps out of bed this morning, empties a generous helping of the usual into my bowl, then heads straight for the shower, and is on the phone and booking our makeover appointment almost before I've finished eating.

Ominously, they can fit us in first thing, so Julie starts to check the novelty pugs-in-stupid-costumes calendar on her kitchen wall that she got in last Christmas's office Secret Santa to check what is on her agenda, then sees she's got nothing else to do today and says, though not particularly enthusiastically, "Great."

She may not be particularly keen to go given how she feels Luke's rejected her and, to tell the truth, I can understand that. When you're a rescue dog, you've been rejected too in a way, which means you're naturally very suspicious of anyone who comes along to rescue you. Partly it's the unsettled feeling—you've been in one place, then another, now you're going to be taken to a third, with no guarantee you're not going to be returned if things don't work out. Also, it's the worry that you might just be going to more of the same—after all, you don't need qualifications to own a dog. Or a license. You can just…get one. And the same is true for relationships.

It took me months of living with Julie before I was sure I wasn't going back to *that* place. Ages before I stopped thinking every trip in the car was the last one I'd be taking with her. The best part of a year until I could finally relax.

And this is why I identify with Julie, sympathize with her situation, feel for her dilemma—because I'd be exactly the same. Her concept of a relationship has come from her time with Luke. She's used to playing second fiddle. Always being an afterthought. Never being taken out for walks, if you like, because that just wasn't an option. So she's nervous.

Perhaps she's even worried that this is just how relationships *are*—because that's been her experience. Remarkably Luke has been her first steady boyfriend—if you consider him as such. And while it's all very well to say that she should just look at the likes of Priya and Sanj in the same way I used to gaze out of the rescue home's window at other dogs and see cared-for canines being walked regularly and believe that that's how it was going to be for me, the reality is that sometimes that's just too big a stretch. And so, like me back then as I cowered in my cage in the kennels, Julie is afraid to go take a chance with someone new in case it doesn't work out. Again.

But the thing is, you've got to start over at some point. Take the odd leap of faith. And somewhere, deep down, I'm sure that Julie knows that.

There's an old Chinese proverb, *Qiānlǐ zhī xíng, shǐyú zú xià,* which is something about the longest journey starting with a single step. And as Julie pulls on her jacket, clips on my leash, then leads me purposefully out through the front door, something tells me we're both taking one this morning.

Doggy Style is at the far end of the High Street, and while from the outside it looks a little like a slightly less-threatening dentist's, the moment we walk in, we're treated like their best—albeit only—customers.

"Julie! *Darling!*" A large, heavily-made-up woman who could be anything from twenty to two hundred years old given the amount of foundation she's wearing greets us effusively. She's got a strange, asymmetrical haircut, with eyebrows that look like they've been drawn on with an indelible marker. And from what I can make out from my lowly position on the floor, a tattoo of a coiled snake disappears down between her cleavage. "I'm *Alexa*," she announces. "Like the personal assistant! Though you don't need to say my name every time you want me to do something. Especially if you're a *man*!" Alexa roars with laughter at this, then envelops Julie in the kind of hug you might see in a bout of Sumo wrestling.

Julie reels back from this woman—though she could just be temporarily overcome by the amount of perfume Alexa's evidently doused herself in because I certainly am—and smiles a nervous hello in return. Then Alexa squats down, grabs me just behind my front legs, and hoists me up to her face height. "And who's this handsome *beast*?" she says, pulling me close and planting a sloppy kiss on my nose.

"This is Doug," says Julie, smirking as I sneeze violently and coat Alexa with a fine mist of snot.

"He's *delightful*," exclaims Alexa. "*Aren't* you, Doug?"

I give Julie a desperate, sideways look, willing her to save me from quite possibly the scariest woman I've ever met. But thankfully, before I become asphyxiated by Alexa's perfume cloud, she places me gently back down on the floor, then returns to the reception desk, peers down at the appointments book, licks her finger, and flicks through the pages.

"Here we are. Julie and Doug Newman. You're here for the dual makeover, yes?"

"Um, yes," says Julie, nervously. "Though when you say makeover, what exactly…?" Her voice trails off as Alexa reaches over the desk to grab a lock of Julie's hair, inspecting it as if it's something she's just pulled out of her shower drain.

"Listen, hon," Alexa says. "Did someone *buy* you this voucher?"

"My friend Priya," says Julie. "For Doug's birthday."

"*Doug's* birthday?"

"That's right."

"Hmm." Alexa leans in and peers at her. "And why do you suppose this Priya bought you a makeover?"

"Well, technically, she bought it for Doug…"

"Oh-kay." Alexa folds her arms. "But why a *makeover*?"

"Pardon?"

"Why not something else. Like a…" Alexa waves a scarily-manicured hand in the air. "New collar. Or a chew toy."

"Well, because…"

Alexa raises an eyebrow. "Mmm-hmm?"

"Because she thought it might be fun?" suggests Julie. "You know, for me and Doug. To…"

"Julie, Julie, *Julie*." Alexa takes Julie's hand in one of hers, covering the back of it with her other. "Sometimes, we buy people presents because it's something we think we might like. Other times it's because we feel it's something they might like. And *then*…"

"Then?" asks Julie, although she looks like she doesn't really want to know what the answer is.

"Sometimes, people buy presents because they think it's what the other person *needs*."

"I...I don't..." stutters Julie, then she stops talking because all of a sudden, it's evident that maybe Alexa is right.

"Been through a breakup recently, have we? Or maybe single for a while?"

"Well, yes. I mean, no, but..."

"I'm no psychiatrist," says Alexa, in a tone that suggests she actually thinks she is. "But my guess is your friend bought this voucher for *you*, not Doug, and probably because she felt you could do with a change. And the fact that you've come along to cash it in straightaway suggests that you feel you do too. Am I right, or am I *right*?"

"Well..."

Alexa clicks her fingers so scarily loud that it makes me jump, and almost instantly, a young woman appears and hands a glass of something fizzy to Julie.

"That's what we do here, Julie. You've been dumped, you come in here and we'll get you to a place where you show him what he's missing."

I almost can't take my eyes off Alexa, so fascinated I am with her performance. Even *I'd* be moved by what she's saying, and there's nothing I want to change about myself.

Then I hear a sound I've heard all too often recently, so I spin round and nuzzle Julie's leg in an attempt to stop her tears.

"That's right." Alexa takes Julie's glass, sets it carefully down on the reception counter, then leans over and envelops her in another huge Sumo-hug. "Let it all *out*."

As Julie does as instructed and bawls at the top of her voice, Alexa strokes the small of her back until the worst of the sobs have subsided. Then she hands Julie's glass back to her.

"Now, you drink that down, and leave everything else to us," she says.

So that's exactly what Julie does.

★ ★ ★

I've been shampooed, conditioned, blow-dried, and combed to within an inch of my life, had any wayward hairs snipped, my nails clipped, and even had my teeth cleaned, and I'm waiting back in reception, slurping my way through a huge bowl of something called "Evian" when there's a loud "Ta-daa!" from Alexa, presumably for my benefit, as there's no one else here. Then she all but pushes Julie into the room.

For a second, I don't believe what I'm seeing. Her hair is shorter, shinier and neater, her skin's positively glowing, her nails are manicured and gleam with a vivid dark polish, in contrast to her almost blindingly-white teeth. All in all, she's the female human equivalent of me. And what's more, I can tell she's pleased with the result.

"Doug, you look…" Julie hoists me up and holds me in front of the full-length mirror so I can inspect myself.

"Doesn't he?" says Alexa, and Julie beams at me, then studies her own reflection.

"And you," Alexa continues. "You look like a *million dollars*!"

"I don't know, I…"

"Of course you do!" Alexa mock-punches her on the shoulder. "Doesn't she, Doug?"

I snort appropriately, and Alexa turns her attention to Julie's mirror-image. "Now, remember what I told you about that new skin regime. And your hair's a low-maintenance style, so you can pretty much just wash and go. All in all, you should be set up pretty nicely for *you know what*!" Alexa winks at her. "And if Doug's got his eye on any lady dogs in the park…"

"Oh, he's been fixed."

"Really?" Alexa fixes me with a sympathetic eye. "Shame. Still, it's the thought that counts. Isn't it, Doug!" She bursts out laughing, which is perhaps a little mean given what she's laughing about. "And you remember what I told you about that man of yours too!"

I prick my ears up at this.

"I'm not sure, Alexa."

"You mark my words! A famous philosopher once said… Or it might have been Dolly Parton. I don't remember." She frowns. "Anyway, the gist of it was, the best way to get over a man is to get under another one. And it sounds like you and this Tom…"

Alexa nudges her, then winks down at me, but I'm still too stunned to respond. Julie's obviously been opening her heart to Alexa, and unprompted she's apparently brought Tom up. What's more, it sounds like Alexa's told her exactly what she probably needed to hear—and while Julie probably doesn't want to take it from Priya, or Julie's dad, or even Sanj, maybe the fact that it's come from someone without a vested interest means this time it might sink in.

"Maybe," Julie says, in a way that suggests she actually agrees. Then she hugs Alexa goodbye, clips my leash back onto my collar, and—a spring in her step—leads me out of the salon.

20

"Come on, Doug," says Julie, in the kind of artificially cheerful voice that's often meant to disguise some sort of not-fun activity like a trip to the V-E-T.

She's still looking like a million dollars, perhaps partly because she didn't consume her usual bottle of wine last night, plus she's traded her jogging-pants-and-loose-sweatshirt look of the past few days for her Zumba outfit—perhaps not the most appropriate attire for our usual Sunday morning park outing. Still, whatever the motive is for the pretend enthusiasm or why we're going out dressed like this, it's a walk.

It's a sunny morning, and there are lots of people milling around the park, but for some reason Julie won't let me dawdle. Though that reason soon becomes clear as we make our way over to the opposite side to the café, and to where a group of half a dozen women are waiting, holding onto various dogs of their own, and dressed like they're off to some high-fashion aerobics class too.

Before I can figure out what's going on, there's an excited

murmur from the human contingent, and to my surprise, none other than a tracksuit-clad *Tom* appears through the park gates. It's then I notice the pile of equipment in the corner, and everything falls into place: we're at *Barkrun*. Julie's obviously decided that in her quest to meet someone new, she could do with losing a bit of weight. And she's decided to do it with Tom—or *for* Tom, perhaps, after what Alexa said yesterday.

Tom bounds over, takes up position in front of us all, then strips down to a tightly-fitted T-shirt and gym shorts combination and fixes a smile on his face. Out of his normal work clothes, he's the human equivalent of a Weimaraner, or one of those other finely-muscled, boundlessly-energetic genetically-blessed dogs. A buzz of appreciation rises from the group.

"Thank you all for coming," he says, oblivious to the drooling that's coming not from the assembled dogs, but their owners. "As you know, fitness for our four-legged friends is very important. The less weight they're carrying, the less strain on their joints, and on the most important muscle of all, which is…" His gaze flicks around the group, finally settling on Julie, who's tentatively put her hand up, and he widens his eyes at her, perhaps in surprise at her attendance, though more likely in appreciation of her new look.

"The, um, *heart*?" she says, without the slightest bit of irony.

"That's right!" Tom beams at her, and there's a ripple of what appears to be jealousy from the rest of the women. "Remember, dogs are active by nature. They're descended from wolves, who typically cover many miles every day in search of food, whereas some of this lot…" He grins. "Well, the only distance they cover is possibly from their beds to their bowls and back again. And not having any opportunity for what's essentially a genetically-programmed activity level can lead to frustration, which may in turn lead to hyperactivity, excessive barking, digging, tail chasing, and even, in some extreme cases, home destruction."

There's a consensus of nodding and mumbled agreement from the group, though I can't help wondering why Tom's referring to the canine contingent, then it occurs to me that apart from one woman with an almost comically-fat Chihuahua, no human here looks like they're at all on the portly side. And then it hits me—this group exercise isn't for the benefit of our owners. It's actually for *us*.

I begin whining in horror, and Julie nudges me with her foot. "It's for your own good, Doug," she says, apologetically, and I snort disdainfully.

"So, as you probably know, I'm Tom," says Tom to the group, a statement that's met with an adoring chorus of "Hi, Tom," and he folds his arms self-consciously. "I see we have a few new faces this week, so why don't we introduce ourselves? Starting..." He peers quickly at each of us, reaches Julie, then gives her a barely-disguised wink. "With you with the pug, if you don't mind?"

Julie smiles back at him, then realizes she's supposed to speak now. "Oh, er, hi. My name's Julie."

"Hi, Julie," says Tom, followed by a seemingly resentful "hello" (and one, barely-audible "teacher's pet") from the rest of the group. "And...?"

"I'm sorry?"

"No need to apologize." He flashes that smile again. "Who have you brought with you today?"

Tom's nodded down at me, and I snort in embarrassment at Julie's lack of manners.

"Oh. Right. This is Doug."

"Doug the pug?" A woman standing next to us with a sausage dog named Frank who's shaped more like a meatball, lets out a short laugh. "Really?" she says.

I sigh pointedly through my nostrils. Julie's surname is Newman, and it rhymes with *human*, and no one ever seems to remark about *that*.

"My dad named him," says Julie.

"Well, I think it suits him," says Tom, and suddenly, I like him even more.

The rest of the newcomers introduce themselves without incident, cxcept for a general eye-rolling at a Westie called Kanye. Then it's evidently exercise time, as Tom tells everyone to begin jogging to the far side of the park and back.

I give Julie my best "seriously?" look. This is particularly unfair on us smaller dogs with our shorter legs, as borne out by the fact that it takes Frank and me almost twice as long as the others. Though when Frank's owner wonders out loud why Tom hasn't thought to introduce categories, like they do in the Paralympics, Tom assures us all it's not a competition.

Next, he leads us over to the corner of the park next to the football pitch, where he's set up a little obstacle course with jumps, tunnels, and some strange vertical sticks-in-a-line arrangement that we're supposed to "weave" through speedily. Tom's demonstration of how to do this makes some of the women pant almost as much as their dogs.

Fortunately, Julie's not the fastest of humans, so it's not too difficult to keep up with her. Actually, I've gone through worse chasing Santa out of our garden, so the course doesn't prove too difficult. So far, Barkrun isn't turning out to be the hour of torture I'd dreaded at the start. And apart from a slightly unsavory moment when Tom tells Kanye's owner off after she tries to tempt Kanye over a particularly tricky jump with a biscuit—apparently, it kind of defeats the purpose of being here—at the end of the hour, I feel fine. Most of us have taken it in our stride, even if some of our strides are a lot shorter than others. Julie, however, is looking a little flushed.

And as the group begins to head off in the direction of the café, Tom, who still looks as fresh as a daisy, jogs over to us.

"How was it?"

"It was…fun," says Julie, looking like she's surprised by her own answer.

Tom squats down next to me on the grass. "And for you, Doug?" he says, so I collapse down onto the grass and roll on my back, to pretend the session's done me in.

"He enjoyed it too, I think," says Julie.

"Great!" Tom gives me a quick chest rub, then leaps athletically back up to his feet, and flashes a smile at her. "So, just remember, no snacking between meals, cut back on the treats…"

"Is that me or Doug you're referring to?"

"Doug, obviously," says Tom, quickly. "You don't need to lose… I mean, your figure's…" He stops talking, having gone as dark in the face as Julie has after the exercise session. "So, will I see you again?" he says, and I hold my breath.

This could be it, I think, righting myself quickly. Julie might be about to ask Tom out, and then all our troubles will be over.

"Well, actually…" she says, perhaps a little hesitantly, though then the worst thing happens, and Tom evidently interprets her nervousness as reluctance. And whether it's to save face—his *or* hers—he quickly holds a hand up.

"Next week," he says, though it's a little difficult to interpret his expression. "Here. At Barkr… I mean, Pets-ercise."

"Oh. Right. I guess so," says Julie, noncommittally.

"Okay with you, Doug?" says Tom, so I snort approvingly up at him.

"But if you fancy a coffee…"

Julie's eyes widen, and I mentally chase my tail in celebration. This is *it*! And I think Julie knows it too, because she takes a deep breath. But before she can get any more out than, "Tom, I'd..." he nods toward the rest of the group.

"We all usually go to Mum's café after the class."

"Oh. Right." Julie's face falls so quickly, it's a wonder the momentum doesn't send her sprawling onto the grass. *How have I got this so wrong?* I can tell she's thinking, and to be honest, I'm wondering exactly the same thing. "Um, no, thanks. I have to, I mean, we..."

Tom grins, though there's not a lot of humor behind it. "Not a problem," he says, even though it quite plainly *is*. "So. I'll see you...?"

"Not if I see you first!" says Julie, then she looks like she wants to face-palm herself. "Sorry. You meant next week, didn't you?"

"Oh. Yeah. Next week." Tom nods. "For, you know, Doug's sake."

"For Doug's sake."

Tom gives a wistful smile, then he bounds off after the others, and I collapse down onto my back again. Next week it'll have to be. And every week after that, until the two of them realize they're perfect for each other. The upside, of course, is that I've now got an excuse to overeat all week.

And while I could do without the exercise part, to be honest, if that's what it takes to get him and Julie together, I'll just have to put up with it.

21

Despite what's just happened, there's a post-class buzz about Julie as we make our way home via the town center, so much so that she seems to be attracting admiring glances from almost every man we pass. While that may simply be because the leggings she's wearing are rather see-through from behind, I can tell she's flattered by the attention. But when a female voice calls her name from the other side of the street, the glow in her cheeks disappears as if a switch has been flicked.

I look up from where I've been sniffing a particularly aromatic lamppost, just in time to see a frantically-waving Sarah waddling across the street toward us. She's dragging a reluctant Luke behind her like a child on his way to the dentist, and given the look on Julie's face, I can tell she feels the same way about their meeting.

"How are you?" Sarah hesitates for a moment, then envelops Julie in a hug. "And, Doug—you must be pleased to be finally rid of that horrible thing."

I snort appropriately, assuming she means my cone, rather

than either Luke or Santa, although the answer's a resounding yes! to all of those things.

"We're…good," says Julie.

"You look better than good." Sarah holds her at arm's length. "In fact, you're positively *glowing*!"

"Oh." Julie looks down at me, and then evidently decides not to share the fact we've both been for a makeover. "We've just been to an exercise class."

"We?" says Sarah.

"Yeah. This guy I met. Tom… Well, long story short, he's a V-E-T, and he felt Doug could do with losing a little weight, so…"

"Tom, you say?" says Luke, though he immediately looks as if he could take it back, but if he's worried that Sarah may pick up on his tinge of jealousy, she doesn't seem to have noticed.

"Doug's not the only one!" she says, rubbing her stomach. "Seriously, though, you look amazing."

"I don't know," says Julie, awkwardly.

"You do! Doesn't she, Luke?"

"S'pose," says Luke, both awkwardly and begrudgingly. "Though she's been off work for the last few days, so it's good to see her looking, you know…surprisingly healthy."

"Don't be so suspicious!" Sarah rests a hand on Julie's arm. "Nothing serious, I hope?"

"I thought it might be, but…" Julie stares at her feet, then up at Luke. "No. Turned out to be nothing serious at all, in the end."

"Good." Sarah reaches across and squeezes her arm, then she smiles down at me. "Listen, it's just occurred to me that it's lunchtime, if you and Doug aren't doing anything?"

We're not, and lunch sounds like an excellent idea, but judging by her body language, Julie doesn't seem to agree. And neither does Luke.

"Sweetie?" he says to his wife, and to her credit, Julie manages to stop herself from responding.

"Uh-huh?" says Sarah.

"I wanted to… I mean…" He checks his watch, though possibly more to give *himself* some time rather than to check what it is. "The footie's on soon, so…"

"And that would be of interest to me why, exactly?"

"Just that I fancied, you know, *watching it*, so lunch perhaps isn't…"

Sarah sighs. "Well, I could do with a sit down and something to eat, so…" She narrows her eyes, then widens them again, as if something's just occurred to her. "Here's a thought. Why don't you go off and watch your game, and Julie, Doug and I can go and grab a bite somewhere. Have a good old girly chat. That's if you don't mind?"

"Well, actually…"

"That last sentence was directed at Julie."

"Right." Luke stares at her for a moment, then at Julie, then down at me, as if he's hoping one of us will come up with an excuse as to why his wife and the woman he's been having an affair with shouldn't head off for a cozy lunch together. Not surprisingly, one is not forthcoming.

"So?"

Sarah regards us expectantly, and Julie's grip on my leash tightens almost imperceptibly, then she fixes a smile on her face, and nods. "Why not?" she says.

And as the three of us head off along the High Street, it occurs to me that Luke can probably think of at least one good reason. But judging from the way he's standing stunned on the pavement, he doesn't seem to want to share it.

We're sitting in the park on a bench, finishing off the remnants of our McDonald's lunch, when all of a sudden Sarah winces, passes Julie the fries they've been sharing, and clutches a hand to her stomach. Julie's acting all concerned, but Sarah waves her away.

"Not to worry. Just a kick. They do this from time to time. Just to remind me they're there, I guess. Not that I *need* reminding!"

Julie shakes her head slowly. "It's amazing. Twins."

"Isn't it?"

"Aren't you a bit…scared?"

Sarah grins in that way that means she is. "Terrified! But also, I can't wait, you know? Because apart from anything else, it'll be such a relief to get them out."

"And how did Luke react?" says Julie after a moment when it's clear to me she's been racking her brain to come up with an appropriate question. "When he heard it was twins."

"Oh, you know him," says Sarah. "He says all the right things, but…" She lowers her voice. "Between you and me, I think it's knocked him for a bit of a loop."

"How so?"

"He's been a bit distant lately. Staying at work longer than usual. For a while, I thought he might even be having… No. Silly of me." Her voice trails off, and she stares off into the distance.

Then out of nowhere Julie bursts into tears.

With difficulty, Sarah edges along the bench and puts an arm around her. "What's wrong?"

Julie drops the fries on the ground and covers her face with her hands. "I'm sorry," she sobs.

"Don't worry. I shouldn't be eating them anyway."

"No, it's not that. It's…" Julie looks up miserably, and Sarah rubs the small of Julie's back.

"Hey—it's supposed to be me whose emotions are all over the place. Not you."

"You're going to hate me."

"Hate you?"

Julie dabs her eyes with a napkin. "I don't know how to tell you. I mean, I didn't want to, but then I got to know you, and you're really nice, and I really liked you, and then I decided I couldn't *not*, especially because..." Her eyes flick to Sarah's stomach. "But then I decided I had to, because of..." She does the eyes-stomach thing again. "Because I'd want to know, if it was me."

"Know what?" Sarah's tone is conciliatory, rather than angry, which seems to upset Julie even more.

"About... What you just said. That Luke might be having..." She swallows hard. "An affair."

"*Second thoughts*, I was going to say."

"What?"

Julie's looking horrified, but Sarah just smiles—which seems a little against the run of the conversation.

"But now you mention it. I know."

"About?"

It's a sensible approach, I think, to find out exactly what Sarah's going to say before putting your foot in it. Again.

"You and Luke."

I've seen Julie cry a lot, you understand, mainly (recently) because of Luke, but now, funnily enough, the mention of his name is the thing that makes her *stop* crying.

"You...know?" Julie blows her nose loudly on the napkin. "When did you...?"

Sarah shrugs. "Since the pub."

"The...*pub*?"

Sarah nods. "I've known Luke a long time. Believe me, you weren't the first. And you probably won't be the last."

"But... How can you?" Julie eyes Sarah's stomach for a third time. "Knowing he..."

"You make an assessment, don't you? Decide what you want. What you're prepared to put up with. This is what I want." Sarah rests a hand on her belly. "And Luke and me… We get on fine. He has his life, I have mine. Occasionally, and probably just about enough as far as each of us is concerned, they intersect…"

Julie's still staring, openmouthed, and—perhaps a little inappropriately—Sarah begins laughing. "I'm sorry," she says. "It's just… Your face!"

There's a pause, and then Julie realizes it's her turn to speak. "But how can you stay married to someone who…" She swallows hard. "Doesn't love you…"

Sarah shakes her head slowly. "Oh, Luke loves me. In his own way. And I'm…fond of him. Really I am. And it's quite sweet, really, the lengths he goes to in order to keep his…dalliances from me. No offense."

"None taken," says Julie, though she looks like she still can't believe the conversation's taken such a surreal turn.

"And to answer your question, I'll stay married to Luke as long as I'm the one he comes home to. And he'd never leave me…" She rubs her belly again. "Especially now. So what if he has a little—and again, don't take this personally—'hobby.' Other men his age waste a fortune on bicycles too advanced for them and spend every Sunday morning in the saddle. Luke… Well, I'm not going to make the obvious comparison. He was seeing someone else when I met him, and men generally don't change, so why should I have expected things would be any different with him and me? And while obviously in an ideal world I'd prefer things to be different, this isn't an ideal world. Far from it."

Sarah peers down at her feet, spots the dropped fries, and seems for a moment to be considering picking one up and eating it. "But somehow, this seems to work for us. Like I said,

I'm getting what I want. I guess he is too. And in the long run, that's all that matters. Don't you think?"

Julie's got a funny expression on her face—somewhere between horror and admiration—and I'm not sure if that *is* what she thinks. I'm not sure she is either, given the fact that it takes a few moments before she can speak again.

"But you and me… You encouraged me to be your *friend*."

Sarah shrugs again. "Why not? You seemed really nice—something you've proved by admitting everything to me just now. Plus, we had something in common, and I felt a bit sorry for you. Luke had obviously caused you some hurt. And in a perverse way, I thought I might be able to repair that."

"Right," says Julie, though in a way that suggests things aren't right at all.

"And it's been fun to see Luke squirm a bit." Sarah lets out a short laugh, then her expression changes. "I'm sorry if I deceived you, Julie. I hope you can forgive me?"

"You hope I can forgive *you*?" Julie's eyes have widened so much her eyeballs are in danger of falling out. "What about what I…?"

Sarah smiles as she shakes her head. "That was hardly your fault. I'm guessing Luke didn't tell you he was married?"

"Not in the early days, no."

"And by the time he did, you were too…involved to do anything about it?"

Julie nods frantically. "I did try to end things. But Luke just kept reeling me back in."

"He's good at that. Once a salesman…" Sarah blows air out of her cheeks. "He did a number on you, didn't he?"

"I'll say." Julie forces a smile. "And I thought I'd get some revenge, but then I met you and realized."

"What?"

"That you probably didn't deserve him. In a good way."

"Maybe not. But I've made my bed, and if he wants to tell lies in it…" Sarah laughs again. "I'm a big girl. Getting bigger by the day. I know what I've gotten myself into. And it's fine. Honestly it is. I'll shout at him later, kick him out for a few days, then he'll practically come crawling back and I'll forgive him, and he'll be on his best behavior until…" She gives a flat-lipped smile. "Well, until the next time. And yes, one day, I might decide to put my foot down, but right now? This is kind of how it works."

She smiles again, though it still looks a little forced, then nods toward the ice cream stand opposite. "Fancy one?"

And whether Julie's genuinely hungry, or simply too shocked to argue, I can't tell. Because she looks at Sarah for a moment, then down at her belly, then at me, and says, simply, "Why the hell not?"

22

I have trouble keeping up with Julie on the walk home—possibly because she's trying to power-walk off the huge waffle cone she's just wolfed down, but more likely, because she's trying to get home before the tears start again. Though to be honest, if I was her, I wouldn't know how to feel right now.

On the one hand, Sarah's admission is *excellent*, because it proves the "it's not you, it's me" thing in that it *wasn't* Julie, it *was* Luke, which means Julie shouldn't feel bad about herself at all. Though on the other hand, not only has Luke duped her, but so has his wife, and if that's the case, how can she possibly be sure about anything ever again?

Fortunately, Priya's coming over tonight, so maybe she'll be able to help. Though by the time she knocks on the door, Julie's hardly moved from the sofa.

"Jesus, Jules!" Priya follows Julie back down the hall and into the front room. "I'd say, cheer up, it might never happen, but by the looks of things, it already has!"

Julie doesn't say anything. Instead, she eyes the bottle of wine that Priya's brought, so Priya hands it over.

"Jesus, Jules!" Priya says again, when Julie unscrews the top and takes a swig directly from the bottle. "Why don't I get a couple of glasses, and you can tell me all about it?"

Julie gives her a suit-yourself look, and reluctantly allows Priya to take the bottle back like a toddler being forced to relinquish its favorite toy, then she follows her into the kitchen, with me trailing behind obediently. Priya retrieves the two wineglasses from where they're still sitting on the draining board after her visit on Friday and pours a generous glug of Chardonnay into each of them. "So?" she says, both eyebrows raised.

Julie sits down at the kitchen table, rips open the bag of Kettle Chips that Priya's just produced, and stuffs a handful into her mouth. "Surumph numph," she says.

"What?"

Julie makes the "hold on" sign with her hand, chews a few times, then swallows, wincing when she realizes she hasn't quite chewed enough.

"Sarah knew."

Priya lowers herself into the opposite chair, and hands Julie a glass of wine. "What about?"

"Luke and me."

"Christ! That's… I don't know what that is." Priya shakes her head as she helps herself to a chip, which she passes to me. "And she still wanted to be your friend?"

I crunch the Kettle Chip as Julie relates this afternoon's encounter to Priya, swallowing it in time to hear Julie's final squirm.

"Crikey." Priya does a little shake of the head to show admiration. "She has just gone *way* up in my estimation."

Julie gives Priya a look, then takes a large gulp of wine. "I tried to tell her. But she said she already knew. Said she's *always* known. And about the others."

"There have been others?" Priya stops herself. "Of course there have been. Are you going to tell Luke?"

"Sarah asked me not to. Said it could be our little secret. Besides, what good would that do?"

"Quite."

"Plus it'd mean I'd have to speak to him again. And it's bad enough having to deal with him on a professional basis."

"And how do you feel about this particular bombshell?"

"I don't know. How *should* I feel about it?"

Priya thinks for a moment. And then a moment longer. "Relieved?" she suggests, eventually.

Julie stares at her for a second or two, raises her glass to her mouth, then puts it straight back down again, just at that point where she'd been about to take a sip, spilling some down the front of her T-shirt. "You're right," she says, frowning down at the stain. "I should. But instead, I feel so stupid. And used. And..."

"Let me stop you there," says Priya, firmly. "You weren't stupid, *or* used. You were conned. And there's a difference."

"And that difference is?"

"You wanted to believe you and Luke had a future. He led you to believe that too. And now you know that was never a possibility." Priya picks her glass up and holds it out toward Julie in the "cheers" position. "If you ask me, you should be celebrating."

"Celebrating?"

"The end of Luke. Now you can finally stop wasting your time with him and find someone more...appropriate."

"I suppose." Julie reaches out with her glass and halfheartedly chinks it against Priya's. "But I don't think I'll ever be able to trust a man again."

"Yes, you will."

"And how do I do that, Miss Smartypants?"

"By finding one you can trust," says Priya, as if it's as simple as that.

And though Julie looks like she doesn't agree, I'm pretty sure she does. Mainly because she already has.

It's nearly bedtime, and Julie and Priya are flicking through Netflix and debating whether they've got the energy to start watching another episode of *Suits* when there's a frantic knocking on the front door. From a standing start, I'm there, barking furiously, in approximately half a nanosecond, and when Julie eventually catches up, her tentative "Who is it?" gets the one answer we don't want to hear.

"It's me."

Julie smiles archly, as if it's something she's been expecting. "I'm sorry. You'll have to be a little bit more specific."

"Come on, Julie!"

"I'm sorry, I still don't..."

"It's *Luke*!"

"Luke who?"

"Julie, please!"

"What do you want?"

"I need to see you."

Julie glances down at me, and I do my best to put on an expression that says, "don't open the door!" but it must only half get through, because she puts the chain on, then cracks it open. Almost immediately, a flustered-looking Luke jams his face in through the gap between the door and the frame. He's obviously not realized the chain's on, so he sort of gets himself wedged in by his ears, much like a child did in the metal fence surrounding the park's playground the other week.

"Do you know what the time is?"

"It's late, I know, but..."

"I was just about to go to bed."

Luke can't help himself. "Excellent timing, then," he says, with a grin, but Julie gives him a withering look, then moves to close the door.

"Julie, please. We need to talk."

He's stuck a foot in the door too, doing his best to keep the pressure off his ears, and I'm willing Julie to slam it really hard. The gap's certainly big enough for me to slip through and chase him down the garden path, and I'm seriously considering it, because that's exactly where I'm worried he's about to try to lead Julie.

"About?"

"You and me."

Julie lets out a long-suffering sigh. "There is no you and me, Luke. On account of there being a you and your wife. Remember?"

"Yes. Well. About that."

"*What* about that?"

"I've left her."

Julie freezes, and so do I. "Left her?"

"Sarah."

As if producing a rabbit from a hat, Luke reveals the gym bag he's clutching, but by the look on her face, Julie's putting two and two together. Instead of this being the huge declaration it might have been before her and Sarah's earlier tête-à-tête, it's more likely Sarah's done what she'd threatened and thrown him out for a few days. And Luke being Luke, he's trying to spin it in his favor.

"I guessed that was who you meant. Unless you have another wife neither she nor I know about." Julie reaches up for the door chain, though only to check it's securely fastened. "What for?"

Luke looks at her as if she's just asked the stupidest question in the world. "For you, obviously," he says.

"Right," says Julie. It's only one word, but I've come to understand it can convey a number of meanings. And Luke looks like he's in no doubt as to the one Julie's assigned to it.

"Just let me in, will you?"

"What for?"

Luke raises his eyes to the heavens—not because he's implying Julie's being obtuse, rather that it's started to rain, and our house doesn't have a porch, so he's getting wet. "So we can talk."

"What about? How you lied to me, led me on, shamelessly slept with me behind your pregnant wife's back?"

"Well, yeah," says Luke, though he quickly follows it up with: "But there was a reason for all of that."

"There was. And it's because you're a dishonest shit." This comes from Priya, who's appeared at Julie's shoulder, her arms folded resolutely.

For the first time, Luke's confident demeanor starts to waver.

"No, it's because I..." He hesitates, then glances down at me. "I was confused."

Julie's folded her arms too. "And you're not now?"

"No!" says Luke, as if he's just found God. "When I saw you earlier, and you were looking so amazing, I knew I didn't want to be with her a moment longer, so..."

"Do you know how shallow that makes you sound?"

"So I decided then and there I had to leave Sarah. For you."

"You're saying it like it's a good thing."

"It is!"

"Abandoning your pregnant wife."

"I'm not...abandoning her."

"Seems like that to me," says Julie. I take the opportunity

to sit down, perversely interested to see how Luke is possibly going to be able to spin this in a good way.

"Okay. Maybe. But it'll be better for all of us in the long run."

Julie frowns at him, perhaps wondering whether "all of us" includes her.

"I mean," continues Luke. "It's no good for children to grow up in an unhappy household. I'll still be their dad. And maybe..." He looks pleadingly at Julie. "They'll have *two* mums..."

"Oh, per-*lease*!" says Priya, from behind me, though she's watching Julie nervously. She knows the kids thing is a big deal where Julie's concerned, that Julie's worried she's left it too late, so maybe a share in Sarah's might be her ideal.

Luke seems to suspect that too, because he's looking like he knows he's played his trump card, and for a moment, I worry Julie might be caving. I've seen this before, in those films she and Priya always cry at, where all seems lost, then the "hero" makes some big, romantic gesture, a declaration of undying love, usually in the rain (and it's raining right now), and the heroine takes him back with open arms.

Except Luke is certainly no hero, there's nothing romantic about lying about how you've left your pregnant wife, and as yet—thank goodness—the love thing hasn't even been touched upon. But fortunately, Julie finally seems to have developed an immunity to his charm.

"And have you discussed this with Sarah?" she asks, matter-of-factly.

"What?"

"This grand plan of yours."

"Not yet. Tiny steps, and all that."

Luke mimes a walking figure with his fingers, and Julie

hesitates, then her expression hardens. "Hang on. Does Sarah even know you've left her?"

"She knows I've..." He swallows audibly. "Moved out."

"And does she know where you're...moving *into*? Do you, for that matter?"

"Well..." Luke looks up at the sky, then wipes the rain from his forehead. He really is getting very wet. "I thought I could stay here," he says, giving Julie his best puppy-dog eyes.

"Of course you can!" says Julie—to both my and Priya's *and* Luke's evident shock, then she nods down at the doorstep. "But I don't think you'll be very comfortable."

"Sweetie..."

"Don't 'Sweetie' me, Luke!"

"Please. Give me another chance."

"No!"

"Why not?"

Julie looks at him for a moment, possibly selecting which of the thousand or so reasons to give him, but then Priya comes up to stand next to her, her arms still folded across her chest like a bouncer, and comes out with one that surprises Luke and Julie almost as much as it does me.

"Because she's met someone," she says.

"What?"

Julie blushes so rapidly, it's as if a switch has been flicked. "That's right!" she says, doing her best not to sound as surprised as Luke looks. "I've met someone."

Luke's mouth flaps open, reminding me of Tessa's goldfish on take your pet to work day. "But... How?" he says, eventually.

"I don't just sit around waiting for you to turn up, you know?"

I look up at her, confused. That's *exactly* what she's been doing for the last eleven months. Though I can see why she wouldn't want Luke to think that.

"But… Sarah?"

"What about her?"

"I've…" He swallows hard as if he needs more throat space to force the lie out. "Moved out."

Julie smiles, though it's more than a little condescending. "And I've moved on. So I suggest you do too."

Ignoring Luke's stunned expression, she puts a palm against his face, gently but firmly shoves him back through the gap, and pushes the door to. Then she double-locks it for good measure, picks me up, and—pausing only to high-five Priya as she passes, marches triumphantly back through to the living room.

23

I sleep like a baby that night, and in fact, every night of the following week. With Luke finally out of the picture, all I have to worry about is being up in time for my usual walk to the park with Julie's dad, and—given that they now seem to be an "item"—a visit to Dot's café. I'm also trying to sneak in as many extra breakfasts as possible, courtesy of Julie's dad, in order that I don't lose any weight so Julie won't stop taking me to Barkrun—all part of my grand plan to get her and Tom together.

Perhaps surprisingly, the rest of the week passes without incident, despite Julie's somewhat nervous return to the office. According to what I heard Julie tell Priya on the phone, Luke's spent the majority of the time locked in his office on conference calls, or out on working lunches that seem to have lasted until dinnertime, which seems to have suited Julie just fine. Though by the time Friday evening comes around (and Priya does too), Julie seems less and less sure she's done the right thing.

"What do you mean, you're not going?"

Priya's frowning across the kitchen table at Julie, and talking about Julie's forthcoming work summer party. She's spent the last few months organizing it, and it's something I suspect has the potential to become another episode in the "Julie and Luke" show.

"I just don't fancy it."

"Won't that look a little strange?"

"Maybe." Julie downs the remainder of what isn't her first glass of wine. "I can just take a personal day."

"Sounds to me like you're taking the day a little too personally already."

"Besides, it's kind of your fault."

"*My* fault?"

"It's going to be mainly couples. And I don't have a plus-one, despite what you told Luke the other night. Which means he's going to be expecting me to be bringing this 'someone' I've apparently met, and when I turn up with Doug instead..."

"I had to think on my feet. Plus it seemed like the only way to get rid of him." Priya makes a guilty face. "You're sure there's no one you can take?"

"What for?" says Julie, desperately.

"Rather than letting Luke see he's winning by you not going, you could turn up with someone on your arm. Just to rub Luke's nose in it."

Julie sighs loudly. "Who, exactly? Apart from my dad..."

"Want me to ask Sanj?"

"That's very kind of you, but I hardly expect your husband to accompany me to my work party just so..." Julie stops talking. "You meant if he knows someone, didn't you?"

Priya nods her head slowly, in the manner you might when talking to an idiot. "There must be someone."

Julie gives her a look to suggest that no, actually, there mustn't.

"You're sure?"

"Yes, Priya. I'm sure."

The two of them sit there in silence for a moment—a rare occurrence, but the perfect opportunity for me to interject—so I run to the middle of the room where they can both see me, yowl briefly to attract their attention, then start furiously worrying at my injured ear.

"Doug!" says Julie, so I freeze midscratch as if we're playing Statues, and Priya lets out a laugh.

"What's wrong with him?"

"He had his stitches out last week. Tom said it might be a bit..."

"Tom?"

"Doug's V-E-T. Well, not Doug's, specifically. From the Park Practice. He's Dot's son. I met him at a barbecue a couple of weeks ago, where he thought we'd been set up, and I think he was just about to ask me out, so I told him about Luke, and he decided to give me a lecture on... Anyway, long story short, when Doug got attacked by that Alsatian, Tom was the one who rescued him and treated his ear, then suggested we go to his Barkrun thing on Sunday morning, which is this exercise class in the park but for dogs. At first I thought he'd only asked me because, you know..." Julie stops talking, perhaps because Priya's looking like she's suddenly seen her numbers come up on the lottery. "What?" she says.

"Tom!"

"What about him?"

"He could be your plus-one!"

As I congratulate myself on my charades skills, Julie pulls a face. "Priya, *please*!"

"Is he single?"

"Divorced."

"Well, there you go!"

Julie sighs exaggeratedly. "If only that was all there was to it," she says, flatly.

"He sounds nice, though. Is he?"

"I suppose. But…"

"But what? Does Doug like him?"

"Why don't you ask him?" says Julie, sarcastically, but Priya takes her at her word.

"Doug? Thoughts on Tom?"

I look up at Priya and wag my tail frantically. I *do* like him. Once you get past what he does for a living.

"See? And Doug detested Luke."

Julie gives Priya a look, but evidently decides not to respond to her last point.

"So." Priya picks her phone up. "Tom, Park Veterinary Practice," she says, dictating theatrically as she types the words, then she widens her eyes at the screen. "Not bad at *all*!" she adds, showing Julie the photo of Tom, dressed in his scrubs, that's just appeared on her screen. "And the reason you don't like him is?"

"I *do* like him. Not *like* like, but 'like' like. And I don't want to give him the wrong idea."

"Which would be?"

"You know." Julie picks up her glass and raises it to her mouth, only to discover she's already finished it. "That I'm *interested*."

"And the reason you wouldn't be interested in a single, successful, good-looking ve—sorry, V-E-T—who it sounds to me is interested in *you*, is?"

"I'm just not ready, P."

"You need to make yourself ready, Jules. When are you seeing him next?"

"I'm not seeing him in that sense," says Julie, crossly. "Doug's got his next exercise class on Sunday morning, but that's as far as it…"

"There you go. You can ask him then."

"Priya…"

"Jules…" says Priya, in a pretty good imitation of Julie's voice, then she grins. "Go on. What have you got to lose?"

"Apart from my dignity?"

"Which you definitely won't lose if you turn up on your own to your work do and Luke sees you *sans beau…*"

"Yes, well, that wouldn't be a problem if you hadn't told Luke I was…"

"Avec?"

I'm not sure why Priya's switched to French, but it seems to do the trick, as Julie seems to be considering her suggestion.

"Okay," she says, eventually. "But how would I…"

"Here's a thought." Priya leans across the table and raps her knuckles lightly on Julie's forehead. "Just. Ask. Him."

"I'm not sure…"

"Your problem is, you've forgotten what it's like to have a normal relationship."

"What do you mean by *that*?"

"Calm down. I just mean that you and Luke… Well, it wasn't a relationship in the traditional sense, was it? All that sneaking around, never being seen out in public together, and if you were, you couldn't be holding hands or anything. You always waiting for him to call, because you couldn't phone him in case his wife was around."

"And your point is?"

"Relationships should be *fun*. What you had… And I'm only saying this because I'm your friend, and because no one else will, *and* because you need to hear it."

"Just get on with it!"

"You and Luke. All it was, was a series of booty calls."

"That's not..."

"Fair?"

"No! Or true."

"Yes it is. You'd be sitting around, waiting for him to ring and say he was on his way, then he'd turn up, and..." Priya does some sort of mime that I assume is supposed to be a representation of inter-human "relations." "Tell me what that was if it wasn't what I said."

"Okay, okay. But that's because..."

"He was a cheating scumbag who was using you for sex?"

As Julie winces, I try not to yelp the dog equivalent of "Yes!" because Priya's summed it up a lot more eloquently and succinctly than I ever could.

"But I loved him, P!"

"Interesting."

"What is?"

"You said 'loved.' Past tense."

"Right. So?"

"Which means you don't any longer."

"Well..." Julie sits upright, then her face goes through a range of expressions, finally settling on one that suggests Priya's just pointed out something that she didn't know.

"So why can't I get over him?"

"Because you won't."

"Huh?"

"You can choose who you fall in love with, you know?"

"You couldn't!"

"Ha ha." Priya leans across the table and pokes Julie affectionately in the chest. "And actually, I could. Me and Sanj were an introduction. That's all. No one put a gun to our head and said, 'you're getting married.' What I meant by that is, you don't have a lot of control over it. Or what you do when you're *in* it. But when you're not..." She sighs. "Despite what he said the other night, Luke chose his pregnant wife over you. Possibly because he realized he couldn't have his cake and eat it anymore, or—probably—because he was scared he'd get found out, but either way, he made what to most impartial observers seems like the logical, rational decision. And the only person who can't see that's the case is you. Because you're in it. So you see it as a reflection on you. That you're worthless. That no one else could possibly fancy you, because you couldn't keep Luke..."

"Thanks very much!"

"But that's *so* not the case."

"How can you be so sure?"

"Because he was never going to leave her." Priya smiles sympathetically. "I'm a dentist, Jules. People come to me suffering, and the trouble with toothache is, it's never going to get better on its own. You get an abscess, you need antibiotics. Your filling's causing you problems, you need it replaced. Your tooth is bad? You need it taken out."

Julie mimes a yawn. "As fascinating as this dentistry lesson is, is there a point to any of...?"

Priya leans over and pokes her again, harder this time. "This feeling you have after Luke? It might get better over time, but then again, it might not. And the only way to ensure it does is to..."

"Take something?"

"Or someone." Priya smiles. "So take Tom. To your event. See how you feel. Have some fun. Rub Luke's nose in it. It may come to nothing, but..."

Julie sighs, loudly this time. "Okay, okay," she says. "I'll think about it." Which is progress, I suppose.

As long as that isn't all she does.

24

A funny thing happens today. It's Saturday, late morning, and we're coming back from the shops when Julie decides to phone her dad to see if he's free for lunch.

"That's strange," she says, holding her phone to her ear. When I give her an inquiring head tilt, she frowns. "Dad's not picking up." Then, with a slightly panicky, "Come on, Doug," Julie changes direction, and we head off toward his house.

It's a five or so minutes' walk from where Julie and I live, though Julie seems a little anxious to get there, and while I've been trying to conserve my energy for tomorrow's Barkrun, she seems keen to cover the distance in maybe half that time.

Her hands are shaking as she retrieves the spare key her dad keeps underneath the large flowerpot to the left of the door for emergencies. Evidently, she fears this is one, so instead of knocking, she uses the key to let us in. The television's on in the front room—a nature documentary—though no one's watching, a fact that makes Julie's panic level increase somewhat.

"Dad?" she stage-whispers, then she checks the kitchen and peers out into the back garden, but there's no sign of him.

Apprehensively, she reaches down and unfastens my leash from my collar. "Where's Dad, Doug?" she says to me, and I stare blankly back at her for a moment, until I realize she's asking me to do my "thing" and locate him for her.

I snort, then hunker down a little and sniff the carpet—more for effect, really, as I can hear movement and it's coming from upstairs—so I pad along the hall, stop at the bottom of the staircase, and rest a paw on the bottom step.

"Go on, Doug," says Julie. "Find him." Then she nods up the stairs, obviously expecting me to go first. But the noises I can hear sound a little like a fight, and my imagination is running riot. The last thing I want to do is go up and confront whoever's up there. Then another somewhat familiar smell floats into my nostrils, and I reframe the scene in my mind and relax a little. I'm still reluctant to go upstairs, though, given what I'm envisioning is actually taking place in the bedroom. But Julie doesn't give me the option. She sweeps me up from the floor and, holding me out in front of her like a firearm, begins tiptoeing up the steps toward the second-floor landing.

"Come on, Doug," she says, possibly more to reassure herself than me, though I start to wriggle in her arms: If I'm right, then this is something I can do without seeing, and I'm pretty sure Julie would say the same thing.

My fears are confirmed when we reach the landing and with a tentative "Dad?" Julie pushes open his bedroom door, then lets out a scream that hurts my ears more than last week's stitches removal. Because Julie's (naked) dad is lying on his back in bed, and straddling him, wrapped in a sheet, is someone we both know well.

"Oh. Hello, Julie, love," says Dot.

★★★

Dot's in the kitchen, making lunch, though Julie's rather curtly turned down her invitation for us to join them. She's wearing Julie's dad's dressing gown, which means Julie's dad's sitting in the lounge swathed in the sheet Dot was wearing earlier. He's fashioned it into a makeshift toga to avoid any lapses of modesty, and looks like an extra from *Gladiator*.

To be honest, it's hard to tell who's the more embarrassed, though maybe it's Dot, because she's—perhaps quite sensibly—staying out of the conversation. I'm not surprised by it all, of course: the way Dot leaped at Julie's dad's offer of a walk by the river the other day, and their subsequent body language on that walk, was something I was watching very closely as I chaperoned them in the hope that I might get some pointers for Julie and Tom. But now I can see that this is an *excellent* development—after all, Luke's out of the picture, Priya and Sanj are a couple, so now with Julie's dad and Dot an item, Julie will have no choice but to go out with Tom, if she doesn't want to be the odd one (not going) out.

"Love…" says Julie's dad, just as Julie says, "Listen, Dad," so they both stop talking, then Julie says, "You first," just as Julie's dad says, "After you," which makes them both clam up again.

They sit in silence for a moment or two, each waiting for the other to say something, then both of them smile at the notion that neither of them is saying anything. Then, finally, they both say, "So…" at exactly the same time, just as Dot brings in a tray with three mugs of tea and a packet of biscuits on it.

She takes one look at the two of them, picks her mug up, and heads smartly back into the kitchen. Julie's dad waits until he hears the kitchen door shut, then he exhales loudly. "I'm sorry, love," he says, much to Julie's evident incredulity.

"What are you sorry for?"

Julie's dad's cheeks darken. "For what you just saw, obviously."

Julie holds a hand up. "Hey, I'm sorry I saw that too. Although that's all I'm sorry about—apart from walking in on you unannounced. But you weren't answering your phone, and I thought something had happened to you!"

"Something *has* happened to me, love," says Julie's dad, glancing adoringly at the kitchen door. "Dot's…" He angles his head, a bit like I do when I'm trying to work something out. "She makes me feel *alive*. Plus she's just so…well…easy…"

From the kitchen, there's a crash of a teaspoon being dropped into the sink. "Hey!" shouts Dot, good-naturedly, and Julie's dad's cheeks darken again.

"*Going*, I was about to add," he says, laughing.

"Well recovered!" says Dot, cracking the door open briefly.

"Dad, *please*," says Julie, sounding simultaneously pleased and repulsed.

"I mean, obviously I feel a bit guilty, given how…"

Julie reaches over and grabs his hand. "Dad, you shouldn't. Mum's been gone for *five years*. And you deserve to be happy."

"Oh. Right. Yes, there's that too, obviously, but I did some thinking, and decided that I should maybe take a leaf out of Doug's book." Julie's dad reaches down and covers my ears. "Remember how miserable he was at the rescue center? What had happened to him? He hasn't let that hold him back. And he's as happy as Larry now." He removes his hands, and scratches me under my chin. "Besides, that's not what I feel guilty about."

"It's not?"

"It's more…" Julie's dad looks down at me again, perhaps hoping I'll chip in, but the best I can do is give him an encouraging twitch of the tail. "What with Dot being Tom's mother, and all that."

Julie's mouth drops open. "What has that got to do with anything?"

"Well, it might make things a little awkward."

Julie raises both eyebrows. "As opposed to how they are right now?"

"I meant for you and Tom."

Julie sighs exasperatedly. "There is no me and Tom, Dad."

"And whose fault is *that*?" asks Julie's dad.

While he probably meant "Luke's," that doesn't stop Julie from giving him an astonished look. "Why is everyone so desperate to fix me up with…?" Julie's dad's pointing frantically at the kitchen door, perhaps to remind Julie again that Dot's Tom's mother, and that she should be careful what she says.

Julie lowers her voice. "First Priya, now you. I've got a sneaking suspicion even Doug's in on this somehow."

The two of them turn to look at me, but I just keep my gaze fixed on the table where the biscuits are, so as not to give the game away.

"Doug's a good judge of character," says Julie's dad, picking his mug of tea up, blowing across the top, and taking a tentative sip.

"You want me to go out with someone based on the endorsement of a *dog*?"

"You could do worse," says Julie's dad, reaching for the biscuits.

"Than Tom? Or to take Doug's recommendation?"

"Both!" says Julie's dad with a smile, though he sounds completely serious.

He picks up a shortbread finger and snaps off a bite-size piece. Before he can feed it to me, Julie lets out an exasperated sigh so loud that Dot can probably hear it from where she's no doubt listening in from the kitchen, a fact proven by how she cracks the door open again.

"Love, are you sure you don't want…" she begins, but Julie holds both hands up.

"Will you all please just stop trying to interfere!" Julie says, enunciating each word for extra effect. Then she leaps up from her chair, scoops me up from the floor, and marches back out through the front door.

"To stay for lunch?" Dot calls after her, though I'm not sure Julie's listening.

I'm starting to worry that that's becoming a common affliction.

25

It's Sunday, and apparently my birthday. While I react excitedly to Julie's slightly off-key rendition of "Happy Birthday" by sprinting excitedly to all four corners of the room with my favorite squeaky chew toy in my mouth, to be honest, I'm pretty ambivalent about hitting the big three-five.

At least I'm not upset about it, I suppose, like Julie was when she turned the same age last year. So upset, in fact, that Priya had to almost drag her out, and then virtually carry her home, complaining drunkenly that her life was over. And even though we still have to go to Barkrun this morning, the best present I can think of is for Julie to ask Tom to her work party.

The doorbell rings just as we're on our way out to the park, and to the surprise of both of us, it's Priya. "Morning, Jules!" she says, pushing her way in without waiting for an invitation. She scoops me up from the floor and plants a kiss on my forehead. "And happy birthday, Doug!"

I shake my head in response and do my best to lick her on

the nose, which sets Priya off into fits of giggles. She's dressed in her workout gear, and Julie's eyeing her suspiciously.

"What are you doing here?" she says. "And so early?"

"I, um, wanted to wish Doug a happy birthday…" says Priya, evasively.

"Oh-kay," says Julie. "And are you on your way to the gym, or…?"

"Not exactly." Priya places me back on the floor. "Thought I might come along to—what was it—'Barkrun'?"

"Pets-ercise," says Julie. "But…"

"But what?"

"You kind of need a pet. To be there. Clue's in the name."

"Really?"

"Yes, really!"

"We can go fifty-fifty on Doug."

"P…"

"Come on, Jules. I just fancied a workout."

"It's not really meant to be a workout for us. It's for…" Julie nods down at me. "Them."

"Even so," says Priya. "I could say I'm checking it out. Seeing whether it's suitable for my dog."

"You don't have a dog."

"Well, maybe I'm thinking of getting one. Besides, Tom doesn't need to know that."

Julie widens her eyes. "So *that's* what this is about. Or rather, *who*."

"What?" says Priya, as innocently as she can muster, which isn't all that innocently at all.

"You're planning to…" She lowers her voice, probably for my benefit, given the next word that comes out of her mouth. "*Vet* Tom. For *me*."

Priya holds both hands up. "Listen, Jules. You need a plus-one for your party. He's obviously interested in you. You said it yourself. For some reason, you don't seem that interested in him. So I thought you might benefit from a second opinion. That's all."

"I don't need a second opinion. I'm quite capable of making my own mind up when it comes to the suitability of the men in my..."

Julie stops talking and Priya gives her a look, then she grabs her by the hand and leads her out through the front door. After all, we all know the veracity of that last statement.

It's a chilly morning, but that hasn't deterred the assembled dog owners, and in fact, some of the women seem to be wearing even skimpier outfits than last week, perhaps in an attempt to garner Tom's attention and counter any favoritism toward Julie and me. Julie, however, in stark contrast to last week's outfit, is wrapped up in her old, shapeless jogging ensemble. As Priya strips down to something she informs Julie is the latest "Sweaty Betty," Tom jogs over to where we're standing.

"Great!"

"What is?" says Julie.

"To see you. In that you came! Back, I mean!"

Julie sighs. "Couldn't stay away," she says, though in a tone that suggests she'd rather have.

"Great!" says Tom, a tad less enthusiastically than a moment ago. "And you look... I mean, have you done something with your..." He reaches a hand out toward Julie's hair, then evidently thinks better of it. "Hey, Doug," he says, bending down to check on my ear, and I give him an affable snort in response.

"Hi, Tom!" announces Priya, who's looking a little put out that Julie hasn't introduced her. "I'm Priya. Julie's best friend. Well, obviously not best friend in the sense of, you know..." She nods down at me, then grabs Tom's hand and pumps it up and down. "Ooh. Firm grip!" She gives Julie the side-eye, then beams at Tom. "Julie's told me all about you!"

"She has?" says Tom, looking about as surprised as Julie is embarrassed.

"Well, not *all* about you, obviously. Just that you're a vet, and recently divorced, and..." She grins. "Well, that, really. And how you run these classes. For dogs. So I thought I'd come and check you...I mean, *them* out. Not that I'm a dog!" She throws her head back and erupts into peals of laughter at this so loudly that Tom takes half a step backward.

"Great," he says, for a third time, reaching a new level of un-enthusiasm. "Although..."

"Although?"

"You kind of need one. A dog. To take part." He indicates the rest of the group, then peers pointedly at the patch of ground Priya's standing on. "And I can't see..."

"No. And you're right. I don't have one. Well spotted. You *are* a good vet! But, if I did, and he got fat—no offense, Doug—I'd want somewhere to take it, so I thought... Well, forewarned is forearmed, and all that."

"Right." Tom's looking like he's wishing Julie had forewarned him about Priya. "Well, if you like, you can observe from that bench."

Priya nods toward the obstacle course. "So I can't join in?"

"I'm not sure you'd be able to fit through the tunnel," says Julie, and Priya roars with laughter again.

"That's so funny!" She nudges Tom. "She's so funny. Great sense of humor. And a good cook, too..."

Tom and Julie exchange awkward glances, and Priya clamps a hand over her mouth. "Sorry," she says. "I'll go and sit down. You have fun now. But take it easy on poor old Doug this morning. What with it being his birthday, and everything."

Tom widens his eyes. "It's Doug's birthday?"

"Five years old today," says Julie, then she mimes a muted "yay!" and Tom hesitates for a moment as if considering whether wishing me a happy birthday is something a little unprofessional for someone in his line of work. Then he evidently thinks, *What the hell?*

"Many happy returns, Doug," he says, reaching down to give me a chest rub. "Though I'm not sure taking him out to an exercise class is his preferred birthday activity."

"Oh, don't worry," says Priya. "He's having a birthday party later to make up for it."

"He is?" says Julie, and Priya nods.

"He is! Three p.m. At Julie's house. Cake, the works!"

I look up at Julie. She's looking a little anxious. Probably because she, like me, knows exactly what Priya's going to say next.

"In fact," says Priya, "you should come."

"What?" says Julie, though before Tom can say anything, Priya's grabbed him by the arm.

"We won't take no for an answer. Will we, Jules?"

Julie's looking like actually, she will and quite happily, but Priya sounds insistent. Besides, judging by Tom's expression, it looks like no isn't going to be his answer anyway.

"In that case, I'd love to!" he says, smiling broadly.

26

It's the aforementioned "three p.m.," and Julie still hasn't forgiven Priya for a) conjuring up a birthday party for me out of thin air for the apparent purpose of inviting Tom and b) inviting Tom. Perhaps that's not surprising, given how "it's for your own good" never seems to be a phrase that makes anyone feel better about anything that's been imposed upon them. But the bottle of wine the two of them have shared while putting hastily-purchased chips into bowls and arranging corner-shop cupcakes on plates has eased the tension somewhat.

Priya's somehow miraculously convinced Julie she needs to flirt with Tom a little, just to see how it feels, and more importantly, to see whether she can get him to agree to come to her work party. And while I suspect that Tom would go with her to anything she asked, Julie doesn't seem to share my confidence.

Today's birthday guest list consists of me, Julie, Priya, Julie's dad and Dot (to make up numbers, I suspect, so Tom doesn't think it's been set up just for him), and of course Tom. It's small, but given the limited party food the corner shop was able to supply, that's probably a good thing.

What's *not* a good thing, however, is the silly, pointy party hat that Julie has just elastically-fastened onto my head and that resembles a smaller, upside-down version of the cone I had to wear the other week. As if on cue the doorbell rings, so I scamper along the hall to welcome whoever it is—Julie's dad, by the smell of it, a fact confirmed when Julie throws open the door. He's holding Dot's hand—though he quickly lets go of it when Julie raises her eyebrows at him.

"Happy birthday, Doug!" says Julie's dad, reaching down to massage the loose skin in the middle of my back in the way that I like, before hauling himself back upright to give Julie a kiss on the top of her head. "Not doing so badly for thirty-five!"

I snort accordingly, just as the doorbell rings again, and this time I smell *Tom*.

"Nice hat!" Tom says as Priya lets him in, and I go appropriately mental, doing my best to show Julie how much I like Tom despite the torture he's just put me through at Barkrun. I even run off and fetch my favorite soft toy to show him—something I've *never* done with Luke—and Tom then embarks on a tug-of-war with me over the toy, an endeavor he's never going to win. Julie's dad and Tom greet each other warmly—obviously there are no hard feelings after Dot's barbecue the other day, or over the obvious fact that Julie's dad's been shagging Tom's mum (Julie's words to Priya, and that no one else hears except me). Then Tom hands Julie a bottle of something for me that makes Julie's dad frown.

"Dog beer?" he says.

Tom nods. "Well, seeing as it's Doug's birthday. He is over eighteen, after all."

Julie laughs. "Almost double!"

"Great!" Tom grins, then lowers his voice. "It's not actual beer. In that there's no alcohol in it."

"Bit like that stuff Julie made me drink when I had that health scare last year," says Julie's dad, and everyone laughs, though at the time it wasn't funny at all. Ambulances are frighteningly noisy, and I'd never seen Julie that worried before.

"It's actually more of a health drink. Packed with vitamins. But we can pretend."

"Maybe I ought to drink it," says Julie's dad, and everyone laughs again.

"Speaking of drinking, would anyone care for a birthday beverage?" says Priya, putting a strange, posh voice on for those last two words. She's holding a bottle of Cava that she's just retrieved from the fridge, and that's apparently "Champagne for people who aren't label snobs," according to Julie's dad.

"Sounds good," says Tom, though Julie's dad makes a face, which makes me wonder if he *is* a label snob until, with an "I'll stick with my usual," he helps himself to a can of *actual* beer from the fridge.

To a chorus of oohs Priya launches the Cava cork out of the bottle with her thumbs, and I dutifully run and fetch it from where it's landed in the corner of the kitchen. She fills up four glasses, hands one to everyone who isn't Julie's dad, then she pops the top off my dog "beer" and empties it into my drinking bowl. To be honest, it's not as tasty as water, but I fake a few enthusiastic laps at it to try to convince Julie that Tom's done another good thing.

"Doug!" says Priya. "You might have waited for the toast!"

I stop drinking and look at her expectantly as she holds her glass up.

"To Doug!" she says.

"To Doug!" choruses everyone else.

"Happy birthday!" Tom says to me, making a special "cheers" effort to clink his glass against my bowl, something that seems to make an impression on Julie. Judging by the smile she does her best to hide, it's a positive one.

With a wag of my tail, I tuck cheerfully into my "beer." After all, if today goes as planned, this birthday might just be my happiest yet.

It soon becomes clear to me that Julie is hopeless at flirting. Maybe it's simply because she's out of practice, but it's a bit like my color-blindness, except where I can't tell the difference between, say, "blue" and "green," she can't tell whether Tom's teasing her or insulting her.

For example, as she hands him a cupcake, he says "so, what do you do?" and she says, "I'm an event organizer." Tom nods, then says, "which means?" To which Julie replies, "I organize events." Tom jokingly says, "Like this one?" and Julie just stares at him, deciding not to dignify his comment with an answer. I wouldn't blame him if he got up and left, except he's not that rude, so he just smiles again and sips his Cava, then he says, "So..." and she says, "So?" too. And while I've been *all over* Tom in an attempt to show Julie just how much I like him, and by deduction, how much she should like him, Julie doesn't seem to be anywhere nearer to asking him to her work party than she was when he first arrived.

I can't help but shake my head in dismay. But when Tom looks at me strangely, I disguise my response as an attempt to get this stupid hat off my head, though all I succeed in doing is getting the elastic stuck around my ears.

Tom looks down at me, and says, "Hah!"

Julie frowns. She's doing it a lot, and I'm worried it's not a good sign. "What's 'hah'?"

"Doug," says Tom, picking his phone up from the table, and quickly snapping my photo. "He's got both of his ears turned inside out!"

Tom reaches down to sort them out, then he shows Julie—though he shows me first, something I love him even more for—the photo he's just taken. Even if I say so myself, the combination of the inside-out-ears action and the silly hat at a jaunty angle means I'm way up there on the cuteness scale.

"We should send that pic to *We Rate Dogs*."

Julie bristles a bit, perhaps at Tom's presumptuous use of *we*. "What's '*We Rate Dogs*'?"

Tom looks at her as if it's her first day on planet earth. "It's this Twitter thing. People send in photos of their dogs, and they, you know..." He nods at her, but she doesn't complete the sentence. "Rate them."

"What for?"

"Well, for cuteness, mainly."

"No, I mean what do people want their dogs rated for?"

"Because it's a laugh?"

Tom's suggested that as if it's something Julie could do with a little more of, and she evidently gets the inference, because she sighs loudly.

"Right."

"It *is*!" He presses a couple of buttons on his phone, hands it to her, and indicates she should swipe through the pictures. "See?"

"Yes, very cute. And?"

Tom does that "patient sigh" thing through his nose. "Take another look."

"At what?"

"The ratings."

"Hang on." She frowns—again—this time at a photo of a Labrador puppy with a flower behind its ear and wearing a soppy expression that would melt the hardest of hearts. "This one has a rating of thirteen out of ten."

Tom glances at the photo. "Yeah," he laughs.

"Thirteen. Out of ten?"

"Yup."

Julie peers at the screen again, scrolls further down, then lets out a scornful laugh. "And this one. The sausage dog."

"The Dachshund, you mean."

Julie gives him a look. "No, the sausage dog," she says in a tone that makes Tom suddenly aware of his place. "In the 'hot dog bun' outfit. Twelve."

"Uh-huh." Tom looks at the photo, grins, then shows it to me and sniggers, though it's not the kind of thing I want to show a positive reaction to in case Julie gets any ideas about dressing *me* up.

"Out of ten."

"Yup."

"That's just stupid."

"Why is it stupid?"

"Because you can't have more than ten out of ten."

"Why not?"

"You just can't," says Julie, exasperatedly. "It's like when those athletes interviewed after a race say, 'I gave it a hundred and ten percent.' It's impossible. That's, like, more than… Well…" Julie frowns again, aware she's tying herself in knots. "Everything."

"It's a figure of speech, isn't it?"

"Well, it shouldn't be."

Tom looks at the photo again. "So, you don't think poor old…" He pinches and expands the screen, zooming in on the Dachshund's face. "*Edgar* here deserves that kind of score?"

"It's not about deserving. It's whether it's possible. And it isn't. Otherwise you might as well give them all stupid more-than-perfect scores."

"They do. That's kind of the point."

"To rate every dog greater than ten out of ten?"

"Yeah."

"Where's the sense in *that*?"

"Because they're dogs."

"And?"

"And..." Tom looks like he's wondering whether he can be bothered to attempt an explanation. "Because it's *fun*."

"Fun," says Julie, with the attitude of someone who's forgotten what the word means.

"Yup. And if you're a dog, it's kind of an honor to be selected. I imagine. At least for the owner, that is."

"Right," says Julie. "And this is popular?"

Tom nods. "Nine million followers can't be wrong."

"Nine million...?" Julie's expression suggests that yes, in fact, they can.

"Anyway." Tom takes his phone back, jabs at the screen a few more times, then places it screen-down on the table, in the manner of someone referring to something that's not up for discussion. "That's done."

"You sent it?"

Tom grins, then nods. "Doug'll be famous."

"They rate everyone?"

"Every dog, you mean?" he says, and Julie gives him a look. "No. I imagine they must get quite a few sent in." He reaches down and carefully takes the hat off me, and I perform a grateful full-body shake in response. "But very few looking as cool as Doug."

"I suppose."

Julie leans down to pet me at the precise moment Tom decides he will too, and their hands touch, though Julie snatches hers away as if she's just received an electric shock.

"Anyway," Tom says after an awkward cough. "You make sure you follow them."

"What for?"

"To see if Doug makes it."

"Even though he probably won't."

"But he *might*," says Tom, then he rolls his eyes, as if to suggest the difference between his and Julie's attitudes to life has just been neatly summed up in that last exchange.

He stares at the coffee table, or more specifically, the spot on the coffee table where Julie's left her phone, then he picks it up and hands it to her. With a sigh, Julie unlocks her screen, navigates to Twitter, makes a show of finding *We Rate Dogs*, and presses Follow.

"Happy?" she says, turning the screen round to show him what she's done.

"Ecstatic."

Tom doesn't exactly sound like he is, though at least it's another reason the two of them have to stay in contact, so I let out a satisfied grunt. Then Tom looks at his watch.

"Well, I suppose…"

There's a loud throat-clearing from Priya from the other side of the room. Julie catches Priya's eye, then her less-than-subtle nod, then even-less-subtly mouthed "Do it," so she takes a deep breath.

"So. Tom. Before you go. There's this…thing."

Tom stands up and slips his phone into his back pocket. "Thing?"

"Like a party."

"A thing like a party." Tom furrows his brow, then scratches his head for extra effect. "Nope. Can't guess."

"A *work* thing."

"A *work* thing, but like a party? Sounds… No, I don't know what it sounds like."

"Well, it's not really work. It's a thing, organized by my office… Well, for my office… An event. That I've, you know, organized."

"What with you being an events organizer, and all that?"

"Tomorrow. After work."

"Like a party."

"That's right. But outside. More of a fun-fair theme, really. With games and things. And it's, um…" Julie stands up too, just as Tom decides to sit back down, and almost headbutts him on the nose. "A plus-one."

"A *plus-one*?"

"Yes, you know, as in I can invite someone…" She moves to sit back down, just as Tom stands up again, so she has to quickly reverse her movement, and nearly overbalances in the process. "Sorry. Obviously you know what a plus-one is."

"So, who are you taking? Doug?"

"Oh. Well, yes, obviously, but I thought that maybe you might… You know, so I could say thank you for saving Doug the other day, and…" Julie stops midsentence.

Tom's angling his head, a bit like I often do.

"No, silly of me. Of course not. What was I thinking?" Her cheeks darken, and she suddenly seems fascinated by a freckle on the back of her hand.

"I'd love to," says Tom, beaming at her. "Let me just check my…" He pulls his phone out of his pocket and navigates through to his calendar app. "When did you say it was?"

"Tomorrow. Six o'clock. In the evening."

"As opposed to six o'clock in the morning?" He grins as he taps the screen. "Fine by me. In fact, I have no plans at all tomorrow night. All night." His cheeks darken too. "Just in case it goes on a bit, I mean."

"Like you're doing now?"

As Julie mimes a yawn, I watch the two of them with interest, enjoying their verbal sparring, realizing to my relief that Julie *is* just out of practice. Gradually, *finally*, she seems to have remembered how to flirt.

"So, what's the deal?" Tom asks, slipping his phone back into his pocket.

"Deal?"

"Yeah, you know." He leans across and elbows Julie gently in the side. "I assume Luke is going to be there. Given that it's a work thing. And how he's your boss."

"Um…" Julie's cheeks have gone even darker than they did during this morning's Barkrun sprints. "Yeah, but…"

"With his wife?"

"I don't know. I suppose so," says Julie glumly. "Seeing as it's couples, and everything."

"Couples?"

"Sorry. Plus-one."

Julie smiles coyly at being caught, and Tom grins. "So, like I said, what's the deal? Do you want me to pretend to be your boyfriend? Act like I'm crazy about you?"

"What? No!" Julie folds her arms and regards him sternly. "Like I said, it's because I wanted to thank you for…"

"Because I could. Pretend. For Luke's benefit. Make him jealous. If that's what you want? Get a bit of the old R-E-V-E-N-G-E…" Tom shakes his head. "Sorry. Don't know why I felt the need to spell that out there."

"It's actually more because…" Julie stops talking abruptly, as if deciding that admitting to Tom that she'd told Luke she'd met someone might give him the wrong idea.

"At the very least, it might keep him off your back."

I look at the two of them, wondering what on earth's going on, and why on earth Tom is pushing so hard for this, then it hits me like a thunderbolt. Tom wants to be Julie's boyfriend, and this will be the perfect opportunity for him to audition. He'll get to show Julie just how good he'd be at it—like on an actual date, but without any pressure. And maybe, just maybe, if she can get over her loathing for Luke, Julie might realize that too.

"You'd do that for me?" says Julie.

"Pretend to be crazy about you?" says Tom, then he shrugs. "I could give it a go."

Which is funny, because I suspect he won't be pretending at all.

27

Tom arrives early, wearing a suit with an open-necked shirt, shoes so shiny I can see my face in them, and with a jaunty dotted handkerchief poking out of his jacket pocket. It's probably the way I'd dress if I had to wear clothes, so I can't help but approve. He smells good too. Or at least, a lot more subtly than Luke.

"Wow!" he says, the moment Julie opens the door. Priya's helped her pick this outfit out via Facetime earlier; a summer dress that flatters (rather than flattens) her figure, heels that could do me a serious injury, and a big, floppy sunhat. "You look..." Tom doesn't finish the sentence, but instead, removes the hand he's been hiding behind his back, and produces a single carnation.

"Is that for me?"

"No, for Doug. I thought he might appreciate a healthy snack." He thrusts it toward her. "Of *course* it's for you."

"Right. Sorry. Tom, I..." Julie stares at the flower suspiciously, as if she's being handed a subpoena, then she shakes her head quickly as if to clear it. "Ah. I see what you're doing. In character. For this boyfriend thing."

Tom looks at her for a moment, then he bursts out laughing, though it doesn't sound very sincere. "You got me!"

"Right."

"Start as we mean to go on. Method acting, and all that. After all, you never know who's watching! And speaking of which, do we need to get our stories straight?"

"Huh?"

"If anyone asks. You know, when did we meet, where did we meet, *how* did we meet? That sort of thing."

Julie slips the carnation into the band of her hat. "How about we tell them the truth?"

"That we met at a barbecue and hated each other on sight?"

"That's not exactly…"

Tom silences her with a grin. "Just kidding! Or, we could say what happened the second time—how Doug was being attacked by a vicious, out-of-control Alsatian, and I bravely ran across to save him. That's a bit more, you know…"

"Romantic?"

Tom nods. "Plus it makes me look like a hero!"

"To any other small dogs, perhaps."

Tom sticks his tongue out at her. "Even so."

"Fine!" Julie sounds exasperated at him, but I can tell she's trying to keep a smile from her face. The two of them stand there awkwardly until he glances at his watch.

"Shall we?" says Tom, nodding toward his car.

"Why not?" says Julie. "Though we're a little early."

Tom shrugs. "It's a nice evening. I thought we might take the scenic route. Go for a bit of a ride."

As Julie shrugs in agreement, I peer through Tom's legs at the car parked in front of the house. It's the Mercedes convertible Dot mentioned, and even though Julie pretends not to be impressed when Tom lowers the roof with a press of a button on his key fob, I sense the opposite is true.

"Madam, your chariot awaits," Tom says, then he scoops me up from the floor with one hand and takes Julie's arm in the other.

He escorts us both to the curb, opens Julie's door for her, then deposits me on her lap, before hurrying round to his side of the car.

And as Tom takes us for a ride, I can only hope that's not what Julie's going to do to him.

Tom's car is great! The equivalent of one massive open window covering the *entire vehicle* means we all get the benefit of effectively sticking our heads out of it. And while Julie almost loses her hat as we speed along the road, I can tell she's enjoyed the journey too.

As we're parking, the mood in the car changes a little. The party's taking place in the grounds of a local hotel that looks more like a castle, and while Tom's got a grin on his face that looks like it'll need to be surgically removed, Julie looks as anxious as a boxer at a weigh-in.

"Ready?" says Tom, once we've made our way to the entrance.

He holds his arm out, and Julie stares at it as if she's never seen an arm before, then she makes an "oh, right" face, and slips her arm into his. Tom and I exchange glances, then—satisfied we've both got her covered—we make our way inside. And then outside, where we're met by a cacophony of noise.

Over in one corner, there's a smaller, inflatable version of the hotel, where what sounds like a thousand-or-so children, given the levels of screaming and whooping, are jumping about in such a frenzy it's as if they've come straight from a sampling tour of a candy factory. Dotted around the grassy area are several stalls featuring an assortment of fairground games. At the far side (and with the biggest crowd) is the bar, while in the middle sit a pair of small platforms, on which a couple of overdressed women sporting the kind of head protectors amateur boxers wear are trying to bash the living daylights out of each other with what appear to be oversize Q-tips.

Tom surveys the scene, then widens his eyes at Julie. "Well, this looks like…"

"A nightmare?" Julie makes a half grin, half grimace face. "Is it too late to turn around and go? If no one's seen us yet, then perhaps we can just…"

"Don't be such a party pooper." Tom fixes her with that smile of his again, and I feel her grip relax a little on my leash. "The first thing you need is a drink, and then we're going to have some *fun*."

"Fun. Right." Julie glances down at their linked arms. "Do we still need to…?"

"Absolutely!" says Tom. "Remember why we're here."

"Sure," says Julie, though remembering why we're here seems to make her even more anxious.

"Now, where's that… What was his name again?"

"Luke. Though at work he insists everyone calls him Lucas."

"Luke. Ass. Got it." Tom grins again, and this time, gets the briefest of smiles from Julie in return. "That's the spirit. Try to look as if you're having a good time, at least."

"Sorry." Julie briefly lets go of his arm, but only to salute him. "Will do."

"And how will I recognize him?"

"Six one, medium build, shortish dark hair…" Julie takes a breath. "Heavily pregnant wife."

"Right." To his credit, Tom doesn't say anything though I can almost hear the cogs whirring in his brain.

I lead us over to the bar, where Tom procures a couple of

glasses of something called "Pimm's"—which I suspect isn't especially healthy, even though it appears to have fruit floating in it—then the two of them sit down on a nearby bench.

"Cheers," he says, so Julie touches her glass briefly against his, then downs the majority of her drink as she anxiously scans the crowd. "Well?" he adds, as Julie stifles a burp.

"Well what?"

"Is he here?"

"I haven't seen him yet. Maybe he's chickened out."

"Like you nearly did?"

Julie gives him a look. "Tom, I…" She shakes her head, then pats him on the arm. "Nothing."

"What?"

"I was going to give you a big lecture on how you don't understand, but I'm guessing that after what you went through you probably do, or alternatively you just don't have any sympathy for me, so I decided against it." She smiles sheepishly. "I know what we were doing wasn't right. I just couldn't see it at the time, and I so wanted it to be different. That's all."

"And now?"

Julie looks up sharply, but it's evident Tom isn't referring to the two of them. "Now I'm doubting myself, wondering how I got it all so wrong."

Tom shrugs. "It happens. I thought I'd met the love of my life. Evidently the feeling wasn't mutual. And you can either let that eat you up, or…"

He stares off into the distance for a moment or two, and Julie rubs his arm. "How long does it take?"

"How long does what take?"

"For you to stop blaming yourself."

Tom smiles flatly. "I'll let you know," he says, and Julie's expression softens.

"Oh, Tom, I'm so sorry."

"What for?"

"Everything. I've been making it all about me, whereas..." She nudges him, then takes a deep breath, and stands up purposefully. "Shall we go and have some of that fun you mentioned?"

Tom shrugs again, then he sets his drink down on the grass. "Sounds like a plan," he says.

The next hour passes without fanfare possibly because Luke's nowhere to be smelled, which is a shame, because giving Julie the chance to compare Luke and Tom side by side can only result in a hands-down win for Tom. To make that happen, though, I have to find him, which is why I've been leading us from stall to stall, sniffing the ground for any sign.

And while I may not be excelling in the tracking department, at least this gives Tom the chance to demonstrate his prowess in the various activities; throwing beanbags into an open hole; hooking rubber ducks on the end of a pole; even punching a hanging ball so hard that the stall owner, perhaps out of fear that Tom might do the same to him, hands Julie a stuffed teddy bear. Though he refuses to take part in a game involving throwing a ping-pong ball into a fishbowl that has a live goldfish in it on professional grounds, and instead spends ten minutes lecturing the woman running the stand why she shouldn't be keeping the fish in such small bowls as they end up swimming around in their own urine, Julie seems to find that impressive too.

Despite me nearly embarrassing myself at the coconut shy when I try to chase every ball Tom throws and end up knocking one of the coconuts off myself in an attempt to retrieve a wayward ball, we all seem to be having a good time. Any initial forced friendliness seems to have changed into a genuine enjoyment of each other's company, and I'm starting to think we don't actually need Luke today. But just as I'm leading Tom and Julie back to the bar while congratulating myself on my plan coming together, a familiar smell from the direction of the Q-tip-fighting raises my hackles.

I dig my feet into the grass and manage to bring Julie to a sudden stop. So sudden, in fact, that she drops the end of my leash.

"Alright, Doug?" she asks, as I look up at her, feeling a little guilty about what I'm planning to do next.

"I thought we were getting a drink?" says Tom.

"Doug's obviously not thirsty." She bends down to grab the end of my leash, just as I take a step backward to pull the handle out of her reach.

"Doug?"

"Want me to…?" Tom takes a step forward in an attempt to stand on the loose end, but I'm too quick for him, and by the time he's regained his balance, I'm already trotting off toward where I've scented Luke.

"Doug!" calls Julie, as the two of them set off in pursuit. They're still holding hands (and in Julie's case, a large stuffed bear), which means Julie's slowing Tom down, and I reach my objective easily.

I let out a low growl, and a wide-eyed Luke wheels round, catches sight of me, and jumps a foot or so into the air. He smells of Pimm's—which admittedly makes a pleasant change from his usual brand of deodorant—and not only because he's carrying a glass of what evidently isn't his first. When he lands, he appears to be a little unsteady on his feet.

"Doug?" he says, and then—almost in slow motion—he looks up, as if he's just realized I can't possibly be here on my own. "And Julie!" he announces, his features morphing into a slightly creepy grin.

To her credit, Julie doesn't flinch. Instead, she fixes a smile on her face, and says, coolly, "Luke," and even though she adds the "arse" part loudly, at the sound of his name, I sense Tom stiffen.

"Having a nice time?" he asks. He's talking to Julie, but his eyes are on Tom, regarding him warily.

"We were," says Julie, curtly.

It's an excellent response, and it makes Luke flinch. "Right. So…" He peers at Tom as if waiting for an introduction, and when one doesn't come, he kneels down to my level. "Doug! How are you, boy?" he says, attempting to pat me on the top of my head, but I'm too quick for him, and take a step toward Tom instead.

Luke hauls himself unsteadily back to his feet, then he gives Julie a slow, deliberate once-over. "You look…" He seems to be reaching in the dark for the word, though it must be very dark, because he doesn't seem to be able to find one.

"Doesn't she?" says Tom, after a moment, then he holds out a hand. "I'm Tom, by the way."

"Right." Luke stares at Tom's hand, then back at Tom, then down at his hand again, then finally shakes it. "And you are…?"

"Tom?" repeats Tom.

"No, I meant…"

"Oh!" Tom lets out a short laugh. "I'm Julie's…" He turns and smiles down at her. "What's the word?"

"Plus-one?" she suggests.

"Though technically, that's two words," says Tom.

Luke ignores him, and scowls at Julie. "You kept this quiet."

"Kept what quiet?"

"About being in a…" He hesitates. "Re-la-tion-ship," he says, making the second syllable the longest.

It's not a question, so it doesn't require an answer, but Julie gives him one anyway, and it's a goodie. "Ditto," she says, archly.

"Right. So..." Luke's voice trails off, and he looks like he wants to leave but—perversely—can't, so Julie takes the opportunity to peer exaggeratedly over his shoulder.

"No Sarah?"

"Sarah?" says Luke, still a second or two behind the conversation.

"Your *wife*?"

"What? Oh..." Luke shrugs. "She's not here. I'm..."

"In the doghouse?" says Julie.

"No," he says, after a moment. "She's not here, because she's..."

"Pregnant?" says Julie, and Luke makes a face.

"I was going to say tired, but the two seem to go hand in hand nowadays. Much like the two of you seem to be doing."

Tom looks down, as if he's only just realized Julie's grabbed onto him again, and he seems rather pleased.

"So what do you do, Tom? Apart from..." Luke nods toward Julie.

"I'm a..." Tom glances down at me. "V-E-T."

"A what?"

Tom reaches down and covers my ears with his hands. "A vet," he says.

"A vet?" says Luke, loudly, and with no thought for my feelings. "That must come in handy. You know. For..." He points down at me, though with the hand that's holding his Pimm's, and splashes the remainder of it on Tom's shoes. "Sorry." Luke suddenly notices the large stuffed bear Julie's holding. "Been having a bit of luck, I see?"

"This? Tom won it."

Luke eyes him suspiciously. "I bet he did."

"Yup," says Tom. "On the old..." He mimes a slow punch

in Luke's direction, and even Luke's not too stupid—or drunk—to get the inference.

"Right," he says, followed by a mumbled, "Good for you."

There's an awkward silence, though it's suddenly punctuated by a loud cheer from behind us. One of the Q-tip-fighting women is standing on her platform, arms aloft in celebration. Luke lets out a snigger, then his face does that classic "I've had an idea!" thing, and his eyes narrow.

"Fancy trying your luck on something a bit less...passive?"

"Huh?" says Tom.

Luke points at the Q-tip fighting. "You and me. On *that*!"

Tom shakes his head. "I don't think so," he says.

"Scared, eh?"

"What? Why would I be...?" Tom folds his arms, as if it's just occurred to him he'd quite like to smack Luke around the head with a large Q-tip—or possibly even something a little less padded. He glances across at Julie, who just widens her eyes in an "if you like" kind of way, then he nods. "Sure," he says.

Wordlessly, Luke hands his empty Pimm's glass to Julie, and beckons for us to follow him across to where the girls have just been fighting. Then, elbowing Vinay from Accounts out of the way, he climbs purposefully onto one of the platforms. The operator hands him his protective headgear, so he slips it on, picks up the Q-tip, then beckons Tom to join him.

With a sigh, Tom hands his jacket to Julie, and leaps nimbly up onto the adjacent platform, though he's barely had time to fasten his headgear when Luke takes a sneaky swing, catching him a glancing blow on the temple.

Tom just about manages to absorb the shot. "Hey," he says, adjusting his now-lopsided protector. "No fair."

"Fair?" Luke sneers at him. "You'll be telling me you weren't ready next."

"I was born ready."

"Yeah? Well *I* was born..."

"Yesterday?"

Luke frowns at him, perhaps not sure whether that's an insult or not, and I take the opportunity to study Julie. Something tells me she's going to find this interesting.

Tom turns to the operator. "So, what are the ru—oof!"

Luke's attacked again, with a sort of forward poking motion this time, catching Tom in the stomach.

"Rules?" says Luke, waving away the operator's attempt to explain, then he lets out a short laugh. "There are no rules. Except that the first person knocked from their platform loses."

"Right." Tom picks his Q-tip up, tests the weight of it, then twirls it round in the manner of a drum majorette. "Well, mind you don't hurt yourself when you fall off," he says, and a look of rage flashes across Luke's face.

With a quick glance across at Julie, he suddenly switches so he's holding the stick at one end, crouches down, and swings it at the side of Tom's knees. Fortunately, Tom sees it coming, and with a loud "Whoa!" manages to jump over it.

"Nothing below the waist," warns the operator, and Luke gives him a dismissive look.

"Anything goes, as far as I'm concerned."

"So I've heard," says Tom, archly.

Luke opens his mouth to answer, then perhaps conscious this is a work event, evidently thinks better of it. Quite a crowd has gathered—possibly because Luke's employees are keen to see their regional manager get knocked on his backside.

"Ready?" says Luke, sarcastically, as he squares up to Tom.

"I am *now*," says Tom, adopting a defensive position.

The two of them begin a series of feints in an attempt to feel each other out, followed by a couple of tentative swings, though nothing connects. It soon becomes apparent that while

Luke has the weight advantage, Tom's more agile, and after one particularly wild swing, an off-balance Luke reels forward, only for Tom to poke him full in the face with the end of his stick.

"Hey!" Luke's eyes are watering, and he puts a hand to his nose, as if expecting it to come away bloody.

"Sorry," says Tom, though he doesn't look sorry at all.

The two of them thrust and parry for a while, until Tom lets fly with a roundhouse swing that connects so solidly with the side of Luke's head that—even through the protection—seems to make his head spin. He drops his stick in shock, then steps off the platform to retrieve it, only for Tom to punch the air with a celebratory "Yes!"

"What do you mean, yes?" says Luke.

"I won."

"No you didn't."

"Yes I did."

"No you didn't. You have to knock me off. I got off on purpose."

"Off is still off."

"No it isn't. I dropped my…" Luke brandishes his stick, evidently unsure what the thing's called. "I was vulnerable."

"Really?" says Tom. "I thought you'd be the last person to worry about going for someone who's…" He glances across at Julie, making sure Luke sees. "Vulnerable?"

"No, I just…" Luke swallows hard. "You have to win fair and square. That's all."

"Fine." Tom shakes his head, then he beckons Luke back up in an exaggerated mimicry of his earlier encouragement. "Give it your best shot. Unless you already have?"

He holds his stick out, perhaps intending for Luke to touch the end of it with his, like boxers do at the start of a bout. Instead Luke pretends he's about to do exactly that, then ducks down and swings the end of his stick up between Tom's legs. Tom winces, and the onlookers groan along with him, but he doesn't fall off his platform.

"Above waist height," warns the operator meekly, and Luke glares at him.

The two of them trade blows again for a few seconds, Tom blocking or ducking Luke's wild swings, deftly replying with accurate jabs of his own. Then as Luke pauses to catch his breath—and in a masterful move—Tom suddenly lowers his stick, half turns away, and pretends to adjust his headgear. Luke looks like he can't believe his luck, so he launches an almighty swing, putting everything into it. But Tom leans smartly back, then—as Luke is off-balance—he pokes him on the shoulder, with just the right timing to add to Luke's momentum. It's not a heavy hit, but it does the trick, as Luke topples from the platform and goes sprawling onto the grass.

Tom throws his stick down in the manner of a victorious gladiator and takes a bow in Julie's direction.

Luke scowls up at him, and for a moment, I fear he's going to attack him for real. Then—perhaps remembering where he is and *who* he is—he scrambles to his feet.

"Best of three?" he says, but Tom shakes his head.

"No thanks," he says. "I've neglected this lovely lady long enough."

Then Tom steps off the platform, struts over to where Julie's still applauding him, and—taking my leash in one hand, and her arm in the other—escorts us away across the grass.

28

"That was…" Julie looks up at Tom, her mouth open, then shakes her head slowly when she can't come up with an appropriate word.

"Wasn't it?" Tom grins, then grabs his belt buckle, and makes a show of loosening the front of his trousers. "Though I took one right in the batteries." He winces exaggeratedly. "Still, I think we made our point."

"Didn't we just!" She rubs Tom's arm affectionately, then perhaps realizes she shouldn't have. "So you can probably, you know, let go of…" She flicks her eyes down at where Tom's hand is gripping tightly onto hers. "If you wanted to, that is."

Tom grins again. "Best not. Not yet, anyway. Wait until we're out of sight. Just to keep up appearances."

"Oh. Okay. Sure." Julie smiles at him tentatively, though she looks like she's not too disappointed.

The three of us walk on in a comfortable silence to find a bench, stopping off on the way at the bar, where Tom gets Julie another drink, and he and I share a bottle of water. Then, when we're sitting in the early evening sun and I'm trying hard not to doze off, Tom clears his throat.

"Listen, Julie, and please tell me it's none of my business..."

"It's none of your business!" she says, then she smiles. "Go on."

"It's just... You and that Luke guy..." He frowns, then takes a second or two, as if he's trying to work out exactly how to phrase his question, then he shrugs exaggeratedly. "What exactly did you see in him?"

I brace myself. I've seen Julie react in a bad way whenever Priya's asked her this question, but for some reason—maybe because of what Tom's just done for her, or perhaps because she's halfway through her second Pimm's—she seems happy to answer.

"I guess the fact that he was just...interested."

"Interested?"

"In me."

"I assumed you didn't mean in stamp collecting."

"Ha ha!" Julie reaches over and pokes him in the ribs. "And I hadn't had that—a man, interested in me, paying me so much attention—for a while."

"I find that hard to bel..." Tom face-palms himself. "Sorry. That sounded really cheesy."

"It did. But thank you, anyway."

"And, at the risk of asking the obvious question..."

"Which is?" says Julie, after an awkward second or three.

"The fact that he was married...?"

"I didn't *know* he was married at first. He didn't tell me until we'd been seeing each other for a few weeks. And even then, he told me he was separated, that it was complicated..." Julie looks up to the heavens and does a silent scream. "But when you're with someone, and you like them, and they treat you like a queen—and trust me, he was very charming, and attentive, in the beginning, at least—then after a few weeks they sit you down and say, 'we need to talk,' and you're expecting the worst, but what they actually come out with isn't quite the worst even though it's still pretty bad, it's a bit of a relief. And so you tend to forgive them, rather than…" She pauses for breath. "And then everything that happened, he always had an excuse for. When I found out he and his wife were still living together, it was because she couldn't afford to move out, and when I asked him why we couldn't be seen out together, it was because he didn't want to hurt her until they'd finally made public the fact that they were separating, and in a perverse way, I respected him for that. Thought he was being caring. Stupid of me, I know."

"And the whole 'getting her pregnant' thing?"

Julie shakes her head. "It's crazy, I know, but even then a part of me wanted to believe him. Or at least, I was prepared to give him the benefit of the doubt…"

She looks at Tom earnestly, noticing his widened eyes. "None of us are perfect, Tom. We all make mistakes."

She takes a sip of Pimm's. "But then when I found out he and his wife had undergone IVF…"

"How on earth did you find *that* out?"

Julie's cheeks darken. "That's not important," she says, perhaps not wanting to bore Tom with the stalking-Luke's-wife episode. "But sometimes, somehow, something happens that means you can suddenly see everything else for what it was."

"So, that was the thing that made you realize things had to, you know…?"

"End?" Julie does that thing where she sticks her lower lip out to indicate that she's thinking. "Yeah. Plus by then, I'd met her, and…"

"You *met her*?"

"Yup. And she was lovely. And I felt really guilty." Julie

catches me watching her, so she reaches down and scratches the top of my head, and I nuzzle her hand affectionately. "I'd just about managed to convince myself that if their relationship was, as Luke had told me, over, then I wasn't actually doing anything wrong. But it wasn't, so—like you so kindly pointed out at your mum's barbecue—I kind of *was*. And it's a dilemma, isn't it?"

"Yeah." Tom nods, then he frowns. "Um, what is?"

"Whether you do the right thing or not. Like I said, I realized how nice she was, and, of course, that she was, you know…" Julie mimes being pregnant. "So I decided I better just walk away and leave the two of them to it. You know, do the decent thing."

"As opposed to the indecent thing. Like he'd been doing all that time."

Julie ignores him. "And then, there was a part of me that thought she deserved to know. After all, she was going to be raising a child with this man, and she needed to understand what he was like."

"So what did you decide?"

Julie shrugs. "Obviously I wanted some revenge, but that doesn't make me out as a very nice person. And if I did tell her, and she left him as a result? I'd be responsible for their kids growing up without a dad."

"Kids?"

"They're having twins," says Julie, and Tom makes a face. "And as someone who's lost a parent, I wouldn't wish that on anyone."

"Fair enough."

"Plus it turns out she knew anyway."

"No!"

Julie nods. "Said she's made her peace with it. So I thought to myself, the best thing I could do would be just leave them to it."

"That was good of you, you know?"

"Maybe. Although it doesn't make me feel very good about myself."

"Well you should. Because you've a lot to feel good about. Not the least of which is how you've shown yourself to be a decent human being, after all. Selfless. And with a lot to offer to..." He looks away. "The right man."

"Tom, I..."

Julie looks like she's about to start crying, and at once, Tom looks like he's fearing he's overstepped the mark. "Hey," he says, nudging her playfully. "You just need to think about what *you* want."

Julie gives him the longest of side-eyes, then she grabs Tom's hand, and stands up.

"I want you to take me home," she says.

29

The drive back home doesn't take that long. Even so, Julie spends it staring quietly out of the window, as if the warm breeze combined with the soporific hum from the engine is making her so relaxed she's in danger of dropping off to sleep. And when she does and, in fact, starts snoring, her head drops onto Tom's shoulder. He has to drive slightly hunched over so as not to wake her, and I can't help feeling there's a connection between the two of them that goes a lot deeper than today's pretending to be together.

When we pull up outside the house, she's still dead to the world. Tom parks the car as smoothly as he can, then lifts me from her lap into his, and sits there for a while, stroking me absentmindedly, looking like there's nowhere he'd rather be. Eventually, Julie snorts herself half awake, so he takes the opportunity to give her shoulder a gentle shake.

"What? Oh." Julie looks shocked to realize she's been resting her head on Tom's shoulder. She sits up with a start, recognizes where we are, and performs something akin to my big stretch. "Was I asleep?"

"I hope so. Otherwise this car's going straight in for a service."

"What does *that* mean?"

"If that noise wasn't you snoring…"

"I don't snore!"

Tom just raises an eyebrow.

"I *don't*!"

"Back me up here, Doug."

At the mention of my name, I let out a short bark, and Julie harrumphs. "You're supposed to be on my side!"

Julie reaches across to pet me, just at the same time Tom does, so she ends up patting his hand like before. It's a little awkward for a second or two, then possibly as an excuse to withdraw her hand without offending him, she looks at her watch.

"So, thanks, Tom."

"For?"

"Everything. Coming with me today. Driving me home. Putting Luke in his place. And pretending to…you know."

Tom smiles broadly, in a way that suggests it hasn't been any trouble whatsoever. "My pleasure," he says.

Julie looks at her watch again. "Did you want to come in?"

"Come in?"

"Yeah. You know. To the house. For a coffee, or something."

Tom stares at her for a moment, then he bursts out laughing, stopping just as abruptly. "Just so we're clear, you mean for an *actual* coffee."

"Yes! What did you think I…?" Julie blushes, then she reaches across and punches him lightly on the upper arm.

"Sorry." Tom rubs his bicep. "I didn't know how far we

were taking this pretend date thing." He unleashes *that* smile again, and Julie swivels toward him in her seat and stares at him for a moment. Then—with a whispered "at least this far"—she leans across and kisses him.

I suddenly feel like a gooseberry, so I carefully hop off Tom's lap and into the back seat, and pretend to be interested in something in one of the door pockets. But then, as Tom begins lightly kissing Julie's neck, and to the evident horror of *everyone* in the car, Julie says the worst thing possible.

"Oh, *Luke*..."

Tom freezes, then he disentangles himself from Julie's embrace, maneuvers himself back into the driving position, and places both hands carefully on the steering wheel.

"Oh god, Tom! I'm so sorry."

"Me too."

We sit in the car in an awkward silence for what seems an age, then Julie sighs. "Tom, I need to..."

Tom holds a hand up in the stop position. "It's okay. I..." He clears his throat, then he turns to face her. "Listen, Julie, I really like you, *more* than like you, and I know you're probably not in a great place right now insofar as relationships are concerned, but the trouble is, I am, and I'd like to have one with you, to show you that not every man is like Luke. We could have a great time together, *be* great together." He glances round at me. "The three of us. I mean, how many couples do you know who get to go on a dress rehearsal for a date like we have today, and have a fantastic time, which must make you think..."

Tom stops talking and makes a face, and I get the feeling it's at the hash he's making of his declaration to Julie. "After what happened to me, like I said to you the other day, I've got what I think might be called trust issues, and so I don't want to risk any of this if you're not truly over Luke. So if there's the slightest chance you and he might…" He shakes his head, then stares straight ahead, as if he can't bring himself to think about it. "It might sound selfish, but I was hurt so badly when my wife…you know…when she…that I just can't…"

Tom seems to be losing the ability to finish his sentences, but Julie obviously gets it.

"Tom…" She mimics his earlier stop sign and rests a hand on his thigh. "I've had a lovely time. Really I have. And I promise you we'll talk about what you just said. *All* of it. And soon. But I'm a little drunk right now, and that's a conversation I think I'd need to be…" Julie hesitates, though only to correct herself. "*Like* to be completely sober for." She makes a "pained" face. "Just know one thing—Luke and I are over. Whatever that little slip was, Freudian or otherwise, it was just a slip."

"It's fine," says Tom, though by the way his voice is sounding, I suspect it isn't. "So, I'll call you? Or you can call me. Whatever works, really. Or I'll just see you at Barkrun. Or, of course, if Doug gets into another scrap…" He looks round at me again, then rolls his eyes at himself. "I'll shut up now."

"Probably best," says Julie, with a smile. "So…"

"So… We might do this again?" asks Tom, as Julie opens the car door, grabs the stuffed bear Tom won for her, and climbs out.

"We might well," she says, hurrying off toward our gate, then she mimes being on the phone. "Let's, you know…"

"Great," says Tom, though he doesn't sound all that convinced.

He reaches for the ignition key, then starts the car, and begins to pull away from the curb, then all of a sudden, Julie stops, midstride, wheels round, runs back into the middle of the road, and begins waving her arms around frantically.

"Tom! Wait!" she shouts, and he slams on the brakes, then hurriedly reverses to where she's standing.

"What?" he says, hopefully, and Julie grins guiltily.

"Sorry!" With a pained expression on her face, she collects me from the back seat, then gives Tom an apologetic smile. "I forgot Doug!"

And though she doesn't catch the look on Tom's face, I do, and…well, it almost breaks your heart.

30

It's Wednesday, two days after the "Oh, Luke" incident, and Tom has not called—something I overheard Julie telling Priya on the phone during their forensic analysis of the "date." And while one option might be for Julie to call *him*—something he might be expecting given their rather ambiguous goodbye the other day—apparently, that would "be ridiculous."

Instead, Julie spends a lot of time staring at her cell phone, hoping it'll ring, a bit like I often sit in the hall and stare at the front door, willing Julie to come home from work. But unlike my sit-and-stare-at-the-front-door thing, where Julie always comes home eventually, her phone stays ominously silent.

Early evening finds us heading to the corner store—Julie's renounced her recent healthy ways and has managed to drink pretty much everything alcoholic in the house. When the bell on the door rings as we come in, Sanj looks up from his usual position behind the till and smiles.

"Evening, Jules!"

"Is it?"

Sanj frowns and looks at his watch. "Well, yeah, unless…" He holds his wrist to his ear, as if to check his watch is still ticking, then realizes it's a digital one. "Duh!" he says, good-naturedly, but the attempt at humor is lost on Julie.

"Sorry," she says, glumly. "I thought you said, 'Good evening.'"

"So your 'is it?' was meant to suggest it isn't?"

"Duh!" says Julie, back at him, though not quite as good-naturedly as his earlier one.

She grabs a cart and makes straight for the wine section, where she quickly fills it with as many bottles of her favorite Chardonnay as she can, then heads back to the register. As she unloads them noisily on the counter, Sanj looks up from his phone, and widens his eyes at the contents.

"Having a party?"

"No."

"Oh. Right."

"What's that supposed to mean?"

"Nothing." Sanj looks down at me, then hurriedly begins ringing the bottles through the register. "That's, um, thirty-six sixty." He nods at the till's display, then his gaze meets Julie's. "For the wine."

"And your point is?"

"Just wine."

Julie's eyes flash, then she grabs a packet of chewing gum from the display next to the register and hands it to him. "Happy now?"

"Well…" Sanj rings up the gum, then realizes Julie's brandishing her credit card at him as if it's an offensive weapon she's using in a robbery, so he gingerly slides the card reader across the counter toward her. "Is everything okay?" he asks, as she presses her card into the machine.

"Why wouldn't it be?"

"No reason." Sanj hesitates as Julie angrily punches in her PIN, then he swallows loudly. "It's just that Priya said..."

"Well, she shouldn't have!" Julie snaps, then her expression softens. "Sorry, Sanj. I'm just a bit..."

"Time of the month?"

Julie's glare reappears almost instantaneously. "No, Sanj. Not every bad mood a woman has is down to her hormones."

"No. Of course." Sanj stabs at a button on the card reader, then waits what evidently seems to him like an age for the receipt to emerge. "So it's..." He swallows again, even louder this time. "Luke?"

"Luke's out of the picture."

"Right. Good. I mean, good if *you* think it's good. Which, you know, we all do."

"And I'm guessing Priya's told you about what happened with Tom?"

Sanj looks like he doesn't know whether yes or no is the right answer, so instead, he just half smiles, which obviously *is* the right answer, because Julie sighs resignedly, and all the fight seems to go out of her.

"And I suppose you're going to tell me I should just call him? Apologize. Promise it'll never happen again. But what if it does? What if I'm not over Luke? It's not fair to Tom for me to lead him on, then break his heart if *I* haven't moved on, and if there's still a danger that I haven't gotten Luke completely out of my system. If I can't trust myself, then it's not fair for me to ask someone else to trust me, is it?"

Sanj looks even more uncomfortable than before, then he glances down at me, and an idea evidently occurs to him.

"What do *you* think you should do?"

It's a master stroke, a brilliant question. Because most people already know what they need to do about whatever their problem is. They just need a little help admitting it.

"What do *I* think?" says Julie, as if her own opinion is one she's never thought about consulting.

"Yeah."

"Well, let me see. I can become a nun, I suppose, which means I won't have anything intimate to do with men ever again, thus sparing me from the likes of Luke and saving Tom from the likes of me. Or I could just refuse to answer my door, get a cat, and go the same way as my next-door neighbor. And I'll tell you something. Right now, that second option is a lot more tempting than ever having to deal with any of this crap again!"

Another customer's just come in, and the look of relief on Sanj's face is evident. "Right," he says after an awkward pause, but one he's evidently decided is less awkward than anything he might say.

"So, mad Cat Lady here I come," Julie says, a little shrilly, and I stiffen. "And in the meantime I'm going to self-medicate with Chardonnay. If that's okay with you?"

Sanj nods mutely, then he produces a couple of plastic bags from beneath the counter and begins bagging the bottles. The moment he's finished, Julie virtually snatches the bags from him, marching out of the shop before he can even get out a whispered, "ten pee."

We hurry home, the bottles clanking in time to Julie's steps, and I can't help thinking they sound ominously like the chimes of doom. How come we're back where we started, after all this work? The irony is, Julie knows exactly what she needs to do. She just won't do it. And working out why that might be is the hardest thing of all. I console myself with the fact that there's Barkrun this Sunday morning, sure that the moment Julie and Tom set eyes on each other again, they'll realize they've both been silly for not calling, get together, and live happily ever after.

Mainly because the idea that they won't just doesn't bear thinking about.

31

It's been the best part of a week, and Julie's back in the same old funk she was in after she and Luke parted company. She's back to phoning in sick at work again, though I don't think she really is ill, even though once or twice she's even thrown up noisily in the bathroom first thing: the vomiting's more likely a result of her drinking herself to sleep every night. More worryingly, she has a general sadness about her that seems to be getting worse. Things are so bad that even when we're stopped by a little girl and her mother on the way to the park, and the little girl is fussing over me and her mother says, "You should ask what the doggy's name is," and the girl puts her face close to mine and says to me, "What's your name?" it doesn't even provoke a hint of a smile on Julie's face.

The worst thing is, Julie still won't do anything about her sulk. It's obvious she's upset because Tom still hasn't called, and yet, for some reason that's beyond me, she won't call him either. And while it's perhaps understandable (and a bit of a relief!) that she doesn't want to take me to Barkrun on Sunday, the knock-on effect (no walks that might take us within a mile of Tom's office, or anywhere near Dot's house, or cross his route to work, or even his running route), is making my life a little awkward.

And this is what I don't understand. If I'm hungry, I go and wait next to my bowl until Julie fills it. If I need a walk, I stand by the front door, until she takes me out for one. If I want Julie to get up and let me out into the garden, I'll scratch on the back of her bedroom door until I get the desired result. But Julie won't do any of this. Instead, she seems to be waiting for the phone to ring, without doing anything to influence it.

I learned from *Frasier* that there's a famous quote from someone called Einstein about how the definition of insanity is doing the same thing over and over again and expecting a different result. Well, inversely, that's Julie, doing nothing over and over again except drowning her sorrows, yet she's still thinking something might happen. This means I have to get involved fast.

Which is why, on Friday evening when Priya comes round for another episode of *Game of Thrones*, I decide I'll play a game of my own. Cleverly biding my time until Julie goes to the toilet, thus leaving me and Priya in the living room, I take the opportunity to run over to the French doors and scratch frantically at them.

"Do you need to go out?" says Priya, though the question's evidently rhetorical, as she's already opening the doors for me.

With a grateful snort, I run on out into the garden to where I've strategically placed my favorite knobbly rubber chew toy behind Julie's huge collection of empty wine bottles that are meant for the recycling. Priya's remained indoors, so—having anticipated this—I start barking. Sure enough, after a moment or two, she comes outside to see what all the fuss is about.

"What is it, Doug?" she says, making her way over to where

I'm sitting in front of approximately a dozen empty bottles of Chardonnay. In truth, the stale wine smell's making me feel a bit queasy, but I keep my resolve, and do that "eye-flicking" thing between my toy and Priya, until she spots it.

"How on earth did your toy get…? Jesus, Jules!"

As Priya counts the bottles, then double-checks them in disbelief, I realize my plan has worked. She was here for my party last week, and afterward, she and Sanj helped Julie take the stack of empty bottles that were here to the recycling bin. You don't have to be a genius to work out that all of *these* bottles are new this week.

She stands in the yard with me for a moment, then she gives me a look, before stepping carefully over them to retrieve my chew.

"Here you go, Doug," she says, so I gently take it from her fingers, and give a wag of my tail. As I gnaw the toy happily, Priya takes one last look at the bottles, then smiles at me.

"Well, someone looks like they've got what they wanted," she says, and I wag my tail even more frantically.

Because I'm pretty sure I have.

32

It's the following evening, and thanks no doubt to my skillful maneuvering the previous one, Priya and Sanj have decided to stage an intervention. Which basically means coming around with Julie's dad and inviting Julie and me back to their house for dinner.

Even though we all know it's an intervention—mainly because Julie's "what's going on?" as they virtually bundled her into their car was met with "we're staging an intervention"—it takes until he is well into his second oversize bottle of Cobra beer before an evidently previously-briefed Sanj dares to bring up the subject.

"Well, if you want a man's point of view, you need to take the lead."

"What's the point?" says Julie, miserably. "He's obviously not interested."

"One way to find out," says Priya. "Just call him."

"Or not," says Sanj. "Send him a text."

"No, just call him. He'll be flattered. Plus you can't ignore a call. Whereas a text..."

Julie stares at her plate for a moment, then she puts down her knife and fork. "As much as I appreciate the benefit of your extensive dating knowledge, tell me again how you and Priya got together?" she says, dismissively, but Sanj just shakes his head.

"I'm sorry, but..."

"But what?" spits Julie.

Sanj takes a sip of his beer, realizes he's finished his bottle, then reaches over and helps himself to Priya's, and maybe because he's technically now on his third beer—as I've certainly never heard him talk like this before—the next sentence that comes out of his mouth surprises us all. "It's just so bloody frustrating."

"What is?"

"You! Especially all that time you were with Luke. And now, this refusal to do something about someone who actually likes you..."

"Luke liked me."

Sanj makes the "ha!" face, embellishing it with a loud "Ha!"

"What's that supposed to mean?"

"Just that you could have fooled me, judging by how he treated you, and yet you hung in there..." He gestures toward her with his bottle, ironically in the way a cobra might before striking. "In fact, I'm beginning to think the only reason you were with Luke was because he was married and not going to leave his wife, so you'd always have something to complain about in your usual 'woe is me' kind of way, with the knowledge that you'd never have to..." he makes a pair of bunny ears "...'woman' up and have a normal relationship.

"And how do I know that? Because the one time you finally get the chance to have one with a normal guy, you hit the first bump in the road—for whatever reason—and you not only run a mile away, but you spend all your time telling anyone who'll listen that it's because of you, and that you'll never find a man…"

Sanj pauses for another mouthful of beer, and we're all still too stunned to say anything in the gap. "And do you know what the *most* frustrating thing is? You're forever asking Priya what to do, and Priya listens patiently, and gives you advice—good advice—but then you *never take it*. I've lost count of the times Priya's come home after a night with you, rolling her eyes at your intransigence, your refusal to accept that it's not them, it's you…"

Priya starts into action. "That's not true, Jules. Honest. I…"

"Yes it is," says Sanj. "Julie needs to hear this, so I'm not going to sugarcoat anything."

He takes another gulp of beer, and turns his attention back to Julie. "Each time you find yourself in exactly the same position, but what changes have you made to try to get yourself out of it? None. So please, tell me something. What is it about being in a normal relationship that scares you so much that you can't—sorry, *won't*—do it?"

I get up from my position under the table by Sanj's feet and pad across to the far side of the room to get a better vantage point. Julie's sitting there, openmouthed. Priya's staring at Sanj with what might either be horror or wide-eyed admiration on her face. Julie's dad is doing his best to keep eating. And Sanj? To his credit, he seems to be holding his nerve.

"Okay. Let me put it another way," he says. "What was it about Luke that made him such an attractive proposition?"

"Well, he… I mean, I…" Julie looks like she's floundering, and not just because she's been put on the spot.

"I knew he was bad news. Priya knew he was bad news. Your dad knew he was bad news. Even Doug could tell."

Julie looks at me accusingly, but I can't meet her gaze.

"We all knew he was never going to leave his wife, mainly because these people never do. So unless the sex was amazing—sorry, Jim—and looking at Luke, I find that hard to believe, I can't think of *one single reason* why on earth you stuck with it for so long. Unless..."

"Unless?"

This comes from Priya, rather than Julie.

"You just don't want to be happy," says Sanj, quietly.

For a moment, we all just sit there, too stunned to say anything.

Sanj is staring at Julie, Julie's staring at her plate, Priya's alternately staring at the both of them, and Julie's dad appears to be fascinated by something on the label of his beer bottle.

"Where on earth did all that come from?" asks Julie eventually, and Sanj shrugs.

"You're not the only one who's addicted to *Frasier*."

Then Julie's face starts to...well, "crumple up" is the best way I can think of to describe it, and her chest starts to heave, then she lets out this wail, and the wail turns into sobs, and before you know it, she's bawling her eyes out.

"Oh, *Jules*..." Priya reaches over and envelops her in a hug, and I rush across and start to nuzzle her leg.

Sanj is looking terribly guilty, but I don't think he should feel that way at all, because he's only said what all of us have been thinking. Besides, Julie's tears don't strike me as upset ones. They sound more like relief. And a release. As if finally, someone's had the guts to call her out.

"That's because... Because... I..." Julie's hard to understand, mainly because she's doing more sobbing than speaking. "Don't...deserve...to...be."

"Don't be silly." Priya's holding her close, and gently stroking her hair. "Everyone deserves to be happy."

"Do they?"

"Of course they do!" says Julie's dad.

"But…" Julie reaches for a piece of kitchen towel from the roll on the table, and blows her nose so loudly it makes me jump. "I'm scared."

"Of what?" says Priya.

"You know!" says Julie, but when it's evident that we don't, she shakes her head. "Falling in love."

"What on earth for?" says Julie's dad. "It's the best feeling in the world."

"Maybe." Julie dabs at her eyes with the kitchen towel. "But when you lose someone, it's the *worst*!"

Julie's dad sits back in his chair, a little stunned. "What's that got to do with the price of fish?" he says.

"You remember how devastated you were when you lost Mum?"

Julie's dad's voice falters a little. "Something I'll never forget, love."

Julie reaches across the table and takes his hand in both of hers. "What if that happens to *me*? What if I meet someone, and fall in love like you and Mum did, and I lose him? I've seen how badly that hurts, and…" She sniffs loudly. "I don't think I could survive it."

"Yes, love, but…" Julie's dad, someone who normally has a quick word or a snappy comeback for all occasions, actually looks as if he doesn't know how to respond. "That's like saying, I don't know, that you never want to get behind the wheel of a car, because one day you might have a crash. I mean, you might, especially the way *you* drive, but to miss out on the pleasure of driving simply because of a fear of…" He sighs, then jump-shifts his chair closer to Julie's so he can slip an arm around her shoulders.

"The truth? When I lost your mum, it was the worst thing

that had ever happened to me. Can't have been much fun for her either, mind," he adds, with a wink. "But I got through it. People are more resilient than you think. And while yes, it was horrible, terrible, awful, I'll tell you something. I'd go through it all again even if I knew what was going to happen. Because however bad the pain of loss is, it's nothing compared to the joy of true love."

I take a pace or two back, feeling comforted by the tableau in front of me. Julie's dad is sitting there, cradling Julie, rocking her slowly from side to side. Priya's sobbing silently next to them, though the slightest of smiles keeps appearing on her face. Sanj looks like he's wondering whether it's okay to go and get himself another beer. Which, after a moment, is what he does.

I'm not a psychiatrist—I don't think it's allowed, and apparently those "therapy" dogs aren't the same thing—but I can kind of see what Julie's been doing. And the problem is how to convince someone that the benefits of love outweigh the potential pain of losing it. Especially if they've got nothing to use as a touchstone.

"Hey," says Julie's dad, after a moment. "All we're asking you to do is take some of your own advice."

"*My* advice?"

"You told me to ask Dot out. 'Because you'll never know, otherwise,' you said."

"I'm not sure those were my exact…"

"And I'm really glad you did." He smiles. "I should never have let what happened with your mum hold me back for so long. And you shouldn't either. Just give it a try with Tom, love. See what happens. Because you'll never know otherwise. And I'd hate for you to miss out. We all would. And if anyone deserves to be happy? Well, after what you've been through with Luke, I think we can all agree that it's you."

There's a murmur of assent from Priya and Sanj, and Julie's dad gives Julie a final squeeze. Then he reaches down to pat me encouragingly on the head, as if he's telling me it's down to me to make sure she and Tom get together.

And although it's in a roundabout way, that's exactly what I do.

33

Perhaps thanks to me fetching Julie her phone from the coffee table and pointedly dropping it in her lap while she's having her breakfast, Julie calls Tom the following morning. While he sounds a little surprised to hear from her, he leaps at the chance to see Julie again. And less than ten hours later, we're all sitting in the pub.

Julie's opted for a small glass of wine, which she's nursing, while Tom's drinking a beer, and the smile hasn't left his face since we turned up.

"Did you always want to be a V-E-T?" asks Julie, after they've got through their initial round of small talk.

"Yeah. Well, not *always* always. I mean, I flirted with the idea of being a rock star, then an astronaut, but you've got to be able to have at least a bit of musical ability for the first one... Anyway. Yes. I loved the five years of training. And I love my job. Apart from..." He lowers his voice. "Occasionally you have to put someone's beloved pet to sleep. And it breaks your heart."

"I bet," says Julie.

"But mostly the job's all about helping people."

"You mean 'animals'?"

"That's a bit harsh!"

"No, I meant..." Julie stops talking, then punches Tom lightly on the arm, and although punching is normally a sign of disliking someone, I'm pretty sure this means the exact opposite.

"So why did you leave it so long?" says Tom, after a brief but comfortable silence.

"Leave what so long?"

"Before you called and asked me out."

"I didn't ask you out."

I peer up at Julie, a little confused, then remember she's probably getting him back for a similar exchange when he stitched me up after the Rambo Incident. Tom evidently gets it too, because he shakes his head, then mimes shooting himself in the temple. "Okay. Got me. Maybe I'm a bit rusty. That's what comes of having been single for a year, I guess."

"A *year*?" Julie makes a sympathetic face. "Because of...?"

"Exactly because of." Tom nods. "It hit me pretty hard, I'll tell you."

"Do you want to talk about it?"

"Not really." He shifts uncomfortably on the bench, then puffs air loudly out of his cheeks. "Though would you believe it was with my oldest friend? He was the best man at our wedding. Turns out my ex thought so too." Tom sighs dramatically. "I miss him," he says, and Julie laughs, then perhaps realizes she shouldn't have.

"Sorry. Shit."

"It is, isn't it?"

Julie half moves as if to take his hand, then seems to have second thoughts at the last minute, and instead, just briefly rubs his forearm briefly. "And since then, there's been no one…special?"

"Nope." Tom's said it definitely enough, but he shakes his head too, as if to leave Julie in no doubt. "When you choose someone to spend the rest of your life with, and it turns out they're not prepared to be that person, it knocks your confidence."

"Too scared, in case it goes wrong again?"

Tom laughs, though it's a hollow one. "Something like that."

"Get us, eh?" Julie stares off into the distance, then she forces a smile. "Want me to tell you more about what a bastard Luke was?"

"If you think it'll make you feel better."

"I was hoping it might make *you* feel better." Julie pretends to be fascinated by a spot on the table. "About us."

"Right."

"Might it?"

Tom wipes a line of condensation from his glass. "A bit."

Julie stares at him for a moment, then she picks up her wine and takes a sip, and he does the same with his beer, and I snort, but neither of them seem to hear as they're too busy trying not to meet each other's eyes. "Oh, Tom," she says, eventually. "This has hardly turned out how I hoped it would. Trying to outdo each other with our tales of misery. I'm so sorry."

"Here's a thought," says Tom, suddenly. "Maybe it's not us. Maybe we're actually both excellent at relationships, and it's just that the people we were with *weren't*."

"Huh?"

"I just realized. I've been spending the last year or so blaming myself that my marriage didn't work out, that it must have been my fault she left me. But maybe… Maybe it was her fault, because that's just what she's like? And Luke—we know he's a dick in relationships, treats his wife terribly, and you've met her, and she seems…"

"Nice," says Julie, begrudgingly.

"Exactly!" Tom grins. "Proof if ever there was proof that 'it's not you, it's me' is true! But, you know, the other way around."

"You think?"

"It's a possibility, at least. I mean, just look at us…" Tom's phone pings, and with an apologetic look, he picks it up. He stares at the screen, gives his head a little shake as if he can't quite believe what he's seeing, then leaps up from the bench to punch the air, nearly toppling the table over in the process. "He's done it!"

Tom's sudden exclamation has made us both jump. Meanwhile, he's staring at his phone as if he hasn't the faintest idea what it is, and Julie's doing something similar to him.

"Who's done it?"

"Doug!"

"What are you talking about?"

"Doug." Tom beams at me, like a proud owner at Crufts. "He's only gone and made it."

"Made what?"

"His photo. It's… Well, it's him!" Tom's talking in the manner of an excited five-year-old struggling to get his words out in the right order. "On here!"

"Do you need me to slap you?" says Julie.

"No, I'm fine. Sorry. It's just…" He's grinning like a loon, while pointing frantically at his phone. *"We Rate Dogs!"* he says, finally.

"What?"

Tom takes a breath, does a strange "top to bottom" gesture up and down his body with his hands as if centering himself in a yoga class, then smiles. "Doug's been rated," he says, calmly. "On *We Rate Dogs*."

Julie peers at me, as if expecting me to confirm the news. "You're kidding?" she says, after the few seconds it evidently takes her to regain the power of speech.

"Nope," says Tom, perhaps a little unnecessarily given his actions of the previous thirty seconds. "See for yourself."

Julie glances nervously down at his phone, as if it's radioactive. "I can't look."

"Why not?"

"What if..." She lowers her voice. "What if it's not a very good score? I don't want him to be scarred for life."

"He's a dog, Julie. He's hardly going to understand what's going on."

"You'd be surprised."

"Remember they all get good scores. So it's unlikely he's about to be traumatized..."

"Okay, okay." Tom sits back down, and Julie picks me up from the pavement, then plonks me down on the bench in between the two of them so I can see. "Show."

"Ready?"

Without waiting for a reply, Tom taps his phone's screen, and as my inverted ears party hat photo appears, Julie lets out a short scream of delight. "What does it say?"

Tom scrolls down with his index finger, then clears his throat. *"This is Doug,"* he reads. *"Having a bit of an ear-mergency on his birthday. Would totally turn them outside in again for him."*

Julie breaks into a wide grin. "And the score?"

Tom doesn't say anything. Instead, he just lifts his phone up and positions the screen a foot or so in front of Julie's face. She narrows her eyes, scans the screen, then her jaw drops open in amazement. "Fourteen!" she exclaims.

She angles the screen so I can see it. I'm still a little embarrassed by the picture, and I'm determined not to get too excited, but it's hard not to get carried away by the mood.

"Told you!" says Tom. "And look how many likes he's got!"

"Does that say...?"

"Ninety-seven *thousand*!"

Julie's jaw drops even further open, so I imagine "likes" must be the human equivalent of "licks" in terms of what they represent.

Then something strange and wonderful happens. Tom and Julie leap to their feet and begin dancing madly next to the table as if they're in some sort of competition, high-fiving each other every few seconds. I leap off the bench to join them, though I'm only able to run around in excited circles, since my leash is fastened round the table leg. Trouble is, as a result, I get it tangled round Julie's ankles, sending her toppling into Tom.

She throws out her hands to break her fall, but Tom catches her instead. He holds her tight, and their faces are inches from each other's, and... I'll leave you to work out the rest.

Though I'm happy to report, there's no humming.

34

"Morning, Doug!"

Tom, grinning from ear-to-ear, is the sight that greets me when my scratching on the bottom of Julie's bedroom door finally provokes a response the following morning. And while I'm not so happy when he scoops me up off the floor, plants a loud kiss on my forehead, then plonks me unceremoniously back down, I still mark yesterday down as what is generally referred to as a "result."

I cheerfully tail Tom into the kitchen, where he begins searching the cupboards, eventually managing to find most of the things needed for breakfast. By the time a bleary-eyed Julie appears in the kitchen doorway, there's French press coffee, toast and jam, cereal, and even some fruit laid out on the table, along with a bowl of my usual on the floor for me too.

Julie catches sight of the spread, opens her mouth as if to say something, then evidently thinks better of it. Instead, she makes her way over to the table, and lowers herself gingerly down into one of the chairs.

Tom wheels round from where he's been inspecting the contents of the fridge. "Morning! I didn't know what you liked. For breakfast. So I did a bit of everything."

"So I see," she says, curtly.

"You must be hungry. I know I am! Although we could go out if you'd pre..."

"Listen, Tom..."

At Julie's interruption, Tom halts midsentence, then he folds his arms. "Nope!"

"Pardon?"

Tom unfolds his arms, but only so he can stick his fingers in his ears. "I won't."

"Won't what?"

"Listen."

"What?"

"Isn't that supposed to be my line? Seeing as I've got, you know..." He removes his fingers from his ears, pulls out the chair next to her, sits down, and begins buttering a piece of toast. "But no, I'm not going to listen. Because you're about to give me the talk, to tell me that last night, while it was fantastic, amazing, and probably the best sex you ever had, has to be a one-off. That you're just not ready for a relationship yet, or how you won't be good for me, and I don't want to hear it, because you're wrong. We're great together. And I think if you give it a chance, give *us* a chance, I know you'll see that too."

He cuts the toast into triangles, places one into Julie's open mouth as if he's feeding a toddler, then he puts a finger underneath her jaw and gently closes it. "So eat your breakfast, drink some coffee, I'll take Doug for a walk, and you think about what I've just said, and if by the time I'm back you still think you and me are a bad idea, well..." He grins. "I'll just have to think of some other way to change your mind."

With that he stands up, kisses Julie quickly on the top of her head, says "Come on, Doug," collects my leash from where it's hanging in the hall, and the two of us head out through the front door.

And as I take a last glance back toward the kitchen, I can't help noticing that Julie's so stunned, she hasn't even begun chewing.

Ultimately, Tom doesn't get the chance to change Julie's mind. Though to be fair, he doesn't get to find out if it needs changing or not. Julie's dad is there when we get back from our walk, which makes for a rather awkward encounter, especially because Tom's bought flowers from the shop on the corner, which he presents to Julie's dad by mistake when he answers the door. Then Tom splutters something about having come to take me for an early walk, to which Julie's dad smiles and says, "I wasn't born yesterday, son."

Julie's dad asks Tom if he'll stay for a cup of tea, and Tom suddenly remembers he has to get to the office, even though today is apparently something called a "Bank Holiday," which means neither he nor Julie need to go to work. When Julie and I escort him along the hall, though she promises him she'll call, their awkward goodbye isn't exactly that of two people who are on their way to falling in love. Especially since he's so flustered, he forgets to give Julie the flowers, and ends up taking them away with him.

And while that's not ideal, there's an upside to it too. He'll have to bring them back.

35

"I slept with Tom."

Priya's eyes widen, and she holds up a hand to high-five Julie, a move I know Julie knows how to do because her dad's taught me to do it *and* takes the greatest pleasure in showing Julie whenever he gets the chance. But for some reason, she seems to have forgotten how to respond.

"When?"

"Last night."

"And?"

"And what?" says Julie, blushing.

"How? Well, not *how,* obviously, rather how did it happen?" Priya's mouth falls open, and she does that little head shake thing to indicate amazement. "Was it amazing?"

Julie picks up her gym bag and stuffs a towel into it. At Priya's behest, the two of them are off to the gym this evening for a Zumba class. I haven't been invited because according to Julie it's nothing like Barkrun, and instead involves dancing, which Julie's dad informs me isn't something I'd apparently be good at since I do, literally, have two left feet. Instead, Julie's dad has come around to keep me company, and so he can watch "the match" on Julie's TV subscription service.

"Yeah," Julie says, quietly, and Priya narrows her eyes.

"I'm sorry. Am I missing something? You've just had..." She lowers her voice. "Hot S-E-X with a hot V-E-T, and yet you look like your world's just fallen in."

"Sorry, P." Julie retrieves another towel from the shelf, then remembers she's already got one, so she hurriedly puts it back. "It's just... This morning, when I got up, he'd made breakfast, then he took Doug for a walk, and when I tried to tell him we should maybe take things slowly, he wouldn't hear any of it. He'd even bought me flowers. Not that he had the chance to give me them."

"The bastard!" Priya grins. "Great sex, breakfast, flowers... So, the anti-Luke, basically. You couldn't get him to have a word with Sanj, could you? Give him a few pointers."

"I know. But after everything with Luke..." Julie shakes her head. "What if he's the one?"

"Luke?"

"Tom."

"Sorry. Now I'm even more confused."

"That makes two of us." Julie sighs. "I'm clearly not over Luke. I've got all this...baggage. And now I meet the most perfect guy, and I'm scared to..." She peers into her bag again, double-checks her towel's in there, then zips it up. "I'm bound to ruin it, P, even though I might not want to. Tom has trust issues because of what his ex did, and the last thing I want to do is hurt him, though I'm probably going to, simply because Luke hurt me. And I know that doesn't sound fair, or make much sense, but..."

Julie swallows so hard you don't have to have hearing as finely tuned as mine to hear it, so Priya reaches across and takes both of Julie's hands in hers. "Jules," she says, shaking her head slowly. "What I'm hearing is, Tom could be the best thing that's ever happened to you, but you're making it sound like it's the worst. Remember, Luke's the cheat, not you, and, in fact, the amount of loyalty you've shown by sticking with him all this time means, perhaps in a perverse way, Tom's probably got nothing to worry about in terms of whether he can trust you. And I know this probably won't come easy to you, given that joke of a—" she does the bunny ears thing "—'relationship' you had with Luke, but d'you know what? You need to just go with it. See that going out with someone in the normal way is fun. Exciting. Enjoyable. Because it can be. Despite what you may think after Luke."

"I just don't know, P…"

"But none of us do. That's the exciting part!" Priya thinks for a moment, then she catches my eye. "Remember that time Doug ate that dead lizard he found?"

"Don't remind me. He was as sick as—well, as a *dog*—for the best part of two days."

"And has he ever eaten another one?"

Julie shakes her head. "Nope. Once bitten, and all that. If you excuse the pun."

"Well, there you go. Luke was—*is*—that dead lizard. And you're smarter than Doug—no offense, fella." She reaches down to scratch the top of my head. "So you're not going to make the same mistake again. Are you?"

I'm good enough at English to know those last two words are normally a question, but Priya's tone has made them sound like a warning.

"No, P. I'm not," says Julie, though not as confidently as she might.

"Besides, I don't see you taking Luke out on Tom, and for one obvious reason."

"Which is?"

"Mainly because it sounds like Tom won't let you!"

Priya grabs Julie by the shoulders and steers her out of the kitchen, so I tail the two of them along the hall, hoping Julie knows that's true.

And that I won't let her either.

It's halftime in "the match," and Julie's dad is just pouring me a bowlful of the usual while pouring himself a third beer, which he accompanies with a wink in my direction and a "don't tell Julie!" when the doorbell rings.

I sprint off down the hall, barking as loudly as I can, determined to ignore Julie's dad's "Quiet, Doug!" as the scent I can detect from outside makes me determined to stand my ground. Julie's dad raises both eyebrows at me, then—perhaps as a consequence of my frenzied barking—opens the door carefully.

"Can I help you?"

"What? Oh, I..." Luke is standing there, obviously nonplussed at the sight of a man he doesn't know answering Julie's door. He takes a half step back and looks up at the house, as if to check he's at the right place, then he frowns. "Is Julie here?"

"Who's asking?" says Julie's dad, in a friendly tone, so Luke—perhaps assuming that means "yes," smiles at him.

"I'm Luke," he says.

Julie's dad seems a little confused, then he looks down to see me still growling, and evidently puts two and two together. "Luke."

"That's right. She might have mentioned me?" Luke grins again. "And you are?"

"Trying to think of a good reason not to slam the door in your face."

"Ah." Luke takes another half step backward. "She *has* mentioned me, then?"

"She has," says Julie's dad, impassively.

Luke is looking a little nervous. Julie's dad is hardly the biggest person in the world, and certainly isn't the most menacing, but Luke's proved himself to be a coward. Between the two of us I think we could take him, and I also suspect Luke knows this.

"So, is she? Here?"

"No."

"Right." Luke hesitates, then peers over Julie's dad's shoulder and along the hall, as if expecting to spy Julie hiding behind the coatrack. "Only, I saw her car, so I thought..." He nods at Julie's Fiat, as if he thinks proving he knows what car she drives might help his case.

"What did you think, exactly? That you could call in for a bit of hanky-panky before heading back home to your wife?"

Luke lets out a brief laugh, perhaps at Julie's dad's old-fashioned description, before realizing perhaps he shouldn't have, and the grin leaves his face so quickly it's as if a switch has been flicked.

"I'm sorry. Who are you again?"

"I'm Julie's father," says Julie's dad. "And it's not me you should be apologizing to."

Luke appears a little confused, as if he's expecting Julie's dad to enlighten him, and when he doesn't, he starts to back away down the garden path, clearly realizing he's made a mistake.

"Oh-kay," he says. "Well, if you could tell her I... Actually, no, don't bother, I'll..."

"Not so fast." Julie's dad takes a step after him, shoots out a hand so quickly I don't see it, and grabs Luke's wrist in an iron grip. "I think you and I should have a little talk. Don't you?"

By the looks of him, Luke clearly doesn't agree. "Actually, I have to..." He tries to peer at his watch, but the grip Julie's dad has on his wrist means he can't quite see the dial. Or get away.

"That's right. You have to," says Julie's dad. Then he stands to one side and, maintaining his grip on Luke's wrist, ushers him in through the door.

Somehow the evening has taken rather a surreal turn. Julie's dad's made tea, and right now, he's sitting on the sofa, while Luke is perched on the front edge of the armchair, looking like he'd rather be anywhere but here. I've taken a strategic position underneath his outstretched legs, where I'm currently growling softly, though not loud enough that I can't follow the conversation, although up until now, it's mostly been polite chitchat about how Luke takes his tea.

Once they've both got a mug in front of them, Julie's dad looks down at me and puts a finger to his lips. Then he sits back in his seat, blows across the top of his mug, and clears his throat.

"So I understand you're expecting?"

Luke nods, even though he looks like he's not sure what he's expecting *at all.* "Yeah. Well, not me, obviously. My w..." He stops talking abruptly, obviously deciding that reminding Julie's dad of his marital status might not be the smartest of moves.

"So you do admit you're married?"

"Technically," says Luke, nervously.

"And yet you and Julie were...?" Julie's dad seems to be trying to find the right word. Unsuccessfully, as it turns out. Though Luke's possibly keen he doesn't either.

"Um, yeah," he says, quickly. "But at the time, I was—my wife and I, I mean—were separated."

"Is that right?"

"Well, we were thinking about it. At least, I was. Because we'd been having some problems."

Julie's dad eyes him suspiciously. "And they're all sorted now? Those 'problems'?"

"Well, that's what I'm here to talk to Julie about," says Luke, a little less confidently. "What with, you know, me about to be a dad, and all that. Because obviously I want to do the right thing. By everyone."

"The right thing." Julie's dad nods slowly. "In that case, may I give you some advice?"

He's said it in a way to suggest he's not really asking for permission, and Luke swallows hard. "Sure."

"Because it can be hard when you're expecting a child. Puts a strain on any relationship, I can tell you. Then eventually this tiny, helpless thing arrives and all of a sudden, you fall head over heels in love. And then you realize you'll do anything to protect them. And that's a feeling that stays with you forever." Julie's dad leans forward, so his face is close to Luke's. "If you get my drift."

Luke swallows even harder. "Sure."

"Good. So. One question."

"Then can I go?"

Julie's dad smiles noncommittally. "Do you love her?"

"Who?" says Luke, though it's a stupid question.

"Julie, obviously. Since it's also obviously not your wife."

Luke opens his mouth to protest, then evidently thinks better of it, and shuts it again. "It's..."

"If you say 'complicated,' you'll end up wearing that," says Julie's dad, pointing at Luke's mug.

"But it *is*," protests Luke, as I move out of the splash zone, just in case. "You're a man of the world. You must know what it's like?"

"What what's like?"

"Marriage. I mean, it's not our natural state, is it, if you think about it. We're men. We're born to procreate."

"Which, correct me if I'm wrong, you're doing with your wife?"

"Well, yeah, but..." Luke gives a shrug, but it's hard to know what he means by it. "You married, are you?" he says, perhaps in an attempt to switch the focus away from himself.

"I was," says Julie's dad, curtly.

"Left you, did she?"

"In a way."

"Right, but you were together, for, what...?"

"Not nearly long enough."

"So you understand the...*ups and downs* a marriage can go through?"

"I understand there *are* ups and downs. And they cancel each other out. The downs certainly don't mean you go running off with someone else. Particularly if you're just leading that someone else on. And especially if that someone else is my daughter."

"I wasn't leading her on."

"You told her you'd leave your wife for her."

"Well..."

"And have you?"

Luke shifts uncomfortably in his chair. "Well, that's kind of why I'm here."

"That doesn't answer my question."

"To see if I...need to."

"I don't understand."

"Yes, well, like I said, it's..." Luke sets his mug down on the coffee table, careful to place it out of Julie's dad's reach. "Complicated."

"So you keep saying. Though in any case, you're too late."

"Am I, though?" says Luke, and I spot a vein in Julie's dad's neck start to throb.

"You are. So I'd suggest you go back home to your wife,

forget all about my daughter, and do your best to live up to those vows you made a few years ago."

Luke makes a face. "Till death do us part, and all that?"

"That's right," says Julie's dad, though there's a tremor in his voice I haven't heard before. "Let me tell you, if you have one bit of the thirty years I had with Julie's mother, you'll think yourself lucky. And you'll thank me for putting you straight."

"Thirty years." Luke winces. "You could have killed her, and you'd have been out five years earlier."

He's obviously meant it as a joke, but the look that appears on Julie's dad's face suggests he hasn't found it funny at all. Luke looks at him like that's a failing, and Julie's dad picks up on that, because he's up off the sofa and looming angrily over him.

"You'd do well not to joke about that kind of thing, son."

"Jeez! Lighten up, old man."

"I'm just trying to give you a little advice. For your own good."

"Yeah?" Luke stands up, so I do too. "Well if you're such an expert, where's your wife now?"

"I..." Julie's dad hesitates. "Lost her," he says, and Luke leers at him.

"That sounds a bit careless, if you ask me!"

He's got a point, though as he stands there, grinning inanely, Julie's dad lowers his voice. "She died," he says, in little more of a whisper, causing both Luke and me to stare at him.

As Luke perhaps contemplates how he can possibly come back from that one, my head is spinning. Julie's mum isn't simply "lost," like Santa next door. She's *dead*. No matter how many posters he might put up on lampposts around town, she's never coming back. And now I understand *everything*.

"I'll tell you something," he continues. "There's not a day, not *one hour* where I don't beat myself up wondering whether

I could have prevented it. Done something differently. Every time I look at Julie, I'm reminded of her mother, and it's simultaneously the best and the worst feeling ever. So to think about someone like you messing her about..."

"Okay, okay. Keep your hair on," says Luke, and it's about now that the evening really takes a turn for the worse. The argument escalates, until Julie's dad is shouting at Luke, who's giving as good as he's getting, even prodding Julie's dad in the chest as he tries to make a series of points that don't seem to be relevant.

I'm on the floor in between the two of them, barking frantically, until suddenly, Julie's dad stops talking, turns shockingly pale, and clutches his chest right where Luke has been prodding him.

Luke starts to protest that he wasn't even prodding him that hard, then Julie's dad tries to say something, but no sound comes out. He takes a couple of steps backward, collapses down onto the sofa, and his eyes sort of do this funny "rolling" thing until they match how white the rest of his face is. Then everything goes quiet.

I jump up onto his lap, snort inquisitively, then give his hand a tentative lick, but Julie's dad doesn't so much as acknowledge me. Then from behind me Luke says, "Fuck!" softly, then once more, then once more still, although a little louder each time.

He hurries over to where Julie's dad is lying, leans in cautiously, and says, "Mister Newman?" softly, as if scared he might wake him. With another "Fuck!" he reaches down, takes him by the shoulder, and gives him a gentle shake, then a slightly harder one, accompanied by a loud "Mister Newman!" leaving me in no doubt he's definitely trying to wake him up now.

Luke looks desperately down at me and then back at Julie's dad. Then he scrabbles for his phone in his pocket and starts to dial a number, but slips it away again just as quickly. He runs both hands frantically through his hair, then says, "Don't judge me, Doug," as he picks up his mug, empties it into the sink, wipes the handle on a tea towel, and hurriedly stuffs it into the dishwasher. Then he turns and sprints for the front door.

I've sat through enough medical dramas on television to know that this isn't a good development, and that now would be an excellent time to summon help. I leap off Julie's dad's lap and—at top speed—chase Luke along the hall, out through the front door and along the garden path, eventually managing to get between him and the gate.

"Out of the way, Doug!" he says, as I block his exit, hackles raised.

Luke reaches down, as if he's thinking of trying to manhandle me out of the way, but I bare my teeth just enough to deter him, then begin barking furiously, the very definition of pugnacity.

"What?" he says, as I let out a fusillade of accusatory yaps. "I can't. I…"

I bark some more, then out of the corner of my eye, spot Miss Harris's curtains twitching next door, and her miserable face appears at the window, so I decide to try a different tactic, just like Julie does whenever Miss Harris is going "off on one." Who knows, maybe I can appeal to Luke's better nature. Assuming he has one.

I stop barking, widen my eyes to their maximum, angle my head so far round that it's almost painful, then let out the most pitiful whine I can produce, and…it seems to work! Luke glares at me, then he says, "Jesus" under his breath, and—as if doing me some huge favor—retrieves his phone from his inside pocket and presses the screen three times.

"Ambulance, please," he says, as I tail him back inside the house.

Julie's dad hasn't moved, and in fact, looks like he's sleeping, though the noises he's making aren't sounding particularly restful.

"What?" Luke says into his phone, followed by "My, um, *friend's* father. I think he's had a heart attack."

He gives our address to the operator, then leans in as if he's about to give Julie's dad a kiss, says, "Yes, he is," and then, miserably, "Right."

Then he calls Julie's mobile, leaves her a brief message, and with a hardly-reassuring, "It's going to be okay, Doug," sits heavily down on the armchair.

And as I run back into the garden to wait for the ambulance, I can only hope he's right.

36

After all of yesterday's excitement, Julie's dad's heart attack seems to have only been of the mild variety. While they kept him in hospital overnight as a precaution, the good news is there's no permanent damage, and as long as he keeps taking his medication (and keeps off the beer) the doctors say he's going to be fine. As is Dot, who looked like *she* was going to have a heart attack when Julie told her what had happened.

The less than good news, however, is that even though Luke doesn't unfortunately smell anything like roses, that's apparently how he has come out of all of this. I've even heard the word *hero* mentioned by Julie herself, along with how he saved Julie's dad, even though Julie's dad wouldn't have *had* the heart attack if Luke hadn't been there in the first place.

"Not all heroes wear capes," Luke had reminded Julie, half-jokingly, and he's right. Some of them wear collars.

What's even more worrying than Julie's dad's mild heart attack is that as a result of all this, Julie seems to have forgiven Luke for most of his past indiscretions. Even worse, when an emotional Julie told him, "I don't know how I'll ever thank you," the glint in Luke's eye suggested he had an idea or two. All I can hope is that the Tom factor is strong enough to prevent this from happening, along with the fact that nothing else has changed: Luke is still married, and Sarah's still pregnant with twins.

"Hey, Doug," Julie's dad says, when we pick him up the following morning. "Did you miss me?"

I jump up on him repeatedly in response, which gets me a bit of a rebuke from Julie.

"Go easy on him, Doug. He's still a bit fragile."

"Get away with you," he says, bending over to pick me up, then he straightens up suddenly and leans against the car.

Julie rushes to his side. "You okay, Dad?" she says, anxiously.

"I'm fine," he says, gently removing the supportive hand she's put on his arm. "Just a rush of blood to the head. Probably from one of the hundreds of pills they gave me. I'm bound to feel a little unsteady."

"Right," says Julie. She opens his door, leans the seat forward so I can jump in the back, then helps her dad into the car. "In?" she says.

Julie's dad rolls his eyes. "Yes, thank you," he says, making a show of shutting the door properly.

Julie gives me a look, which I do my best to return, then she hurries round to the driver's side, jumps in, and jabs a finger toward the gym bag next to me on the back seat. "I've picked up some clothes from your house, and made up the bed in the spare room, so..."

"We're not going home to mine?" says Julie's dad, as we make our way out of the car park.

"Nope." Julie lowers the window and feeds her ticket into

the machine, accelerating before the barrier comes back down. "We thought it would be better if…"

"We?" Julie's dad swivels round to fix me with an accusing stare, and Julie laughs.

"Not Doug—although he's pleased you're staying with us. Dot and me."

"What's Dot got to do with…?"

"The price of fish?" Julie keeps her eyes fixed on the road. "You've had a heart attack, Dad. Like it or not, you need to be some place where someone can keep an eye on you. I've taken a couple of days off work. And between me and Doug…"

"But…"

"It's not forever. The doctor said you just need to take it easy for a few days. Let someone else look after you for a change. Get a bit of light exercise in," she adds. "Eat properly. Which means if you see Dot, no…"

"I think what two consenting adults get up to is none of your…"

"Muffins," says Julie, dryly.

"Julie, love…"

Julie shuts him down with a look. "I've already lost one parent," she says. "I'm not keen on losing another just yet, if it's all the same to you?"

Julie's dad opens his mouth to protest, then shuts it again. Secretly, I think he's quite pleased with the arrangement, and so am I. After all, with Julie's dad staying with us for now, Luke surely won't be darkening our front door anytime soon.

And even if he does, that's about as far as he'll get.

My feeling of relief that Luke's out of the picture lasts less than a day. That evening, just as I'm sitting in Julie's dad's lap while Julie cooks dinner, there's a knock on the door.

"I'll get it," says Julie—perhaps a little needlessly, as Julie's dad is under strict instructions to stay in his chair. The next thing I hear is the sound of Julie's awkward cough from the doorway.

"Dad," she says, leading Luke into the front room. "You remember Luke?"

I leap down onto the rug, riding it like a surfboard on the polished wooden floor for a foot or so before scuttling warily over to where Luke's standing, as Julie's dad does a double take from his chair.

"Luke?" he says, as if trying to place the name.

"How are you, Jim?" Luke takes a step forward, hesitates, as if he's not sure it's appropriate, then resumes his journey to where Julie's dad is sitting, so I follow him across the room and lie protectively at Julie's dad's feet. "You don't mind me calling you Jim, do you?"

Julie's dad nods. "Suppose," he says, gruffly, though Luke takes it as the most enthusiastic response in the world.

"You're looking… I'm going to go with, better than the last time I saw you!" Luke laughs nervously, then he seems to realize it's not exactly appropriate.

"That wouldn't be hard," says Julie's dad. "I suppose I owe you a thank-you?"

He's phrased it like a question, and Luke doesn't seem quite sure how to respond, though to his credit, his mumbled "don't mention it" does the job.

"How much do you, you know…" Luke clears his throat noisily. "Remember. About what happened."

"Not a lot," says Julie's dad, to Luke's evident relief. "Why?"

"I just… Well… Sometimes, people…" Luke glances down at me, as if he fears I'm about to give the game away, and if I could, I would. "It's traumatic, isn't it, a heart attack? And it might make you recall things…differently."

Julie's dad shrugs. "All I really remember is someone at the door…"

"That was me," says Luke. "I'd, um, come to check on Julie. She hadn't been in to work, so…"

"Followed by lots of barking. And then an ambulance ride."

"Also me," says Luke, visibly relieved. "Calling the ambulance, I mean. Not the, um…"

"Barking?" Julie's keeping a respectable distance, as if she doesn't dare get too close in case she might fall under Luke's spell again.

"Yeah." Luke lets out a nervous laugh. "That was Doug. The barking. He was obviously a bit…agitated."

"Understandably." Julie smiles flatly. "So, what are you doing here, Luke?"

"I just came to see how Jim was."

"He's doing okay. You're doing okay, aren't you, Dad?"

Julie's dad nods. "Doing okay, son. Thanks."

The three of them stand there awkwardly, then Luke half inclines his head toward the kitchen and inhales exaggeratedly. "Something smells nice."

"It's chili con carne," says Julie's dad. "My favorite."

"Mine too!" says Luke, in a *what-a-coincidence* way, ignoring Julie's dropped-open jaw as he does. "Right, so…" He looks at his watch. "I'd better leave you to your dinner. Take care of yourself, Jim."

"Will do, son. Thanks again."

Luke shrugs. "My pleasure. Happy to help. Lucky I was here, come to think of it. Otherwise…" He puffs air out of his cheeks, and slowly shakes his head. "Anyway. Enjoy your chili."

He glances longingly at the kitchen door, then licks his lips for effect—behavior that would be over the top even from me. Julie's dad opens his mouth as if to say something, then he looks at Julie, and sighs.

"Did you want to stay for dinner?"

"What for?"

This is from Julie, not Luke, but it's Julie's dad who answers the question. "So we can say a proper thank-you. You know, for..."

"For saving your life?" suggests Luke.

Then something really unexpected happens, because Julie's dad says, "Well, yes," then he starts *crying.* And while it's probably due to the stress of what he's just been through, rather than any sadness at forcing Luke and Julie together for an evening, I can just tell Luke's going to seize hold of the situation as hard as he can.

"*Of course* I'll stay," says Luke, ignoring Julie's eye-roll, while peering at me defiantly. "That's if Julie doesn't mind?"

Julie hurries across the room to place a comforting arm round her dad, and evidently decides she doesn't have an alternative. "I suppose not," she says.

"That's settled, then," says Julie's dad. "There's enough chili, is there, love?"

"Oh yes," says Julie, archly. "Enough for Luke to have an extra-large helping."

"Great!" says Luke, a little too overenthusiastically.

"Can I get you a drink?" says Julie's dad, and Luke nods. "Please."

"Would you do the honors, love?" says Julie's dad, as Luke makes himself comfortable on the sofa.

Julie stalks into the kitchen, opens the fridge door, and inspects the contents. "Right, well, we've got orange juice, or..." She frowns, and moves some things around on the shelf. "Well, orange juice, really."

"What kind of orange juice?" says Luke.

Julie shows him the carton, and Luke wrinkles his nose up. "Ah," he says.

"What's 'ah'?"

"It's got 'bits,'" Luke says. "Got any beer?"

"No," says Julie, flatly. "On account of Dad having had a heart attack and not being allowed to drink."

"Some wine, perhaps then?"

"Same answer. And you didn't bring any, so…"

"Didn't know I should, on account of this thank-you dinner being a surprise, and all that." Luke grins sheepishly. "I can go and get some, if you…?"

Quick as a flash, Julie seems to sense an opening for an escape. "That's okay. You stay here and keep Dad company. I'll just nip down to the corner shop and…"

She stands there for a moment, and even I can see she's waiting for Luke to put his hand in his pocket and give her some money, but when he just grins vacantly up at her, she sighs resignedly.

"Doug? Shall we?"

Always keen on the idea of a walk, I stand up and big stretch (though it can't be that big a stretch, seeing as no one mentions it), then change my mind, deciding I'd better stay and make sure nothing more happens to Julie's dad with just him and Luke in the house. So instead of joining Julie, I hop up onto the sofa, from where I can keep an eye on proceedings.

"Suit yourself," says Julie—a little harshly, I feel—then she grabs her bag and stalks off along the hall.

"So," says Julie's dad, once Julie's slammed the front door behind her. "Did you really come around here to inquire about my well-being? Or did you think you could use the fact that you, you know…"

"Saved your life?"

"…to get back into Julie's good graces?"

I frown up at the two of them. It's obviously not just Julie's good graces that Luke's trying to get back into.

"Because she's met someone," Julie's dad continues. "Someone who could be good for her. Rather than somebody who's just trying his luck on somebody vulnerable because he's not getting enough at home. So if there's a shred of decency in you, son, you'll leave my daughter be so she can start to think about her future, rather than trying to hang on to the fantasy of something that can never be."

"Sure," says Luke, though it's not really a valid response.

"Sure?"

"Uh-huh."

"You don't sound it."

"No, I… This person would be *Tom*, would it? Julie's new man?"

I peer up at Luke, not sure if he's making a joke about Julie's surname.

"It would," says Julie's dad.

"Right."

"Right."

"Good."

"Isn't it?"

"Uh-huh."

Julie's dad has his arms folded.

Luke's drumming his fingers anxiously on the arm of the chair, no doubt willing Julie to hurry back with the wine.

Then suddenly the doorbell rings, and Luke reacts like it's the bell at the end of a boxing match he's losing. "I'll get it," he announces enthusiastically, leaping up from his seat.

Thinking it's probably Julie, who's forgotten her keys in her haste to get out, I leap down from the sofa and tail Luke along the hall, just in case he decides to try his luck privately with her there. But when Luke throws the door open, instead of a wine-bearing Julie, it's Tom. With a bouquet of flowers. The same bouquet of flowers he tried to give Julie unsuccessfully yesterday morning.

"Ah," Tom says, after a moment's speechlessness, and I'm not sure who's the more thrown of the three of us. Unfortunately, it's Luke who recovers his composure first.

"Tim, isn't it?"

I know he's got Tom's name wrong on purpose, and though I suspect Tom knows it too, he doesn't rise to it.

"Tom," he says, patiently.

Luke nods at the bouquet. "They for me?"

Tom stares at him, then glances down at me accusingly, as if my standing at Luke's feet is the worst form of treason. "Is, um, Julie in?"

"Julie?" Luke squares up to him, as if the two of them are facing off with the giant Q-tips again. "Nope."

Tom frowns, then glances back over his shoulder at Julie's car, which is parked right outside. "You're sure?"

Luke nods, but when he doesn't elaborate, Tom clears his throat awkwardly. "Right." He looks down at me again, though sadly, I'm powerless to help. "Do you know where she is?"

"Went out to get some wine. We're about to have dinner."

"Right," says Tom, again, evidently growing less confident with each utterance.

"Can I give her a message?" Luke suggests, though in a tone that suggests he's in the process of delivering a powerful one himself. And it's evidently hitting home.

"Yes, just… I mean, no. Thanks." Tom looks down at me a third time, then peers over Luke's shoulder and along the hall, as if he's hoping this is all some elaborate joke, and that Julie's about to leap out from behind the door with a loud "Gotcha!"

Of course, Julie's dad could appear at any moment and put

a stop to this, but Julie's dad is under strict instructions not to move from his chair. In any case, Tom's already backing away along the path, and a part of me wants to go and grab onto his trouser leg with my teeth and drag him inside so Julie's dad can clear up this whole thing.

"Right. Well, I'll just..."

"Oh-kay! Good seeing you again, Tim."

Luke reaches a hand up, and slowly waves goodbye, a small gesture, though one that suggests a finality. And though I take a step after him and whine plaintively at the rapidly-departing Tom, he doesn't even look round.

Luke ushers me back inside with his foot—a little roughly, I have to say—then swaggers back along the hall. I follow him reluctantly, trying hard to resist the temptation to snap at his ankles.

"Who was that?" asks Julie's dad, as we walk back into the front room.

"What? Oh. Some guy." Luke lowers himself smugly back onto the sofa. "Probably trying to sell something. I told him to get lost."

"I hope he got the message," says Julie's dad, and I snort indignantly.

Because I fear he got the wrong one.

The rest of the evening passes without incident. Julie comes back a few minutes later with a bottle of Chardonnay, pours herself an extra-large glass, then leaves Luke to help himself to wine while she helps him to an extra-large plate of chili.

Luke's on his best behavior, perhaps deciding to play the long game. And though he's polite, attentive, eats all his chili (while making the same noises he used to make when kissing Julie), and only gives Julie a chaste hug when he leaves, I'm sure that's only because Julie's dad's watching. He doesn't mention to Julie that Tom came around while she was at the store—*of course* he doesn't.

And while Julie seems a little miffed when Tom doesn't call for the next few days, I'm not at all surprised.

37

True to form, and probably *because* Tom doesn't call Julie, Julie doesn't call Tom either. She does call Priya, though, to tell her that Tom hasn't called, and that she thinks it's because he's the same as all the rest of them, and that he can't be bothered getting in touch now that he's already got what he wanted, and how she's left the ball in his court.

And because she doesn't know that Tom's already picked the ball up and attempted to throw it back to her, only to have Luke throw it back in his face, I fear she's in danger of spiraling down into her old depression. Which is why I'm desperate for her to see Tom. So he—or she—can explain.

In fact, I'm *so* desperate for Julie to see Tom again, that I decide to fake an injury. I've seen it done before—the footballers that Julie's dad likes to watch do it all the time. Which is why, when Julie takes me for my walk this morning, I put on a limp.

"What's the matter, Doug?" she says, as she sees me staggering along the pavement behind her.

In response, I put my paw down gingerly, then let out a whimper, and Julie frowns.

"Have you hurt your leg?"

She kneels down in front of me and gently inspects my paw, so I yowl—an Oscar-winning yowl if ever there was one—then she beckons me forward. I manage a tentative step before reverting to a three-legged hop, and Julie sighs.

"Right," she says. "Better get you off to the V-E-T."

I'm so pleased my plan is working, I almost do a happy dance, before I remember that I'm supposed to be hurt. And as Julie scoops me up from the pavement and carries me back home, I congratulate myself on how easy it's been.

Of course, as I've learned over the last few weeks, the path of true love never runs smoothly, because it's not long before I discover the fundamental flaw in my plan is that there's more than one V-E-T in town. Perhaps it serves me right for trying to interfere, but Julie, of course, takes me to a non-Tom one. As she carries me into the waiting room, I suspect I might be in danger of being found out.

I also realize I have to think on my feet and decide there's nothing else I can do but pretend my leg's okay again. Seeing as Julie doesn't seem to want to put me down, I can't quite find a way to show her.

I wriggle frantically, making myself as impossible to hold as I can. After trying to contain me for a second or two, Julie sets me down on the floor, where I proceed to run as far as my leash permits—which is pretty much only in circles around her feet. While Julie is watching my strange behavior, the receptionist looks up from her computer screen.

"Can I help you?"

"I phoned earlier. The pug with the limp?"

The receptionist looks over the counter at me, where I've stopped circling in order to catch my breath. "Oh yes. Doug, wasn't it?" she says, smiling in a way that suggests my *We Rate Dogs* celebrity has preceded me.

"That's right. Only he seems to be okay now."

"Oh." The receptionist frowns. "Did you still want the vet to see him?"

"I'm not sure," says Julie as I do my best to demonstrate how I'm fine now by repeatedly hopping from one front leg to another, as if I'm trying to play an invisible pair of bongos. "Doug does seem to be acting a bit…odd."

"You say he just started limping this morning?"

Julie nods. "When we were out on our walk. But now…" She peers down at me, where I alternate between intensely staring at the door, then looking back up at her to suggest it's time to leave.

"Does his behavior seem funny to you?" Julie says.

The receptionist leans over the counter and examines me from the other side of the desk. So I stop the intense staring and do my best to act naturally, which of course I now worry looks unnatural since I'm trying so hard.

"Not really. But perhaps the vet should take a look. Just to be sure?"

I snort frustratedly, and Julie hesitates. "Doug's never behaved like this before. Do you think he needs an X-ray? Or maybe one of those…" She lowers her voice. "*Cat* scans?"

At the mention of the *c* word, I look up so quickly it almost gives me whiplash. There's no way I'm going to have any kind of feline-related therapy.

With an aggrieved bark, I give Julie a look. Then, using all four legs at their maximum capacity, I pull her unceremoniously toward the door.

In a strange coincidence that makes me think Santa might be Luke's spirit animal, the cat next door is back. I'd feared the worst, but when Julie and I spot Miss Harris systematically removing all the Missing Cat posters from our street, the look on her face tells us everything we need to know.

"My baby's home!" announces Miss Harris, enveloping Julie in a huge hug that surprises us both—and almost squeezes the life out of her.

"Oh, that's..." Julie hesitates. Then when she sees just how relieved Miss Harris is, she breaks into a huge smile, perhaps having realized how she'd feel if I went missing. "*Fabulous* news."

Miss Harris makes like one of those nodding bobblehead figures you sometimes see on car dashboards. "Isn't it?"

"Any ideas where she's been all this time?"

"Someone around the corner had been feeding her so she'd decided to stay there for a while. They'd assumed she must belong to someone in the neighborhood and that his owner must be away. So they just kept feeding her, and she thought she'd move in for a bit and, well, long story short..."

Miss Harris pauses for breath just as Julie's eyes begin to glaze over: the story's already ventured into "long" territory. "They said they only saw my posters this morning," she continues, "so they phoned me right away, and..." She forces a smile now, even though she looks as if she's on the verge of tears, perhaps unsurprisingly. Santa evidently had decided the grass looked greener at someone else's place and stayed there until she got found out.

I gaze up at Julie, wanting her to see the similarity, the *irony*, in her own situation, but apparently she doesn't.

"Cats, eh?" Julie says. But instead of a friendly agreement, Miss Harris bristles. "What do you mean by *that*?"

"Well, just that..." Julie looks like she's already regretting stopping for a chat. "I mean, they say they're not, you know, that, um, *loyal*..."

"Rubbish!" spits Miss Harris. "My Santa was just...confused. Let's face it, you turn up in a strange environment, someone gives you everything on a plate…"

"Or in a bowl…"

Miss Harris glares at Julie for having the temerity to interrupt. "As I was saying. They're only animals." She flicks her eyes down at me as she says this. "It's in their nature."

I have to stop myself from placing a paw on Julie's shin to get her attention. *This is Luke*, I hope she realizes. He fancies a change of scene, to—if you excuse the phrase—eat out of someone else's bowl, and then, when he is found out, off he goes. Only now he's trying to wheedle his way back in as if he's never been away.

"Still." Julie reaches over and pats Miss Harris on the arm. "She's back now. That's the important thing."

"It is," agrees Miss Harris.

I follow Julie home, stunned into silence. If that's truly how she feels, then I've got a long and uphill battle ahead of me.

38

There are two ways to get those people in the park who spray-paint themselves gray and pretend to be statues to move. One is for someone to put some loose change into the collection box they've positioned in front of them; the other is for me to make the mistake of thinking they're *actual* statues and pee on their feet. And while I'm more than a little embarrassed at my *faux pas*, it seems to amuse both Julie and Julie's dad, so I don't feel too bad.

It's Julie's dad's first proper walk after his heart attack, so we decide to take it slowly, so despite my keenness to get away from Angry Statue Man, I refrain from my usual straining-at-the-leash activities. Julie's been insisting her dad holds onto her arm for most of the way, and though he protests, you can tell he's actually quite glad for the support.

When we get to the pond, Julie points at the nearest bench. "Did you want to wait here while I take Doug for his circuit?"

Julie's dad shakes his head. "I think I can make it as far as the café," he says, winking at me.

Julie tries, and fails, to hide a smile. Her dad and Dot have hardly been off the phone to each other since his trip to the hospital. Given how she reportedly makes him "feel alive," that's probably a good thing.

"Fine," says Julie.

The three of us stroll over and find a table on the café terrace, Julie looping my leash around the table leg. Dot catches sight of us through the window and, leaving another customer half-served, she rushes out to say hello.

"Jim! How are you feeling?"

Without waiting for a response, Dot leans down and throws her arms around his neck. Julie's dad sits there awkwardly for a moment, then he reaches up and gives Dot the briefest of embarrassed hugs in return.

"Oh, you know..."

Dot nods, as if she knows *exactly* what it's like. "What can I get you?" she says. "And I hope you're not going to tell me it's all health food from here on in?"

Julie's dad laughs. "Not much point in surviving a heart attack if salad's all you have to look forward to for..." His voice trails off, perhaps because he's aware of the look Julie's giving him. "Just, um, bring us a couple of coffees. Oh, and make mine decaf," he adds, glumly.

"Coming right up," Dot says and, true to her word, she's back in a couple of minutes with coffee for Julie, decaf for her dad, and a bowl of water for me. Plus a huge slice of frosted cake.

Julie frowns at the cake. "We didn't order..."

"It's carrot cake. So it's healthy. And it's on the house," says Dot, with a wink. Then she takes Julie's dad's hand and gives it a quick squeeze. "It's good to see you up and about," she says, as she leans down to hug him again. "*Really* good," she adds, as if she's trying to tell him something. Judging by the way his face flushes, he understands.

Dot rests a hand on Julie's shoulder. "And how are you, love?"

"Oh, you know."

"Tom…" Dot begins, but Julie holds her palm out.

"Dot, please."

"I don't know what's happened between the two of you, but…"

"Nor do I, Dot."

"All I know is that he's back to moping around the house…"

"Yes, well, he's got no right to mope!" says Julie, angrily.

Dot makes eye contact with me, as if she doesn't know where else to look, then she glances back toward the café where a number of people are waiting impatiently in a line by the register.

"Well, I'd better…"

"Of course," says Julie's dad, reassuringly.

"No rest for the, you know…"

It's the first time I've seen Dot flustered, but fortunately, Julie's dad is there to save the day.

"Wicked?" he suggests, with a raised eyebrow.

A smile returns to Dot's face, and with a loud "Cheeky!" she heads back inside. Then, after a somewhat uncomfortable silence, Julie's dad clears his throat.

"I really don't want to talk about it," says Julie, before he gets a chance to launch into his speech. "And I suspect you don't either. So can we just…?" Julie rearranges the items on the table, though not by much, but Julie's dad won't let it go.

"Julie, love…"

"Dad, *please*. Tom's just… He's probably decided… I mean, he's not… I gave him a way out, and on reflection he's decided to take it. And it's for the best. He's probably still trying to sort himself out, and I'm... You know, after Luke, and all... Well, I'm sure the last thing Tom wants to do is to have to deal with the fallout from that. And I can't blame him, really."

"Don't sell yourself short, love."

"I'm just being realistic."

"Really? Because it's not always easy to tell. You know. How someone feels about you." Julie's dad swallows audibly, and glances over to where Dot is standing behind the cash register, occasionally glancing over in our direction in a way that she's pretending she isn't watching us, although she's doing a bad job of it. "Look at me and Dot, for example. All that time, it didn't occur to me that she... Well..."

"Had the serious hots for you?"

"Well, yes. I thought she was just being... Friendly."

"The free muffins weren't a giveaway?"

"Maybe." Julie's dad grins sheepishly. "And I worried I was off-limits because of your mum, and I thought Dot knew that too. But it can take a while for reality to sink in. For you to see a way out. Especially if you're...resistant to it."

"A way out of what?"

Julie's dad looks at her earnestly. "Whatever's holding you back," he says.

Julie seems to bristle a little at this, then she picks up a knife, though it's only to slice the cake into bite-size pieces before sliding the plate across to her dad.

"Here."

"Love...?"

"It's what you used to do for me when I was a little girl, remember? Cut up my food when I wasn't well? Told me I had to save my energy for chewing? You did that for Mum too, when she got really bad. She didn't like it, though."

"I remember." Julie's dad smiles wistfully. "Your mother hated being ill. And with good reason."

"Yup," says Julie.

"I tell you." Julie's dad picks up his decaf, blows on the top of it, takes a sip, and grimaces slightly. He reaches for a packet of sugar from the glass on the center of the table, then—as if he senses Julie's disapproval—hurriedly changes his selection to a sachet of sweetener. "Life's too short," he says.

Julie reaches across the table to squeeze her dad's hand, then she frowns. "For?"

"Everything. What happened to your mum should be a lesson for both of us. As should Doug."

"Doug?" She glances down at me, and I wag my tail in response. "I don't..."

"He's only here for a seventh of what we get, and is he unhappy about it? No, he lives each day to the fullest."

"Even though he spends most of his day asleep?"

"That's not the point," says Julie's dad, then he hesitates, as if he's trying desperately to work out what the point actually is. "All I mean is... Watch this."

Julie's dad picks up a chunk of cake, but instead of handing it directly to me, he places it just out of reach on the edge of the table.

Though we all know I can't possibly jump that high, I understand Julie's dad's using me as a metaphor right now. And since the last thing I want to do is let either him or Julie down, I spend the next thirty seconds doing my best to defy the laws of gravity.

"See?" Then, with a whispered "Good boy, Doug," Julie's dad feeds me the piece of cake. "Doug spots something he wants, and he goes for it, no matter how far out of reach he thinks it might be, however hard it is to get, no matter what the obstacles are. And more importantly..." He holds a hand out to me now, and I give his fingers a friendly lick.

"He doesn't hold a grudge." Julie's dad pats me on the head. "There's a lesson there for us all."

"Okay, okay! Enough of the lecture. From both of you!" Julie rolls her eyes at her dad, gives me a look as if I'm a traitor, then reaches down and scratches my chin in a way that tells me she forgives me.

But despite her dad's lecture, I'm still not sure she'll forgive Tom, though. And how on earth I'm going to make her understand she's got nothing to forgive him *for*, I'm just not sure.

39

It's Sunday morning, Barkrun time, but despite me eating everything I've had the opportunity to, so much so that Julie's had to loosen my collar a notch, she's decided we're not going to class. And while that's possibly a little selfish—after all, it's my well-being as well as hers we're talking about—Julie's pride won't seem to let her make any moves where Tom's concerned.

Julie's dad's moved back to his own house—something about living with us "cramping his style." He's also wearing a huge, Dot-inspired grin most of the time, though Julie hasn't pressed him for details. When she reported the goings-on to Priya, Priya suggested Julie's dad and Dot might get married, and if that turned out to be the case, Julie and Tom would be brother and sister, which Priya seemed to find hilarious, even though it would be a major barrier to them getting together. And there seems to be enough of a barrier there already.

It's a sunny morning, and we're back home after a brief walk along the river. Julie's changed into her bikini and she's just setting up her lounge chair in the back garden sun, no doubt planning a day of doing nothing, when the doorbell rings.

"Round the back!" she shouts, then she unlatches the high wooden gate by the side of the house, perhaps assuming it's her dad. Instead, a familiar if unwelcome smell comes wafting through the air, and a moment later, the gate swings open, and Luke appears. What's more, the look on his face on seeing how Julie's dressed (or undressed, to be more accurate) suggests he's just won the lottery.

"Looking good, Julie!"

"Do you mind!"

Julie grabs the nearest towel, and does her best to cover herself with it, but it's *my* towel, so it's a little small and not quite up to the job. Something Luke seems to be taking great pleasure in.

"It's nothing I haven't seen before."

"And you're not going to be seeing it again! What are you doing here?"

"Thought I'd come and see how your dad was?"

"He's not here." Julie seems a little uncomfortable as he realizes she's just admitting she's alone in the house. "And neither should you be."

"Come on, Julie." Luke's showing no sign of taking the hint. "What's with the hostility? After all, if I weren't here the other night, hadn't called an ambulance…"

"And I'm very grateful for that. We all are. But not *that* grateful."

"Don't I at least deserve another chance?"

"Luke, I… We can't."

"We can! Unless…"

"Unless what?"

"That Tom is still on the scene?" Luke's phrased it as a question, though something tells me he already knows the answer.

"Not that it's any of your business, but no, he isn't."

"Oh. Right. I'm sorry to hear that," says Luke, though his face gives the opposite impression.

He takes a step closer, then another, and moves to take Julie's hand. "Come on, Julie. We were good together."

"*Were* being the operative word."

"And we can be again."

"Luke…"

Julie seems to be frozen to the spot, perhaps in fear, so I start barking, as loudly and frantically as I can, and prepare myself to leap to Julie's defense. Although in the end, I don't have to, because, in that weird way that life sometimes surprises you, it's Miss Harris who comes to our aid.

"He's doing it again!" she shouts, from the other side of the fence.

"What?"

Miss Harris could of course be referring to Luke, as he's so obviously back to his old ways, but she's staring accusingly at me, so I stop barking.

"Not now, Mary, please," says Julie.

"That dog of yours." Miss Harris points a gnarled old finger at me, as if keen to make sure Julie knows she means me. "Has a screw loose."

Julie sighs. She's still trying to hold the towel up to protect her modesty, though it makes her look like a half-naked bullfighter. "What do you mean?"

"Some guard dog he's turned out to be."

"I'm sorry, I don't…"

Miss Harris shakes her head. "Most dogs bark to stop people coming into the house. This one…" She points at me again, just to leave Julie in no doubt whatsoever. "He barks to stop them leaving."

"Huh?"

"The other night. All that commotion..."

"If by commotion you mean the ambulance that came and saved my dad's life..."

"Before that. The raised male voices through the wall. Then this young man." She turns her attention to Luke. "Doing his best to flee the scene. I thought he was a thief, the way he came running out the door. And he wouldn't let him out of the garden."

"Who wouldn't?"

"Doug." Miss Harris points at me a third time. "Stood at the front gate blocking his way, barking his silly head off."

"I'm sorry. Which young man?"

"Him." The finger comes out again, though this time, it's aimed squarely at Luke. "Then he reached into his pocket... For a moment, I thought he was going to pull out a gun and shoot Doug!"

Thought, I think. *Hoped*, more like.

"But instead, he got his phone out and dialed someone. Next thing you know, it's all sirens and blue flashing lights. It's lucky my Santa wasn't here, otherwise she'd have been quite traumatized by it all."

"But..." Julie stares at her, then at Luke, then she says, "But" again, and Luke's mouth flaps open.

"What?" he says, as Julie folds her arms and glares at him.

"You were *running away*?" she says.

"No, I...I can see how you might think that, but..."

"Tell the truth, will you, Luke," Julie says, "for once in your life!"

Julie's shouted that last sentence, and so loudly, so forcefully that Luke actually does what he's told.

"We'd had a simple argument, okay? Your dad tried to tell me to leave you alone, and I told him I wouldn't, and the next thing I know he's clutching his chest, and all..." Luke lets his tongue loll out of his mouth, and mimes someone having a medical episode. "And I panicked, so I ran, and..."

"Left him for *dead*?" Julie says.

"Well, no. I mean, that's what it might have looked like. I was going to call an ambulance. Really. I just couldn't get any decent phone reception in the house, and..."

Luke's voice trails off, probably because his excuse isn't getting a decent reception either. And it's at that precise moment—thanks partly to the range of expressions that pass across Julie's face, from disbelief to realization to anger, though mainly because of the way she pulls her arm back, drops the towel, balls her hand into a fist, then punches Luke squarely in the nose—I realize I've *won*.

"Julie, what the...?" Luke staggers backward, puts his hand to his face, then stares at her incredulously.

"You..." Julie looks like she's struggling for the right word. While I can think of a few, miming them is a little beyond me.

"You *hit* me!" he whines, then he turns to Miss Harris, who's watching the whole show from the other side of the fence with the intensity of someone seated in front of the season finale of their favorite soap opera. "Did you see that? She *hit* me," he says as if he still can't believe it.

Miss Harris nods. "I'm guessing you probably deserved it."

Julie's making a fist again—and ominously for Luke, with both hands. "How could you?" she says, advancing angrily toward him.

Luke takes another step backward. "I was...confused," he says.

"Confused," says Julie, though the look of disbelief on her face suggests that, finally, she isn't.

She feints another punch at him, smiles as he flinches, then she crouches down to pick me up, and nods toward the gate.

"Don't slam it on your way out," she says, then she turns her back on Luke, and carries me toward her lounge chair.

I'm gloating a little as I watch him over her shoulder, I have to admit, but after all I've been through, I think I have the right to feel pleased with myself.

"Think about what you're doing, Julie," he warns.

"Oh, I am," she says.

Luke touches his nose gingerly, then he scowls at the two of us. "I can make things difficult for you at work, you know?" he says, but Julie just shrugs.

"Backatcha!" she says. "Although..."

"Although what?" snaps Luke.

"I can make things difficult for *you* at work too. Oh, *and* at home."

With a final glower in our direction, Luke turns and stalks wordlessly out of the garden, accompanied by a slow hand-clap from Miss Harris.

"Good for you, dear," she says.

Then—and with a smile on her face—Julie lowers me gently to the grass, picks up her headphones, sticks them in her ears, and lies down to enjoy the sun.

As Julie dozes off, her bikini top untied to avoid tan lines, a contented look on her face, I crawl beneath her lounge chair and analyze what's just happened.

As I see it, there are two big pluses to the end of the Luke situation. The first, and obvious one, being no more Luke, which means he won't be able to mess Julie about anymore (and *I* won't have to put up with any more of his fake throws, which—by the looks of the lines he'd been feeding Julie for the past few months—was exactly what he'd been doing to her too). The second is that Julie's finally emotionally free to go out with Tom. And if there's one thing I've learned over the last few weeks, it's that Julie *needs* Tom to help her get past the Luke phase of her life.

Trouble is, Julie doesn't seem to want to call Tom, and Tom doesn't seem to be calling Julie. Probably because he thinks Luke's back on the scene. And despite my best efforts, I can't seem to find a way to get the two of them together.

Or can I?

A creaking sound from elsewhere in the garden catches my attention. It's not Miss Harris's arthritic joints. Rather it's that Luke decided to take Julie's instruction not to slam the gate on his way out a step further, and hasn't actually shut it closed. Which means anyone can come in. Or go out.

It's nearly lunchtime, which means Barkrun will be finishing soon, so I creep out from underneath the lounge chair and take stock of the situation. Julie still seems to be napping, plus there's a tinny sound coming from her headphones, so I'm pretty sure my movements will escape detection. Under the pretext of a security patrol, I trot over to where the gate's swinging gently in the breeze and peer through the gap.

With a final glance back at Julie, and before I have time to think about what I'm doing and perhaps lose my nerve, I squeeze through the gap, making it out just as the wind slams the gate shut behind me.

I swallow hard as I hear the latch drop back into place—*no going back now.* Then, with a hop and a skip, I'm out on the pavement.

I check up and down the road, careful I don't lose my bearings after the excitement of my Great Escape, as this adventure will no doubt be referred to in the future. The park's to the right, so all I have to do is navigate the three-minute walk without being run over, or dognapped, or getting lost. I've done it a thousand times with Julie, or Julie's dad, after all, so making it on my own should be a piece of cake.

Which, hopefully, is what I'll get as a reward, once Julie and Tom realize what I've done for them.

40

Being outside on my own feels exhilarating if a little bit scary, but apart from a slightly hairy moment on the crosswalk, when none of the cars stop for me so I have to wait for a gap in the traffic and make a desperate run for it, I make it to the park unscathed.

Sure enough, I'm just in time to see Tom clearing up after Barkrun as the usual band of breathless women make their way to the café. Excitedly, I run toward him and let out an insistent bark. The second Tom catches sight of me, he breaks into a huge grin, then straightaway he scans the space behind me for any sign of Julie, and there and then, I know I've done the right thing.

"Hey, Doug!" He reaches down to scratch the top of my head. "On your own?"

I bark again in an attempt to convey that yes I am because I've come to get him. But for some reason, the message doesn't get through.

"Is Julie in the café with Mum?" He gets his phone out,

then something seems to occur to him, so he slips it away again. "You haven't *escaped*, have you?"

I spin in circles, first one way then the other, this time trying to make him understand Julie's at home and he should come back with me. But even though these exaggerated mimes always seem to work for the likes of *Lassie* and *Flipper*, Tom doesn't seem to get it.

As I claw the ground anxiously, wondering whether I should start writing the words *follow me* in the dirt, he hurriedly stows the last of the Barkrun equipment in the boot of his car.

"Well, whatever it is you're doing here, I think I'd better get you home. Don't you?"

I high-five him (more commonly recognized as offer him a paw) as I mentally punch the air, then allow myself to be lifted onto the passenger seat of Tom's Mercedes. I sit there patiently as he starts the car and steers us quickly out of the park. The roof's down, though I'm too focused on my end goal to enjoy the short, breezy drive back to the house.

This could be it, I remind myself. *Tom and Julie get together, and live happily ever after, and by extension, so do I.* I'm so excited by the prospect, it's all I can do not to wee a little on Tom's leather upholstery. And to be honest, I'm not sure I don't.

Tom parks behind our Fiat, then climbs out of the Mercedes and lets me out, pausing briefly to inspect Julie's car as I run excitedly toward the house. The gate leading to the garden's still shut. So even though I run up to it and begin scratching at the bottom, Tom doesn't take the hint and break it down like he might if this were the movies and not real life. Instead, he makes his way to the front door and rings the bell, though when there's no answer, he bends over and pushes the letterbox open.

"Julie?" he shouts through the slot.

He tries the doorbell once more, then shouts, "Julie"

through the letterbox again, though a little more anxiously this time. Then he peers back over his shoulder at Julie's car, and frowns down at me.

"Is everything okay, Doug?" he asks, and I wag my tail as if to suggest that yes, it is, because Luke has both been given his marching orders *and* punched in the face, but that doesn't seem to reassure him. He starts banging loudly on the door, and the next thing we hear is a haughty, "Can I help you?" from next door. Though it's quickly followed by a coquettish giggle, and "Oh, hello, Doctor Tom."

"Hello, Mary," says Tom. "I didn't know you lived here."

"I didn't know you made house calls on a Sunday."

"I don't. Normally. But, you see…" Tom appears to be floundering, so I bark to remind him I'm here, which seems to do the trick. "Doug turned up at the park. Without Julie. So I'm a little worried that she's, you know, not…okay."

"Oh-kay," parrots Miss Harris.

"I don't suppose you've seen her?"

"She's in the backyard. Looks dead to the world."

"What?" Tom sounds panicked. "I don't suppose you've got a spare key?"

"No," says Miss Harris. "But if you want, you could come through to my garden and peek over the fence. Just to check."

"Just to check. Sure."

Tom hesitates, perhaps fearing if he disappears into Miss Harris's house, he might not make it out again, and perhaps he has some justification given the adoration with which she looks at him.

"Okay," he says, perhaps a little nervously, scooping me up from the path.

We make our way into Miss Harris's front garden, and Tom hurriedly carries me through her house. Santa's nowhere to be seen, fortunately, but it's dark and smells so much of cat

I almost can't stand it, and when we finally emerge into her barely-cultivated jungle of a backyard, I'm nearly gagging. Then I hear a hissing from the far corner, and spot Santa: she's shut in her cat jail, glaring malevolently at me through the bars, and I can't help but let out a smug snort. Miss Harris is obviously punishing her for her indiscretions, which explains why she hasn't been trespassing in our garden since her return. While it's perhaps a fleeting victory, I have to see it as a good omen.

Tom sets me down, so I run over to the fence and peer through a crack, and he does the same. Julie's still lying on her lounge chair, sunglasses on and headphones in, only like Tom's car, she's now topless.

"Julie," he shouts, but her music is turned up so loud we can all hear it. After a moment's deliberation, he picks me up and hoists me over the fence, dropping me gently the five or so feet onto the grass, where—and credit where credit's due—I land with the agility of a cat.

It doesn't occur to me to let Julie know Tom's on his way—I'm more interested in ensuring he escapes Miss Harris's clutches—so I stand and wait for him. After a moment, there's a "one-two-three!" from the other side of the fence, and the next thing I know, Tom comes flying over and lands in a heap in the middle of the lawn.

I bark excitedly, and Julie sits up with a start, removes her sunglasses and her headphones, and peers curiously at me. Then she catches sight of Tom, flat on his back by the birdbath, and lets out a piercing scream.

"Tom! What the..."

As she leaps up from the lounge chair, Tom hauls himself into a sitting position. He's obviously winded himself, though his discomfort is evidently from something else.

"Julie, I..." He puts one hand over his eyes. "You're..."

"Are you hurt?"

"No, I..." Tom's doing that thing where he's doing his best not to look, though I can tell he desperately wants to. "You might want to..."

He's pointing in the vague direction of her chest, but Julie seems to have forgotten she's removed her bikini top. And in fact, it's only when I retrieve it from where it's draped over the end of the lounge chair and present it to her that she remembers, shrieks again, then does her best to cover herself up with her forearm.

"What are you? Some sort of peeping..." She stops talking, evidently realizing how stupid what she's about to say will sound.

"Everything alright over there?" Miss Harris is peering anxiously over the top of the fence, so Tom waves at her.

"Yes. Fine."

Julie's expression implies the opposite. "Well?" she says.

"Doug turned up at the park. On his own."

"Doug did *what*?"

"Came to the park."

"He's been here all this time!" Julie stares at me. "Haven't you?"

"Actually, he hasn't," says Tom, getting slowly to his feet. "It was almost as if he'd come to get me."

With a twirl of her finger, Julie indicates he should turn round, and when he does, she takes the opportunity to slip her bikini top back on. "Why would he...?"

"Well, maybe because... I mean, I thought something might have happened..."

"Which was why you decided to climb into my back garden to scare the life out of me?"

"Well..."

"To be fair, that was my idea," says Miss Harris from the other side of the fence.

"Thank you, Mary," says Julie, in the tone she uses when I chew something I shouldn't.

"You're welcome," says Miss Harris.

As she disappears from view, Julie holds one hand up toward her and extends her middle finger, which gets an indignant "Charming!" from the other side of the fence, where Miss Harris is obviously still watching the goings-on through a gap.

Julie's angry too, and as I trot across the garden to hide behind Tom's legs, her terse "Stay!" seems to be directed at both of us. She nips toward the open French doors and inside the house, I imagine to get dressed, so Tom perches on the end of the lounge chair to wait.

"I think we're in trouble, Doug," he says to me, so I sit down next to him and give him a look to say, *actually, you might be surprised.* A moment later, he is when—after the quickest outfit change in history—Julie marches back into the garden wearing her best sundress. Interestingly, she appears to have refreshed her makeup too.

"So tell me again what you're doing here?"

Tom makes to stand up, but Julie's glare means he quickly changes his mind. "Like I said. I thought something might have happened..."

"And something might have, Tom. But instead, you heartlessly slept with me, then never called, despite it being the best sex of your life, of *my* life, even after you gave me that big romantic speech..."

"...to *Doug.*"

"To Doug?"

"Yeah." Tom reaches down to pet me. "If I hadn't brought him home. Because he was on his own. In the park. And he might have been run over, or dognapped, or fallen in the pond."

"Right." Julie's cheeks have darkened, and I suspect that's nothing to do with the fact she's been lying in the sun. "Well, you've brought him back now, so it's fine."

"Great."

"So you can go."

Tom stands up. "Okay."

Julie's sounded like she hasn't meant it, and Tom looks like he doesn't want to, but even so, he starts to tentatively backpedal toward the gate, just as she circles warily round to the lounge chair, almost as if they're sizing each other up in a boxing ring.

"Julie, just..."

Julie pauses, sunglasses in hand. "What?"

"Is that really how you see...?"

"How else can I possibly?"

"Right."

"What does *that* mean?"

Tom sighs. "Nothing."

"No, go on. What were you about to say?"

"Like I said. Nothing. It's none of my business."

"What isn't?"

"Your, you know..." He gestures vaguely toward her. "Love life."

"It certainly isn't!"

"Quite. So I'll just..."

"Good."

Julie slips her sunglasses back on in a that's-the-end-of-the-matter way, so Tom turns on his heel, strides purposefully toward the French doors, and heads into the house. Julie watches him go, then stares at the space he's just been occupying as if still imagining him standing there. Then, with a loud sigh and a snort not unlike one of mine, she sits down heavily on the lounge chair.

"It's just, well... Luke." Tom has just come bursting back

out through the French doors, and his sudden appearance has made both Julie and me jump.

Julie peers at him over the top of her sunglasses. "Luke?"

"He's never going to leave his wife."

Julie pulls her glasses off, folds the arms in, and sets them down next to her. "I know that."

"So why are you still seeing him?" says Tom, desperately.

"I'm not."

"Because all he's… Hang on. You're *not* seeing Luke?"

Julie widens her eyes and shakes her head slowly, as if explaining something to a five-year-old. "Nope."

"Right. Good." Tom narrows his eyes. "So why…"

"Why what?"

"The other night. When I… I mean, after we'd…"

Julie sighs exasperatedly. "Perhaps if you could try a full sentence, I might actually have some clue as to what on earth it is you're trying to say?"

"Right. Sorry." Tom takes a deep breath. "When I came around the other night, Luke was here. And…"

"You came around the other night?"

"Yeah. The day after we… You know. Anyway, Luke answered the door. And he left no doubt that I absolutely was not welcome, and that you and he…" Tom looks as if he's trying to mime something with his hands, then it turns into something rude, so he gives up and stuffs his hands into his pockets. "Were an item."

"He's right."

"Oh. But you just…"

"We *were* an item. In typical Luke fashion, he'd only come around to give my dad the opportunity to thank him for calling an ambulance when he had his heart attack."

"That was big of… Your dad had a *heart attack*? Mum didn't…"

Julie holds both hands up. "He did. A mild one. He

doesn't—well, didn't—want anyone to know, so he swore Dot to silence. But he's fine. No thanks to Luke."

"I don't understand."

"It appears that Luke may have actually caused my dad to have the heart attack in the first place." Julie reaches down to pat me on the head. "And possibly wouldn't have bothered calling an ambulance if it hadn't been for Doug here."

Tom's looking even more confused. "Right," he says, perhaps deciding now isn't the time for twenty questions.

"So."

"So."

"One question," Julie says.

"Which is?" says Tom, when she doesn't elaborate.

"Why did you come around?"

"I told you. Doug turned up at the park on his own."

"I mean the other night."

"Ah." Tom stares awkwardly at the patch of grass between his feet. "Well, because…"

"Because?"

"Because, I wanted to ask you whether you'd, you know…"

"Whether I'd what?"

Tom's still staring at the grass. "Go out with me," he mumbles.

"What are you? Five years old?"

"No, I just…" Tom looks up, and smiles *that* smile. "Actually, yes. Or rather, that's how you make me feel."

"Tom, I… The reason I might have come across as reluctant that morning is…" Julie swallows hard. "I've got…baggage."

"Who doesn't?"

"Yes, but…mine casts kind of a big shadow."

Tom removes his hands from his pockets and folds his arms. "If you're referring to Doug, I think that's a little harsh," he says, with a grin. "Especially since…"

"I wasn't." Julie smiles back at him. "Though since what?"

"Since he's the one who brought us together."

Julie looks at Tom for a moment, then she frowns down at me, and I will her all the encouragement I can. It seems to work, because she widens her eyes, then pats the space next to her on the lounge chair in a come-and-sit way, so I hop up and onto her lap, just as Tom virtually leaps across the garden to sit down too.

Trouble is, the lounge chair's built for one, and it's old, so the upholstery isn't quite up to supporting the three of us. Suddenly there's a loud rip, and I just about manage to jump clear before the part Tom's sitting on gives way. For the second time today, he lands on his back on the grass, and a split second later, the rest of the material splits down the middle, and Julie falls on top of him.

"Well, *that* was smooth," says Tom after a moment, and Julie starts to laugh. Then he joins in and before long, the two of them are virtually rolling around the garden in hysterics, and it's at that moment I know everything's going to work out just fine.

I'm so happy about this, I have a sudden urge to start chasing my tail. After a couple of spins, and for the first time *ever*, I actually manage to catch it.

Given how things seem to have turned out, I suppose I shouldn't be surprised.

★ ★ ★ ★ ★

ACKNOWLEDGMENTS

Thanks be to:

Superagent Hayley Steed and the fantastic team at Madeleine Milburn (without whom Doug wouldn't even have made it out of my laptop, let alone the back garden), and Kathy Sagan and everyone at MIRA/HarperCollins for giving him a US (pet) passport!

The Board. We're still standing!

The usual suspects—Loz, Tony, John, et al.

The lovely Tina, for being there every step (and occasional misstep) of the way.

Joan, Karen and the Menorca Mob. Biking, boating and beer(ing) have been a blast!

Mekdi, Hector, Cristian, Dior and everyone at Barych in Mahon. Because everyone needs a "local."

And lastly, especially to you, dear reader. This is my fourteenth novel. I couldn't—and wouldn't—have written it without you.